SELECTED

BOOK ONE

R. M. MULLER

WILLOW
HOUSE
—— Publishing ——

For more information, or to book an event, contact:

authorrosemariemuller@gmail.com

Book design by R M Muller

Cover design by R M Muller

ISBN eBook - 978-1-7635496-0-9

ISBN Paperback - 978-1-7635496-1-6

First Edition: October 2024

*For those who always
challenge the status quo.*

The love between sisters
will always outshine
everything else . . .
Even on its worst day.

.

SELECTED

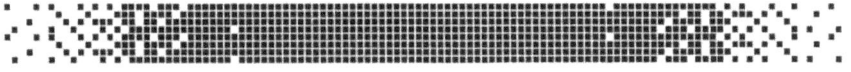

1

CLARA

TESSA'S HAND, identical to my own, slips through my fingers. My stomach plummets. I place the hand still tingling with her touch, over my heart and suck back tears.

Shoulders back.

Eyes forward.

Anything to lessen my chances of being sent to the Engineering Sectors.

Head high, Tessa starts toward the two other twenty-five-year-olds gathered for the Elite side of the oversized yet suffocating shed. Everything about us is identical, being the only set of twins in the outer Province. The only siblings. The only anomaly. I relax. My fate will be the same as hers. A tall grey-haired woman scans me up and down, her face lit with curiosity as my sister walks past her.

The empty warehouse gives no indication of what lies outside, with the back wall marking the border between the Province and the central Sectors. Beyond the door on the far wall, transport waits for the Elites. Whizzing them into the city via the Electro-Rail, they will work using their academic talents to further society. Never to return home, or to the Sectors, for that matter.

What my sister, born mere minutes before me, is walking toward. And so too, will I. The taught face of the guy standing beside me waivers a little. His toned, muscular build strains against his dark skin. If he wasn't so obnoxious he would be stunning. Deep brown eyes shoot me a glance of disgust, it's the same one he's always offered up. The selectors and their ever-scanning eyes don't catch it.

Woman and clipboard halt, toe to toe with him.

"Name and number," the grey-haired woman says.

"Nathaniel Prendergast, 67823," he punches out, standing taller with each digit. Her eyes track down the clipboard in her hand, pen tapping the sheet.

"Engineer, Metal Sector," she says, nodding him toward the door behind us, the way we came. Nate's jaw clenches, but he nods and spins, heading out. Couldn't have happened to a nicer guy.

Engineers make their own way to their relevant Sector. He has three days to arrive, report and make it to his first shift, before officials start hunting. Deserters are exiled to the Wastelands.

She steps toward me, clip board swinging in her left hand.

"Name and number, girl."

"Clara Bendall, 29457." I force my gaze to meet hers. She

2

glances back to Tessa before consulting her clipboard, eyebrow raised, running the pen down the page. She frowns and snaps her head up.

"Engineer, Textiles," she drawls with a sigh.

My heart stops.

Engineer?

No.

No. That can't be right. Tessa and I are identical in every way. Identical genetics, same strawberry-blonde wavy hair and small nose from our mother, matching blue eyes and crooked smile from our father, and flawless academic scores.

Everything.

We are remarkably hard to tell apart. Which used to work in our favor as children.

Now . . .

"Th--there must be a mistake," I splutter.

Her face hardens, lips pulling into a thin line. "No mistake, young lady. Engineer. Textiles!" She points a long arm ending in a manicured hand to the door behind us, her dull green eyes drilling into mine.

"But my sister is in the Elites. I should be on the same list."

She takes a step toward me, clipboard gripped in her hands. "No mistake. Move. Now."

I stare at her, heart thundering in my chest. Six guards, who have been pressed against the grey walls, step forward with hands on their weapons. Tessa's widen eyes hold mine.

Hands shaking, my breath turns ragged. I swallow and turn toward the door behind us. My sister's soft whimper echoes through the cold metal space as I drift toward the external door Nate went through.

I refuse to let the tears burning behind my eyes spill. I turn back, Tessa wraps her arms around her body, chin wobbling. My chest tightens. I hesitate. This is the last time I will ever see her.

A weight forms between my ribs as I press the handle down and push the door open. Blinding sunlight hits like fire, and I walk into the gathering of freshly appointed engineers now chatting.

Ringing fills my ears.

My vision blurs and my knees falter.

Hard, dusty ground hits my palms as I throw them out to save myself.

I cycle through short breaths before pushing back on my heels, fingers dragging through the dirt. Sontaria and the Sectors don't mix. Not only have I lost my parents today, never being able to go home, but Tessa has been torn from me too. With shaking hands, I sweep the hair from my face and try to summon the courage to stand.

And . . . fail.

A small hand drops into my blurry vision, and I push up on my arms. Crouched down in front of me is a girl from the group of Engineers. Small for her age, nobody ever expected her to make the Elite cut. And my gut twists with a realisation—maybe others thought that of me, too. At least now they would be right.

"Come on Clara. Chin up, Textiles is better than Agri at least." She smiles and tilts her head the way people do when they feel sorry for you. I slap a hand into hers, and she tugs me to my feet. I have seen her around; she lives in the settlement close to mine.

"Thanks, Vivi," I utter.

She points to my face and scrunches up her nose. "You have a little something."

"Oh." I wipe the dust and dirt from my face before dusting off my cargo pants and beige shirt. "Thanks, again."

"You can repay the favor when we reach the factory."

"Your Textiles too?"

"Yup. So glad I'm not Agri. Those jobs are the worst."

The Engineers now organise themselves into groups. Nate stands with his hands folded over his chest, the disdain in his eyes from earlier still apparent. It must burn him up not making the Elites. He absolutely has resting bitch face. Or is it resting *bastard* face? Tessa would tell me.

The ache grows in my heart with the thought of my sister being whisked away and into the city turns to fire. Stupid as it was, we had our whole lives planned out together. Land jobs in Sontaria. Buy everything we had ever dreamed of and play house with handsome men who don't take to drink or roughing us up when the mood strikes. Simple plan.

Now, it's just foolish. And I would give anything to have her back.

Anything.

"Clara, over here!" Vivi calls. She stands with a small group of people who I assume are the rest of the Textile Engineers. I walk to where they stand. Another officer with a clipboard. Another list of names.

When roll call is done, we pile into a busted, old bus. The driver, middle-aged and overweight, smokes as he stares straight ahead. Vivi sits next to me. Chatting about her parents. Pointing out anything she finds interesting as we make the journey to Sector Two.

The bus ahead of us heads to Sector One, Metals. It takes a left as we take a right, and drive through the razor-wire-topped enormous metal gates. A twelve-foot fence runs along the perimeter. To keep us in, or the other Sectors out? The surrounding land is sanctioned into small farming allotments. Textiles, like every other Sector, is self-sufficient. Agri supplies ninety percent of its produce to the Elites.

Vivi's head lolls, resting on my shoulders. All her talking wore her out. I smile at her. Her short brown hair is cropped into a bob, her dark brown eyes, when open, are quick and curious. Her slight frame and skinny build are common in the outer Province. Where resources, food being the most monitored, are rationed.

When the factories come into view as we wind through the shallow hills, I nudge Vivi.

6

"Oh crap," she mutters. "Please tell me I missed nothing important?"

I chuckle. "Nope, just more of the same."

She leans across me, peering out the window. "Oh wow, the buildings are much bigger than I imagined."

They are gigantic. The turnover in a place like Textiles must be extraordinary. "I wonder what the quarters are like?"

"Yeah," she says, smoothing her hair now messy from sleep.

"Do you know anyone else in Textiles?" I ask.

"One other person, but he's . . ."

"He's what?"

"Well, he's a few years older than us. I may or may not have slept with him a few years back. With a bit of luck, we won't run into him in a place this size."

"Let's hope we don't then," I say, but my face pulls up into a grin and she smacks my arm. "Ouch!"

"Not funny, Clara. It's just, well—" The bus lurches to a stop. We snap our heads to the window in tandem. A giant stone building stands on the right side. Three Textiles officiates stand, hands clasped behind their backs, in front of a hangar-sized sliding door.

The vehicle's twin doors swing open, and a man steps up into the bus by the driver. "Welcome to Textiles. Everybody out!"

We file out and line up against the bus. Vivi nudges my elbow with hers before tilting her head to the officer in the center standing by the building. His blond hair is shaggy around his face. His eyes burn into Vivi. Oh, that must be him. So much for avoiding him.

Her cheeks flush, and he snaps his gaze away, sending his focus down the line. I don't like him already.

The man who herded us out of the bus a moment ago walks up and down the line carrying out some sort of inspection before coming to a standstill in front.

"Right! First day. So, rules first up. This is your new life. Abide by Sector rules and curfews. Do as instructed, when instructed. Follow *every* safety protocol. Make it through the probation period. At the end of probation, we will keep the top ten percent of probates. The other ninety percent will be reassigned to a lower Sector. If you accumulate more than three strikes, you are for the Wastelands. Do I make myself clear?"

"Yes, sir!" The line chants.

"Walk!" He swivels on his feet and marches inside. The start of our line hurries after him, and we all file in behind. As we cross the threshold of the building, the artificial fluorescent lighting burns my eyes. I squint, holding a hand up. We walk through a long, white corridor. Two metal doors stud the walls halfway down. Dormitory A, and Dormitory B are stencilled on them in green paint.

"When I read your name, walk through this door." He opens the door to Dormitory A. "Jonathan, Miranda, Heather, Clara, Matthew . . ." He goes on as I follow the others into the massive utilitarian living space. Narrow bunks line the three walls of the biggest, barest room I have ever seen. In the center is a row of showers, separated by tin walls and flimsy doors. Behind me, on the front wall, are toilet cubicles. Four.

Painted over the bunks on the left wall is a green sign, WOMEN. On the right wall, MEN.

The only thing separating the men from the women are the absurd, inadequate shower stalls. The only person I've shared a room with is my sister. When the last of the Dormitory A personnel file in, I count. Twenty twenty-five-year-olds in one unisex dorm.

And Vivi's not with me.

I don't know a damn soul in this place. The officer from before strides in waving a hand, indicating we should claim a bunk and settle down. "Listen up. Today you will settle in and go over your schedules. You will find your documents which contain everything you need on your bunks. They are labelled."

One by one, we check our papers and swap bunks in a messy shuffle of 'excuse me' and 'sorry, I think that's mine'.

A moment later, the officer blows a small silver whistle. Every single one of us stands to attention, waiting for what comes next.

"Your schedules, as I said, are in your paperwork. On top of your Engineering duties, you will work a rotating roster between cleaning, kitchen and laundry. Engineers are the backbone of Ring 2. You will no doubt know the success or failure of any given ring comes down to the collective effort of its citizens. Today, you become an integral part of said system. In three months' time, you will find out if you stay or move on. We have curfews. Lights out and physical training sessions for every officer in Sector Two. Failure to appear at any of your given itinerary items results in a strike against your name. Three strikes, and you're off to the Wastelands, no questions asked. Do you understand?"

"Yes, sir!"

"I will see you at supper. Eighteen hundred hours."

He turns on his heel and disappears through the door. The girl beside me throws an expectant glance my way before uttering, "Hey, I'm Trina."

"Clara."

"Did you get a squiz at the guys? This facility has some ripe pickings. Thank Heavens, we didn't end up in Mining. Urgh, these nails weren't made for dirt."

"Hmmm." I tamper a disdainful face as she bends her neck to ogle the guys on the other side of the room. I'm sure they use machines to dig up the metals and minerals, not their actual hands. But I let her prattle on about the cons of every other Sector. She jabbers on about how being sent to Textiles is a good deal. I don't know who she's trying to convince.

Me or herself?

TESSA

HISSING three rows down startles me from sleep, and I rub my sore, puffy eyes. The bullet train, lined with velvet blue seats and waiters wandering through the aisle, slows on its tracks. People around me gather their possessions. Assignment folders, cream with the golden emblem of Sontaria embossed in the center, are gripped in their hands as if this dream could be ripped from them at any second.

The seat beside me is empty. Cold. For the first time in my life Clara is not with me. My sister is not right next to me. Excitement fills our carriage as the train stops alongside the Sontaria platform, every person in this fast-moving metal tube is ecstatic to be here. Except me.

Becoming an Elite is the best possible scenario, but without Clara, I don't want it. I stand and gather my duffle bag, snatching up the cream folder with my name and number under the city's emblem. I run a finger over the type. Tessa Bendall, 48716, Elite ~ Aeronautics. The very thought of being suspended in the air ties my stomach into knots. Proving academics aren't everything. Who assigns these positions? If they bothered to know any of us, they would never have given me this job.

The crowd on the platform moves like a swarm, an urgent energy that could ignite a fire-retardant blanket in a blizzard. I push my way through the horde of excited probationary folk, hoping to get a glimpse of some sign as to where I'm supposed to go.

A man stands on the platform wearing a navy military jumpsuit, aviator glasses stuck in his greased-up hair, his stance wide. The card he holds is printed with the words 'Aeronautics'. His immaculate dark hair tops his thin face with a long nose and light blue eyes that search the platform. I push through the hustling bodies toward him. Stopping briefly to adjust my long, wavy strawberry-blonde hair into a ponytail, straightening my shirt and running a hand over my creased pants.

"Hello," I say reaching him, "Tessa Bendall, Aeronautics."

"You're with me," he turns on his heel, walking briskly through the crowd. Up close, his uniform is immaculate. His standard issue boots are polished to a shine. A security access card swings at his hip. He smells clean and pleasant. Not like the working men of the Province. His arms are bulky, stretching out his rolled-up blue sleeves, the muscles in his back flex under the top half of his jumpsuit.

He doesn't turn back, weaving through the crowd with

long strides. There's no one else? I follow, pulling myself and duffle bag through the thick mass of bodies. He ushers me into the back seat of a large black vehicle, taking the front passenger seat for himself.

Shoving my bag to the other side, I slump into the buttery leather seat. A seat belt slides over my chest, securing in place below my hip with a soft whoosh and click. The whistle of the vehicle murmurs behind us as glistening skyscrapers fly past on every side.

City-dwellers wander the streets of Sontaria in luxurious clothing. Handbags and jewellery dangle from their arms, their fingers smothered with outlandish rings. Dogs trot past with their owners, necks dazzling with sparkling collars. Glass buildings jut through the skyline, a vast contrast to the basic housing in the Province, where every home is the same standard-issue beige, wood-panelled building.

Standard-issue clothing.

Standard-issue families.

But not Clara and me. We are the anomalies.

Non-standard offspring.

Siblings who shouldn't exist in a world of 'only child law'.

The vehicle swerves to the right, and we round another shining glass building. This one is half the height of the others, more spherical than most. A handful of wide, stone steps lead up to massive doors. Chrome railings flank the steps. It looks important.

I lean closer to the window; the glass is so clean you hardly remember it's there.

"That's the Aeronautics training hub. You will be there most days until your probationary term is complete," the officer says from the front seat.

"It's incredible." Ridiculously affluent, but still incredible, nonetheless.

"Over two hundred trainees go through those doors every year. Ten percent stay on. Don't get attached."

I lean back into the seat. For a moment, the grandness and opulence of the city had me in its gnarly grasp. Like a small child with an empty pantry on ration day. And I shake my head, dislodging any trace of appreciation for the city. The last thing I plan on doing is getting attached.

When the vehicle slows and we duck under a thin chrome-encased building, blue lights snap on overhead. The driver taps a button, and the vehicle rolls to a stop. The officer exits his door, swift and precise. I scramble to get out of the vehicle, tugging my bag from the back seat, and follow him to the building. An older man stands by the double glass doors, offering a dip of his head and a smile as we cross the threshold.

Much like the outside of the building, the inside is chrome and shined to a polish. Walking across the foyer we reach an elevator. The doors swish open, and we step in. Bright white light throughout the small space has me ensorcelled. I stand, staring at the blue dots that run across the top of the doors. As we ascend, they light up sequentially.

When the last number glows blue, level forty, the elevator whooshes to a halt and the doors hiss open.

The officer steps out, hands clasped behind his back. "This is you."

I follow him down a well-lit hall, grey soft carpet lines the floor, and doors to what I assume are apartments stud the long walls. The officer stops at the door marked 4008. He turns and swipes the access card that is attached to his hip. The door clicks and opens instantly. He steps aside, gesturing for me to enter.

The large white room is sparsely furnished. A slimline bunk sits on the left by the only oversized window that resembles a bent out of shape triangle. A small dresser. At least I think it's a dresser, on the other side of the window against the wall. By the door I just came through, a compact silver desk sits against the wall with a white lamp. A screen of some sort, with the Sontaria city emblem spinning on its axis as a screensaver, sits on the desk. All resting on more of the soft grey carpet. To the right is some kind of technology embedded into the wall, and a long rectangle silver wall, or is it a small room? It goes to the ceiling, with a door. I lower my brows. "All of this space is for me?"

"This is your allocated quarters while you are in probation, yes."

"Okay . . ." I dump my bag by the desk, running a hand over the smooth silvery surface. Everything is so white, so shiny.

So clean.

"Your schedule and access card are on your bed. You will report tomorrow morning at zero eight hundred hours for your induction. Punctuality is mandatory. All details are on the paperwork." He nods. "Officer Bendall." Backing out into the corridor, he closes the door.

I wander around the sparse, luxurious apartment. The machine in the wall glows to life as I move in front of it. The small rectangle screen to the side rolls through images of meals. This must be where the food arrives? I wave a hand in front of it, and it beeps, low and slow. A white image of an access card flashes up. Oh, you need to use your access card to order?

Leaving the machine, I pad to where the large silver rectangle room is attached to the same wall. There is a small, blue-lit panel halfway up the wall by the door. I press a finger to it and the door slides open silently. Inside is an opal-lined shower. It is the most eloquent looking wash space I have ever seen. Three shower heads protrude from the walls, two either side and one on the back. Just inside the door is a larger screen with the settings.

I read down the options.

Hydro-clean.

Ambient wash.

Steam clean.

What am I, a load of laundry?

Soap dispensers and something with an image of hair on the front is embedded into the back wall under the shower head. I guess that's the soap? No glycerine bars for the Elite.

Tripping backward, I turn back to the empty space, so silent, the white of it all burns my eyes. I wander to the window. Along the sterile wide ledge there is a long grey cushion. I sink onto it and gaze out into the sparkling city around me.

The sun has started her descent, lighting up every single building like a prism. It's stunning. It's too much. Tears prickle behind my eyes. Clara was supposed to be here with me. To see all of this. To have all of this. For the last fifteen years we worked our asses off to get the best test scores, make the biggest impact in our settlement, for the greatest chance to become Elites.

Together.

We were supposed to be here *together*.

People mill about forty floors down. They look like ants, but without purpose or hustle. Citizens of Sontaria lead meandering, absurdly padded lives. And for a moment, I try to remember why Clara and I wanted to be part of it . . . I close my eyes, and the images of rationed lives, desperation and hunger flood in. My gut twists, and acid burns from hunger just out of habit. Maybe I should try to work the food machine again.

But instead, I take one last look down on the city. The material wealth that surrounds stuns me into silence. The most brilliant minds live here, and all they can think about is the next treasure they will earn. Like a game. Not striving for world peace, cheating death or living amongst the stars. This city is powered by pride and competition. All they want is the next shiny object, dangling from the proverbial stick.

Nothing good happens here.

I feel dirty just by being a part of it. I didn't expect to feel this way. But without Clara, I can't seem to find the desire to be here. That carrot we were chasing for over a decade just turned, rotted and shrivelled. Dropping from the sill, I pad to the bathroom and wave a hand in front of the panel, and the door opens. I peel off my clothes and press a thumb to the first setting, hydro wash.

All three heads burst to life, hot steaming water streams out, hitting the pearlescent tile floor. I step into it, letting the heat burn my skin. Every inch of me trembles as sobs spill from my lips. I let her down. I let Clara down. When my legs wobble, I slide down the back wall and pull my knees to my chest. What is she having to cope with in Sector Two?

The worst part is, without Clara, half of my life is missing. I huff a strangled laugh with that thought. We are the only siblings in existence in Ring Two—the highly curated Ring led by General A B Beswick. A visionary, albeit a ruthless one. Literally nobody else had ever had this problem. I feel grateful and spiteful all at once. There is no one who could possibly understand what I have lost.

Mom used to say busy hands means a calm mind. The only option I have is to put my head down, do my best and keep busy. Even if I screw up my probation period on purpose, I would be sent to Sector One, not Sector Two. And who's to say Clara would be there if I did eventually work my way down the ranks?

Nate was sent to Sector One. Maybe I could get word to

him somehow? Do neighboring Sectors communicate? I need to hunt down information. As much as I can about every Sector. The levels each one takes from the academic scores. No, I can't even sabotage my way down the ranks. Each candidate is tested with biometrics technology. There is no way to lie to the tech.

I push off the shower floor and hold a hand under the soap dispenser. The floral scented soap lathers well and I wash and rinse off before washing my long, wavy hair. When I step out of the shower, I wander to the slimline dresser by my bunk. Each draw has a small line of lights in the top left corner. On the top of the dresser, corresponding rows of lights, one, two and three also light up white. I tap the top row and it turns blue. The top drawer slides out seamlessly.

Inside are underwear, something that looks like sleeping attire and socks. I push it closed and tap the two white lights in the middle row.

Uniforms.

Blue jumpsuits. My name and rank already stitched into the right side of the shirt top. A charcoal belt, with a silver buckle is curled up beside it. I slide the drawer shut and tap the last row of white lights. The last draw pops open. Boots, slippers and something that looks like polishing gear line the last white drawer. They really take this minimalism approach seriously. I guess less really is more.

I shut the draw and open the top one again, plucking out sleep attire. When I'm dressed, I finger brush my hair. Did they forget that part? Surely, not . . .

I pad back to the bedroom. Nothing.

Then it hits me, I haven't seen a toilet. I wander the perimeter, until I find a small white door in the back of the room. I wave a hand in front of the access button, and it slides open. Inside is a wall-mounted slimline toilet. Pristine white makes up every surface, every item. To my left is a vanity. Toothbrush, paste and hairbrush sit to the right of the one flat, arched faucet. They are lined up like soldiers. An inch from the edge, half inch apart. I pick up the brush. It's light, tinny, but feels nice as I pull it through my wet hair.

I pad back to my bed, still untangling the wet mass with the tinny brush. I flick the cream, embossed folder open. As promised, the access card and schedule sit on top. I run a finger down the page. Breakfast, oh seven hundred. First up is induction for three hours. Then I skip down the page to where the word flight simulator glares at me from the page.

I know it's not real heights, or even a real aircraft. But my gut roils under the weight of the two words. Terror snakes up my spine. Bile surges up my throat.

I can't do this.

Not one bit.

3

CLARA

THE NOISE of the machines is deafening over my earmuffs. Vivi weaves back and forth beside her machine, sending colored fabric through it. So many yards run through her now yellow stained hands, it may as well be miles. My own hands are a sickening shade of green. The fabric not even completely dry before it reaches us after being dyed.

The factory floor houses twenty printing machines. Vivi and I were lucky enough to be assigned neighboring ones. A floor supervisor stands rigid, his hands clasped behind his back in the center of the factory floor. They oversee the output, as the newly printed materials are spooled and rattled into crates, ready for shipment to Sontaria.

Vivi is waving a hand. Her mouth makes my name, but I don't hear a thing. I raise both hands in a gesture I hope she receives as 'what'. She points. Her pallet of dyed fabric is down to its last roll. And the roll currently feeding her printer is about to run out. I double check mine is feeding in okay, still with plenty to go, and rush over to help her lug it up and into the metal saddle rests. It's heavy, like dead body heavy.

We grunt under the weight and struggle to get each long end into the waiting saddles. When her end drops in with a clunk, I lower mine down. She smiles at me and waves me off. I jog back to my machine; it's making a whirring sound I haven't heard before. The fabric twists and jams.

Dammit.

I duck under the long, wide sail of green as it tugs and grinds against the machine. I pull it back with both hands. It doesn't budge. I put my weight into it. The machine clunks hard. I growl and duck out from under the fabric.

I hit the red stop button and the supervisor marches over. They'll be wanting an explanation for why I am losing productive minutes. Every inch we produce tallies toward our ranking.

"Problem, Bendall?" he says, his dark eyes scan me before tracking to the fabric-strangled machine.

"I can't get it to release. It's stuck fast."

"You try tugging it backward while it's running?"

"Yup." I watch as he runs a hand through his dark, tufty hair. His stitched-on name badge says A Remmins. He looks around thirty, at least. His stubble-lined jaw clenches as he tries to adjust the fabric. His arms flex, the muscle in his forearms cord and settle when he lets go of the material. He shoves a metal lever at the side of the rollers, and they split apart.

"Try to pull it back again and feed it through," he says, still eyeing the machine.

"Clear?" I glance at him, double checking his hands are nowhere near the mouth when I hit the start-up button. The roar drowns out the rest of the machines around us. With a soft clunk and a whir, the fabric starts to feed through; a little crooked it straightens and processes fine. "Thanks, Remmins."

He smiles, nodding softly before striding back to the middle of the floor where he runs his gaze over the rest of the machines. Vivi catches mine and winks. I roll my eyes at her, and she huffs a laugh I don't hear and returns to her work. The roll of green starts to rattle and jump as the fabric runs out fast. I whistle and Vivi somehow hears me, appearing by my side to load up the next.

I slow the machine and when the last inch of green disappears through the metal rollers, I feed the new sky blue in behind it. I wonder how many of the city's citizens will end up wearing this particular blue. Would Tessa find it? Her favorite color has always been light blue. She would look wonderful in a summer dress made from this fabric. Or maybe a shirt . . .

The machine growls. The fabric unravels and hits the floor.

Heavens above.

I slam a hand over the stop button. What is it with this damned fabric. The slippery feel of it washes over my skin as I try to bundle it up, acutely aware of Remmin's gaze on me.

Of the minutes that fly past and my dwindling quota. My cheeks flush as I try to roll the material back onto the bolt. It slips and pools at my feet.

"Shit."

A hand rests over mine.

Brown eyes topped by lowered brows stare at me. "Roll it back, Bendall."

"I know," I snap.

His face doesn't change. With quick hands he rolls the bolt back, smoothing it over as he goes. He makes this look easy. When the bolt is neat, he nods and walks back to the center. This time he folds his hands over his chest, not meeting my gaze.

What the hell's that about?

I turn back and start the machine, ensuring the blue is stretched out properly, and dial the speed right back. Quota be damned, I am not going to be needing his help every other minute. I watch the blue fabric sway and dip as it feeds into the rollers. Something black jumps over the stretched blue as it moves toward the intake. A dead cockroach. Its flattened wings splayed out.

The good people of Sontaria would be horrified to find dead insect in their opulent garments. I flick at it with a hand. It slides toward the intake. Jumping as the machine tugs the fabric into its greedy mouth. I swipe at it again and my fingers brush it. It flicks toward the shining, heaving metal rollers.

I reach over and swipe at it again. My fingers hit the

rollers. It pinches them, dragging my pinkie and ring finger between it.

"Ah! Shit!!"

Fire bursts through my fingers, hand and up my arm. Vivi is at my side instantly. Her hand slams the stop button. I hold my wrist with a shaking hand.

Every breath burns.

Remmins rushes to the machine, shoving the metal lever at the rollers upwards with a heavy grunt. Why didn't I think of that? Vivi holds my upper arm, as if I need holding up. I suck in ragged lungfuls of air and retract my hand from the rollers. My two fingers are a little flatter. Blood lines the sides.

"Infirmary now!" Remmins barks.

He plucks a radio from his hip and jabbers something followed by a number. He nods for Vivi to return to her machine. It takes everything I have not to sit down. My head is spinning. Remmins puts a hand on the elbow of my good arm and leads me off the factory room floor. When we reach the corridor, another officer replaces Remmins, taking a stance in between the rows of machines.

"What happened?" Remmins says, his voice void of emotion.

"There was an insect. I tried to sweep it off."

He looks down at me as we walk along. His mouth turns down, brows following.

"What? Can't have the good people of Sontaria wearing dead bug . . . sir." A slight tweak of cheekiness creeps into my voice. Despite the very real chance of reprimand, I don't try to take it back, only looking ahead, trying to ignore the pain now shooting up my arm. But when I glance over to Remmins, his face is cracked into a small smile. Did he just find my joke funny?

"Maybe I should have left it to its fate?" I say dryly.

He turns me toward a closed door. Green stenciled letters are painted to the left of it—INFIRMARY.

"Thanks, I can take it from here."

He looks down at his hand still on my elbow and drops it instantly. "Depending on what the Medicos say, I will see you back on the floor tomorrow, zero eight hundred hours, Bendall."

"No, I need to finish my quota. I can't get ranked down."

"You're out for the day."

"No, sir. With all due respect, I need to finish my shift. I can do it with one hand."

His head tilts and he schools his face. "Not a chance."

He opens the door and a nurse in green military pants and shirt greets me.

She takes one look at my hand and glances toward Remmins. "Inside, please."

I turn back to protest, only to see my supervisor's back receding down the corridor. I follow the nurse inside and she sits me on a stretcher. She puts a pillow on my lap and rests my hand on it. A second later, something sharp bites my neck. A male Medico stands behind me with a forced smile and a depressed syringe. The pain that had turned to throbbing on the walk here fades quickly. The nurse in front of me rests an icepack on my hand and walks away.

Half an hour later, she cleans and bandages my fingers. "I've seen much worse. This should be okay in a few days. I will write you up for some painkillers. Take two twice a day for the next week. Back here for review in seven days. You should be good for shift in two days' time."

I nod.

She lets me go.

I walk toward the door. But as I turn back to thank her for her help, I take in the long stretcher-lined room. Half of the beds are occupied by other factory workers. But they don't appear injured. No casts or bandages. Nothing. Like they are sick, not injured. When she looks up from her paperwork and I am still in the doorway, I smile and back out, shutting the door softly.

Two officers walk down the hall ahead of me, chatting. I follow them, making my way back to the factory floor. Maybe I can convince Remmins I'm not useless?

"Another one yesterday," the officer on the right says, shoving a clipboard under his arm. Their conversation piques my interest.

"How many does that make the month?" The other says.

"Nine in total. But there are more in the infirmary. Most of them are not showing signs of improving."

"Damn, I was hoping they would keep it in the south where it came from. Must have rolled in with the recruits from south Province last month."

"We will keep them contained. No need to spread it around."

"This stays between us. We don't want that sort of information leaking to the factory workers."

I fall back a little, hyper aware of making my footsteps silent. But I have just overheard something I wasn't supposed to. I take a right turn and head back to the factory floor. The hum of the machines drifts out under the door. I push my way through, slipping around as quick as I can, hoping they don't recognize me at least. I turn back after ensuring the door closes properly, and smack into blue. A solid wall of it. Arms across his chest.

Brown eyes look down at me, a frown etched onto Remmin's face. "Go back to your quarters," he says, nodding to the hand I'm absentmindedly nursing.

"I'm fine, let me finish out the shift, please?"

He shakes his head. "Nope."

"Honestly, I—"

He grabs my arm and walks me back through the door and into the corridor. He's close. He smells like soap, not a glycerin bar. And something heady and masculine. My heart flings in my chest as I look up at him. His Adam's apple bobs, and he releases me after a heartbeat. "Now, Bendall, or I'll escort you." He doesn't put space between us, and I study him. A broad face, angled jaw.

He holds my gaze, his not changing. Stoic. Stone.

"Fine, but can I do extra tomorrow?"

"How many days off did the infirmary give you?"

"None," I lie.

He raises an eyebrow. "Fine."

He waits until I walk away, heading toward our quarters, before slipping back inside the large factory space. I make my way to quarters. Inside I decide on a shower, I'm sweaty from rushing and hauling heavy bolts for six hours. With no one else around, I can take as long as I like.

Stripping off I take the longest shower I have since we arrived here a week ago. Feeling a little guilty, I twist the tap off and wrap a towel around myself. A minute later, I'm pulling on my standard-issue pants and t-shirt. Wet hair hangs in tangles around my shoulders, soaking my shirt.

A blaring alarm starts. Oscillating loudly through the quarters. An amber light by the door flashes.

What the hell?

I grab up my boots and fly out the door, sprinting down the corridor for the factory floor. Amber lights flash every hundred yards. The sound getting louder with every stride. Officers run down the corridor toward me from the infirmary. Their medical issue uniforms familiar from earlier. They rush through the doors to the factory floor I just left. I follow them through.

The machines hum on idle and every worker crowds around in the center of the room. I push through. Weaving, I negotiate my way to the front of the crowd. Remmins crouches by one of the new recruits. Trina. She is on the floor, barely breathing. Her face is red. Her arms curled over her chest—hands cramped to claws. Her body trembles.

"Stay back," he says before turning back to meet my gaze. "Can't you follow basic instructions, Bendall? You're supposed to be in your quarters." He stares at me for a heart-beat, eyes stuck on my wet hair and the soaked through shirt that does nothing to cover my hard peaks in the cool factory room.

He tracks his focus back to Trina. She is mumbling something incoherent. The Medicos swoop in and move her to a stretcher.

Remmins stands. "Clear a path!"

He's waving both hands. The crowd disperses and Trina is carried out. Vivi steps over to where I stand. "What the hell was that?"

"I wasn't here, what happened?"

"She just went all rigid, then her face got red, and she had some kind of fit . . . It was—" She shudders and shakes her head.

The disease?

And it's on our factory floor.

I catch Remmins's gaze. He stares at me for a long, slow second. His radio squawks and he snatches it up, snapping out a reply. Another voice responds. He closes his eyes, clenching his jaw.

When he opens them again, he looks around the room. "Everybody out! Quarantine, now!"

CHAPTER 4
TESSA

INHALE.

Exhale.

I stare at the shiny, silver door to the simulator. Flight simulation, the first of many. What I wouldn't do to have the floor open up and swallow me whole right now . . .

"Enter the simulator, officer Bendall." Smooth syllable seep through my headpiece.

His voice is like molten caramel. Like the delicious steam in my shower room that curls around my skin. Instantly, I relax. I have been hearing his voice on the recordings we used in induction and in the training materials. My attending trainer up until this point has been a woman, so this man remains a mystery. An audibly divine mystery . . .

I have his face already envisioned. His hands, strong. His hair, soft as I run my hands through them—

"Now, Bendall."

I shake my head and open my eyes, waving a hand over the small, blue-lit panel. It flashes. "Yes, sir."

The door whooshes open, revealing a darkened cockpit. A single pilot's chair sits behind a console of screens, dull-lit panels and so on. I step into the space, and I swear it shrinks around me. I drop into the seat and the harness slides over my lap and shoulders, securing around my waist. Strapped to the seat there's no escape.

"Welcome to the simulation," a robotic woman's voice hums.

It does nothing to settle the panicked hummingbird behind my ribs. My heart rate and breathing are displayed on the screen. Great, now it's on record that I'm a flake.

Awesome.

"We will start with basic pre-flight checks," the velvety voice says through the headset.

"Okay."

I assume he hears everything I say.

"Good. I will walk you through the process. There is also a checklist on screen in front of you. To access that, you can tap the check icon. Do you see it?"

"Yes, I see it." I tap the check icon and the list fades in on center screen.

"You should be familiar with each item on the list from your training manuals. Can you confirm this?"

"Yes, I recognize them all."

"Good. Good."

I release a ragged breath.

"To test the first three items on the list, you can do a visual check and tap them when you're satisfied they are sufficient. Then they will disappear."

"Okay," I say, running my eye over the fuel cell gauges, the disrupter settings, lateral, and vertical thrusters. Tapping the items, as he said they disappear, the list moves up. Cool. The nervous twist in the pit of my stomach unravels slightly, and I drag in a breath. Maybe I can do this?

"Now, next on the list are biometrics. Rest your palm over the small rectangle to your right."

I press my palm onto it, and it scans quickly. The item on the list disappears automatically and my baseline metrics fill a small box to the left of the screen.

"Good." His voice is softer.

I glance up and see my heart rate is elevated. Urgh, how embarrassing.

"What's next?" I say, desperate for us to move on to the next part.

"Next is navigation. For this exercise we're going to run simulation one, from Headquarters to dock one at the Province. N1. It's pre-programmed. Tap the number one in the auto-nav list."

I do so and a map appears over the bottom of the screen.

"Good."

I soak up that one word like it's the last drop of water on the earth.

"Now, Bendall, you can start her up."

My breathing deepens and . . . it displays on the biometrics.

Shit.

"Take a long, slow breath. You can do this, Tessa."

A strangled laugh huffs through my lips. He has no idea. My tangled, conflicted emotions surge through my veins. This sim. His voice. I can't tell anymore which is sending the electricity through my veins.

Smashing the heel of my palm over the power button, the simulator drones to life, and the sound fades to a low hiss. A control panel slides from the bottom of the display.

Controls.

The seat under me vibrates a little, like it would in a real aircraft with the movement of the engines. Four disrupter engines to be precise. Maneuverable, from vertical to horizontal and back and forth as needed. The thought of take-off sends bile into my throat.

"Excellent. You will see on the control panel are your orientations?" he says.

A large arrow fills the screen. A horizontal bar on the left of it. Four round icons, one in each corner. A large red bar lines the bottom of the panel.

"Yes, got it."

"The arrows are directional control. The sliding bar to the left is altitudinal control. The four icons are for controlling different aspects of your craft which we cover in the later weeks. The large red bar is ammunition. Don't hit that one unless you are planning on blowing something, or someone, up."

"Okay?"

Warm, throaty chuckles filter into the headpiece. My insides melt, sending butterflies into flight through my center. I cringe, hoping my heart rate and breathing didn't spike. This is going to take some getting used to. Find some self-control Tessa. Urgh.

Can he see me? My face flushes with the thought. Clearing my head with a shake, I resolve myself to learning this job the best I can since I'm in no position to screw up. Not if I want to climb the ranks and have a way to find my sister.

Self-sabotage and falling down the rungs of the ladder is not an option, with getting sent to the Wastelands such a risk. As I found out from a few cautionary tales we were told in the first day of induction.

You screw up in Sontaria then your only option is no-man's land. Without a transferable skill to the Sectors you're dead weight.

"Bendall, focus."

"Sorry."

"Let's run through the checklist again and then we will go through the start-up procedure once more."

"Yep."

I sit straighter in the chair and glance around the screen. It's not like I can actually see the ground below us in the cockpit anyway. Right?

"Start the process of pre-flights, saying out loud what you're doing."

Homing my focus back to the screen, I scan the barely familiar display, but it is still on the run through we just did. "How do I go back to the start?"

"Tap the power down icon twice."

Two taps on the power button fast with my pointer finger. The screen goes black for a moment, and I hold my breath as the last of the light disappears from the small space. The silence is too much. I open my mouth to ask if something went wrong when the screen flashes and the blue-lit panel steadies. What was that about?

"Sorry, hold on." The trainer's voice is strained.

My heart rate elevates, blood rushing fast. If the controls fail does that mean the cockpit door won't open?

Oh shit.

"Right," his voice snaps me up from the shrinking space. I force myself to listen to his tone, hanging on each velvety syllable. Anything but the fact that I'm stuck in a small, confined metal tube that may or may not let me out. Eyes stuck on the panel that opens the door, I try to memorize where it is in relation to my seat, to my hand, my body.

"Hit the check mark again and run me through the procedure."

Running through the checklist again, I explain everything I'm doing and why. Everything that's outlined in the training manual I've been pouring over for the last week. When I finish, he simply says, "Good."

I wait for more, but he doesn't say anything else. "Hello?"

"Sorry," he finally responds.

If I had nerves before, they are cranking back to life again with every moment that passes in this too tiny cockpit.

"Bendall, power up, please. The only white icon on the dashboard."

Pressing a finger to the white circle with a half line through it, the sim whirs to life. Engine specs light up across the dash, undulating through the gauge markers before settling. The control panel slides out to me automatically and I hover a hand over it, waiting for my next instruction.

Nothing comes.

"Do I shut it down?" I ask the void.

"Hold." Is his only response.

What the hell is going on? Is this some kind of mental tactic to see how pilots react to uncertainty? Trying to tamper the thundering in my head, I take slow steadying breaths and the bounding in my veins settles. The screen in front of me flickers then stabilizes. I slap my hand to the door panel. Just as my fingers brush its smooth surface, all light disappears from the cockpit.

Oh hell.

I run my hand up and down the small panel, frantically. Nothing happens. The darkness invades every sense, until stars begin to creep into my periphery.

Shit!

Banging on the door with a fist, the harness tugs around me.

Dammit, that's also electric.

I'm trapped!

"Hello! Please, help!"

With two trembling fists and fast evaporating nerves, I bash on the door. The harness bites into my right shoulder and hip. My breaths shallow out. And the stars that were creeping in now flood in with full force.

Something hits the sim.

That's right, there's other people here. The trainer knows I'm in here. I push a palm over my chest, trying to steady my stupid racing heart and huff a tangled laugh before stifling a sob.

My head and my left hand come to rest on the door. *Please don't take forever to get me out of here.*

A familiar voice calls to me from outside the sim. "Bendall?"

"Please, get me out." It's pathetic, I know. Scared of a small space. It literally can't hurt me. Tell that to my body.

Something hits the door. A small groan and a sliver of dim light splits the pitch black that's engulfing me.

The scrap of light is like looking directly at the sun. It's blinding but I can't look away after being in the swallowing darkness. A hand weaves around the door. At least I think it's a hand. With a grunt the door slides open halfway. Outside the sim is almost as black as it was a moment ago inside it. What the hell is going on?

A man in a uniform, similar to the one I wear, fills the doorway sideways. His hand reaches through and hits a button at the side of my seat. The harness releases and sags, and I exhale a breath of relief. The hand rises and waits for me to take it. Hesitating for a heartbeat, I place my shaking one into it and push out of the seat. The man moves back out of the door, pulling me through the dark's icy grip. I stumble my way through the confined space and down the steps, away from the sim.

"Power outage." His voice is the only thing I recognize about him. My trainer.

"Does this happen a lot?"

"No."

He drops my hand and walks toward the way out. I follow, wrapping my arms over my chest, trying not to let him slip too far ahead. I don't want to lose him in the dark.

He stops to open the door, hand fumbling for the small panel. But nothing is lit up and nothing happens. He pulls out a small metal bar, inserting it into the gap between the door and the jam. When he inches his hand through, he slides the door back and he holds it for me as I step through. We clear the training building, and the entire city is out. The usually bright lit streets of Sontaria are in darkness.

I glance at the trainer. In the dim light I can make out his basic features, his full head of messy dark hair and a square jaw. I can't tell his age or what he looks like. Only the shape of him, really.

It's three blocks back to my quarters.

"You can't go back alone," he says, striding toward my building. The high-rise is a blackout like all the rest when we make it back. He wanders around the side of the tall building and pushes through a door. A normal handle. Thank Heavens.

"Which level are you?" he asks.

"Forty."

Entering the stairwell I didn't even realize the building had, he waits for me to follow.

"I can go the rest of the way by myself," I offer.

"In a dark stairwell for forty floors?"

"Sure," I breathe. I don't want to be rude but I also don't need his protection. I grew up in the Provinces for Heaven's sake.

"Suit yourself, I can stay behind you if you like. But your safety is my responsibility until you clock off training. That's another hour yet."

Walking up the stairs, I don't reply. Him behind me is a little weird. After the first ten flights I turn back. "You can walk up front if that would suit you better?"

I can't really see his face, but I swear he smiles. He takes the stairs two at a time until he's in front of me. We continue to ascend. Now, I'm staring at his ass in a darkened stairwell almost short of breath. This isn't any better.

I hurry to catch up and step beside him. He turns and I think he offers a smile through the dark. He smells so good. And I clench my jaw, forcing the thought from my mind.

His aftershave, or whatever, is woodsy with a hint of

caramel. Or maybe it's my overactive imagination that's already latched onto his voice. If my heart wasn't already thumping from climbing a ton of stairs, I would think he has some kind of effect on me. An absolute eon later, we reach the last door in the stairwell. Floor forty.

He opens the door and I walk past, not looking back.

I could . . .

I can't.

I want to . . .

I won't.

"Goodnight, Tessa."

My heart skips a stupid beat. Nodding, I wave a hand over my door. In my daze of wood and caramel intoxication I forgot it's not going to open. His hand presses to my hip, moving me to the side. Heat floods my face.

I force air past the stone that introduced itself to my airway as he jimmy's the door open with the metal bar. Obviously, he's had to do this before.

He stands holding my door back. I will my feet to move. My eyes to pull away from the outline of him the dark offers up.

Finally, my feet move.

Crossing the threshold, the door slides closed as his hand drops away. The last thing I see is his stare. With my eyes fixed on the dimmed white door, my whole body hums.

Damn.

4

CLARA

REMMINS stands in front of me. His jaw tight, brown eyes burning into mine. For some reason whenever I look at him, all I see is sadness. Right now, though, it's midnight. I'm not supposed to be on the factory floor. Nor is he. But here we are. Me trying desperately to catch up on my quota. Him, standing in my damn way.

Unlike me, he doesn't need to fulfil a quota, so I stand my ground. His hand is clasped over the start button of my machine, he stands in my space. Hate to break it to him, but he won't win this one. I'll be making up for my lost quota from my half-day with the injury and then the twenty-four-hour quarantine. I'm doing this, with or without his permission.

"Go back to your quarters, Bendall."

"No."

"You are absolutely defiant. You know that, right?"

"Whatever, move, I can't miss my quota."

"Leave. Before I drag you out."

"Nope, not going anywhere."

"What if I told you, you don't have anything to make up?" Moving closer, his face is inches from mine. I narrow my eyes. What the hell is he talking about?

"What do you mean?"

"Your quota is full for your half-day."

"How? I wasn't here!"

"I was."

Stunned, I glare at him. He did my work? Why? What are the other Engineers going to think? And say?

"Don't worry it's not blackmail, Clara. Just wanted to help." His voice is softer, eyes tracking to where my hand rests on his still from trying to pry his fingers off the button.

Clara.

Remmins called me Clara.

I tilt my head. He wanted to help me? Really? His eyes are trained to my face. It's possible he's telling the truth.

"Why would you do that, Remmins?"

"Don't—" He runs a hand through his hair. His focus drops to my mouth, and something like hurt flashes in those brown eyes. "Forget it."

Oh.

Ohhhhhh.

Pulling his hand out, he makes space between us. "Do whatever you want. If another senior officer catches you here, I can't help you." Turning away from the machine he walks away.

As the doors swish closed behind him, I lean on the machine. He did that for me? Does he do that for all his Engineers? The hurt that flickered through his eyes sends my gut into a twist of knots.

Hell. I'm an ass.

A world-grade ass.

I stride from the factory and push through the doors, listening for his footsteps. When his familiar stride echoes away from me to the right, I turn and jog to catch up to him. As I round the corridor, he swipes his access card for his quarters. I stop short. Does he expect something in return for his help?

Maybe.

Do I want to be under this man?

Not only under him . . .

He turns back, noticing me. I wander closer but when I open my mouth to thank him nothing comes. His hand slips from the door handle and he pads to where I stand.

At least six inches taller, he crowds me against the wall. So close. He drops his gaze to mine, raising my chin with his hand. I swallow hard and his fingers fall away. He searches my face for a handful of heartbeats, and I want to say something. Anything. Still, nothing comes.

Instead, I study his face, the angles the dark eyes and messy hair. The uniform, tight rolled-up sleeves over toned arms. The start of lines on his face, older than me by at least a decade, his clean-shaven face is already shadowed. He's sturdy and grounding, simply being in his orbit.

I want to.

My breath catches when I look up to his darkened brown eyes. He tucks a strand of my wavy hair behind my ear. My insides melt as I breathe him in, letting my eyes wander over his broad shoulders, and his throat as it works. His hands now hang by his sides. His chest heaves.

"Clara, you can come in. But please know I don't expect you to because—"

Smashing my mouth to his I swallow his last word. He smiles against my lips. I send my hands through his hair, and he spins, pressing my back to the wall beside his door. I want to rip his uniform from his toned, muscled body and drown in every inch of him. It's been so long since I've wanted this.

To let myself take what I need from a man. No strings.

He crowds me against the wall further and I open my mouth, letting him claim it with his tongue. His body presses against mine hard. His hands are around my face, then they travel down my neck. His rock-hard length rubs my center. Heat pools deep in my belly.

Not close enough.

Too many clothes.

Not enough—

Footsteps march down the corridor toward us, and he releases me. His head snaps toward the sound. "You should go."

What?

"Um, okay?"

He turns back, eyes void of whatever was burning us both alive only a second ago.

"Sure," I utter and push a step forward. Did he change his mind? It's his prerogative, I guess. Supervisor-Engineer relations would be frowned upon anyway. His loss.

Fixing my hair and straightening my shirt, heading down the hall toward my quarters, I don't look back. No harm, no foul. He did make up my quota, so I guess I can't be angry at him.

Maybe he was trying to be a gentleman? Or he has a partner. At any rate we got carried away. It will *not* be happening again.

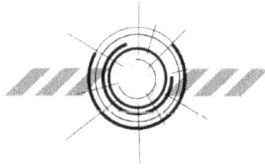

AFTER TWO WEEKS of being on the Textiles floor and meeting our first tier of quotas, sitting around the mess hall, we wait for the ranks to be announced. Remmins stands at the front with three other officers. His uniform is less decorated than theirs. Only a single bar of grey across the top part of his right sleeve whereas the others have three.

Remmins scans the room. His glance washes over me as it does every other Engineer. Something like disappointment rolls in my gut, and I train my eyes to the senior officer who steps forward. Evans.

"This fortnight we have had some impressive numbers. We have also had some mediocre ones. More machine faults have been lodged this fortnight than any other period in the past twelve months. So, listen now and listen well. An Engineer is only as good as the machine they tend. Blaming your equipment for your poor quotas doesn't stand. Complaints and perceived faults are not taken into consideration for this round's tally."

My heart races, sending a stone sinking through my belly. My machine faltered. I lost time and quota because of it. Not to mention acquiring an injury in the process.

Hell.

Murmurs start up around me. Obviously, I am not the only one would has issue with this.

"Quiet down!" Evans says.

The hall goes silent.

"The following ten Engineers are staying on in this facility. Jamieson, Alex. Henders, Eve . . ." He continues down the list.

My name isn't on it.

Stiffening, I grip the edge of the metal bench seat. Vivi's name wasn't on there either. She sucks in a breath beside me.

"The following are on probation for another two weeks, pending a further quota. Meers, Vivi. Johnson, Nigel. Sanders, Jake. Bendall, Clara . . ."

I release a pent-up breath and turn to find Vivi. She is white as a sheet. Nobody wants to be demoted a Sector, and absolutely nobody wants to be sent Wastelands way. Vivi's head hits my shoulder. She mutters a curse word.

"Tell me about it," I whisper.

She huffs a small laugh into my arm.

We have another chance. But now we have to prove ourselves all over again. Half of the Engineers in our intake will be sent to other Sectors. After more preliminary testing, they will reallocate them accordingly. I glance around the room searching the faces of the people I have bunked with for the last two weeks. It occurs to me that I haven't really talked to any of them, let alone made any friends. Vivi being the only exception.

I should try harder. With the Engineers that are staying at least. I turn back to suggest to Vivi we should celebrate still being here, and I find her chatting with the blond guy beside her. They smile at each other. He is a little shy or coy. Maybe somewhere in between. It's sweet. Evans dismisses us for the day, and we file out of the hall. Vivi and her friend are stuck fast to the metal bench.

I lean over. "Hey, you two coming?"

She spins back, her face flushing. Oh shit. I stifle a laugh and she slaps my arm.

"Ouch, what was that for?"

"I'll see you later," she says, turning back to her friend. His hands trace the studs on the metal seat as he smiles at her. I straighten up and walk back to the dorm. Roommates mill around, some stripping off for the showers, some laying on their bunk. Half of our dorm, however, starts to pack.

The half that didn't make the cut.

That could've been me. It almost was. I'm going to have to work even harder to keep my tentative spot. Can't have Remmins covering for me every time I get behind. I have to work smarter, that's all there is to it.

The bell for supper blasts through the dorms and the last of my roommates file out. I slip my boots off and lay on my bunk, letting my eyes drift shut. I'll wait for the crowd to die off before making my way to the days last meal.

The shower is still running. Not unusual. Someone else must have the same idea as me. When the water stops, I realize it was on the men's side of our dorm.

Water drips on my bed, then onto my arm and I open my eyes. One of the guys stands over me, a towel hanging from his hips precariously. Johnson, I think. His name was on the tentative list also. I so don't have the mental space for this.

"You waiting for me, Bendall?" His eyes rove over my body.

"Screw you, Johnson."

"*Or* I could screw you instead." He runs a hand through his dripping blond hair.

My burning stare meets his blue eyes, he narrows them, as if challenge excepted.

"Yeah, nope."

"Really? Is that what you told Remmins?"

Bolting up to my feet I'm in his space in a heartbeat.

How dare he talk about Remmins as if he is some low life, opportunistic sleaze bag.

"My life, my quotas, my body, are *none* of your business. If I was you, I'd watch my mouth. Slurring off about a senior officer will have you kicked off the temp list. I'm sure you'd fit right in somewhere in the heart of the Wastelands."

He squares his shoulders and folds his arms over his wet chest. "You know it's funny, how someone with an injured hand could have made the cut. I mean, you missed half a shift of quotas. Yet somehow, you miraculously still had a solid count. You only screw the supervisors, hey Bendall?"

I slam my good fist into his nose, and he staggers backward. The towel drops from his hips as he grabs his nose to stem the bleeding. My knuckles burn but I ignore them. Now, I run my eyes down his body, slow. Making sure he's watching me do it. Then I step into his space again. "One, stop keeping tabs on me. Two, no, I only screw gentlemen. And you Johnson are not one."

I stalk for the door. All of a sudden, the supper crowd doesn't sound so bad.

"You know you won't last another two weeks, Clara!"

I let the door close behind me.

Asshole.

Rushing out into the corridor I slam into a wall of man.

Seriously?

I mumble an apology, but the wall doesn't move. When I lift my glare, I can't believe how this day went from bad to worse. Standing inches from me, jaw clenched, eyes narrowed with annoyance is Nate freaking Prendergast.

Nate.

Of all people.

I scan him, and back up a step. *Why* is he here?

So much for Sector One, Prendergast.

Screw my life.

5

TESSA

I TILT MY HEAD, dislodging the ridiculous thoughts of the man with the voice that gets under my skin with one syllable. He's my trainer. He was being responsible. Don't over think this, Tessa.

Just. Don't.

If Clara was here, she would be shaking me, telling me to use my head and not end up trapped in every ache that squeezes my stupid heart. I mean our parents loved us. They loved us well. Why do I do this? Always search for something that doesn't exist . . .

I shove my head into my hands. Stars burst into my dark vision as I press the heel of my palm into my eyes—hard. The black fades only a little, as I lift my head. With the power still out, I slide down the door onto my butt and let my head fall back. Why would the most prestigious place in our Ring struggle with power outages?

Why were they unexpected? Why was no one prepared?

Something doesn't make sense. The gadget on my wrist beeps. Supper. I guess there will be no dining hall today. And with the food dispenser dormant, the snacks on my desk will have to suffice.

A half-eaten bag of carbo snacks sits open. Snatching it up, I pour some of the crunchy pieces into my mouth. They are slightly salty, but the crunch is so satisfying. Resting against the desk on one hip I finish off the packet and wash it down with a bottle of water. With my door jammed, I can't go out, so I decide to go back to my studies.

Sliding onto the chair, I flip through the print outs we were given at the induction. All of the materials are on my Visi-Screen, but now it's a lifeless chunk of rectangle glass staring back at me. I drag a finger over the information until I come to the part I was up to last time I sat in this chair. Aerodynamics of the Viper978.

The schematics are so familiar. They're almost burnt into my brain at this point. The thin blue lines scrawled over the page in the shape of the aircraft that has more technology embedded into it than the main Headquarters of Sontaria. The fact that the city trusts me with one of these still blows my mind. The Elite's are given so much that Engineers will never have—and never see. My thoughts cease, and Clara's sweet face floods my mind.

If only there was a way to send her a message, or a comms without both of us getting hauled over the coals for it. Maybe, I could send a message to Textiles, attention to Clara Bendall. Would she understand it? Would they punish her for my infraction? I'm an Elite, she's an Engineer, there is no doubt where they would lay the blame.

None.

With a sigh, I push from my chair and pad to the large window. Plopping onto the long cushion I cradle my knees with my arms. Laying my head on the glass I peruse the city. Dark smothers most parts of the city. The central building, Headquarters, is lit up like a search light amongst the dimmed structures that circumvent it. They must have an alternative power source.

That's it!

If I can make it to Headquarters, I can send a comms to Clara. With the power outage it's likely it will be missed, at least long enough to make it through to her end. But my door is wedged shut.

The trainer had a flat bar to open it last time. I hunt around my room for something long and flat; the right shape to wedge between the door and the jam. I stalk to the bathroom. Nothing. Back to the drawers. I fling each one open with force, the power not there to hold them closed.

Nothing.

I move to my bed. The white linens are tucked under tight.

Underneath . . .

Rushing the mattress, I flip it up. Slender, thin metal slats hold my mattress above the frame.

Yes!!

I tug one up, grab my access card from the desk, and

head for the door. Sliding the slat between the door and the jam, I pull. Wrench it back. Wriggle it forward. Push with my weight.

It doesn't budge.

I dig it in as far as it can go and push it forward.

The door slips backward, and I let out a squeal of delight. It slips and clunks shut.

Damn.

Again. This time, I hold my body still, my focus is homed between the jam and the door. The door slips back, and I shove a hand into the gap opening it further and drop the metal. As soon as I can fit my body through the space, I duck past and let the door slide shut behind me. Should I have brought the slat with? Too late now, I guess.

I head for the stairwell. Going down forty flights is less work than up, but by the twentieth floor my legs shake. I'm a bundle of nerves and take a break on the stairs. Everything is so quiet. Too quiet.

Running down the last few flights of stairs, I push out into the darkened street. The central building is like a beacon leading the way to its flame. Drawing this little moth in.

Breaking into a sprint I keep to the shadows. Even in the city of glass bad things can happen. They don't report on things like that in Sontaria, but stories, gossip, spread like wildfire amongst those bored by a cushy life. I've lost count of the tales I've heard in the dining hall when nobody thinks anyone is listening. I sometimes think all this wealth and advantage makes the city a worse place. A more dangerous place than the Provinces and the Sectors.

I come to yet another small alley. Only one block from Headquarters, I turn into it and follow the trail of light. A figure rushes toward me. I flatten against the wall beside me. He gains on me fast—hoody up. Black clothes clad his large frame. My heart thunders, my mind reeling with panic. Do I run? Or stay still and hope he won't see me? A foot from where I stand his head snaps up, and dark brown eyes drill into mine. My breath lodges—stuck tight.

His shoulder brushes me as he runs past, but he doesn't stop, ducking his head. He doesn't turn back. It's like he didn't want me to see *him*. I peel myself from the wall and suck in much needed air.

Refocusing myself to the task at hand, I take off at a jog, and close in on the central building. Still in the alley, I settle my breathing. If I'm going to walk into Comms, I need to at least appear like I'm supposed to be there.

Setting my shoulders back I slip out of the shadowed side street. I walk across the street between the hushed swooshes of the vehicles still moving between the curbs. When I reach the bottom of the thirty-odd steps that precede the glittering glass doors of Headquarters, I stop. Ensuring my uniform is still neat and tidy, I hold my head high and walk up the stairs. It's after nine at night, but it's not unusual for Elites of all departments to frequent HQ.

I pass a handful of Elites from the Medico branch. One of the girls smiles at me. Her uniform is the same as mine;

but where Aeronautical Elites have light blue, hers is deep red. A pair of Elites from Leadership stand discussing something heated. Their grey uniforms immaculate, still, at this hour. I push through the rotating glass door. No automatics here. Ironic as it is, they have minimal technology to remind the good people of Sontaria of their once humble roots.

The foyer is packed, like it never has been before. People from all departments are chatting to city officers. Most likely arguing their problems are more pressing than anyone else's. At least they are all distracted.

I make a left turn before the front desk and slip past a group of men discussing which part of the city is the most affected. Making it to the stairwell, I glance back before ducking inside. From memory, as part of our induction tour, Comms should be level three.

Easy.

At the third level entrance, commotion is muffled somewhere behind the thick, heavy door. It sounds like lots of people. Hopefully they won't notice me in the hustle? I walk through the door, head high, like I am meant to be here. Despite my blue uniform amongst their navy ones, I appear calm. Maybe no-one will pick up on it? Giant screens are lit up at the front wall of the most enormous room I have ever seen.

Rows and rows of slimline white desks fill the floor. Elites occupy most of the desks. An earpiece, so small it's almost missed, sits snug tight in their right ears. Every single one of them taking some kind of call. Or relaying information at speed into their Visi-Screen. My breathing shallows and my hands shake.

Making a B-line for the last row of Visi-Screens I slink down into the seat. My access card on my hip catches on the chair. I rip it off and drop it onto the desk. Plucking the earpiece from the glossy white surface, I slide it into my ear. Static squeals and I cringe.

Skimming over the long list of correspondence, I search for anything relevant to Sector Two. A comms with the subject 'Rebel Militia' catches my eye. Rebels? In the city? Another one about the unscheduled power outages. So, the city isn't in control of the power outages then . . . Curious. For a city that claims to be perfect with ultimate control over everything within its walls that seems nefarious.

Someone calls out a few rows in front of me, and I tap out of the comms and back to the list. Scanning. Hunting. The messages seem to be in order of Sector.

No time to waste, I tap the screen and bring up Sector Two comms. Tens of orders make up the list of communications, a few medical messages. Most of them are addressed to an officer, Commander Evans. A few have been sent to an A Remmins, Supervisor, Sector Two. One is about the last set of receipts.

I copy his comms address and start typing. But a few letters in, I still. What do I even say?

Finally, I tap out a message only she would recognize. Being the only set of siblings in our entire ring we have always had this familiarity to our advantage. She will know that what I type is false. And who sent it. Only her and I know such things. Only her and I would see through this ridiculous message.

I double check my spelling, and make sure her name is clearly at the top of the comms.

My hand trembles in front of the Visi-Screen.

"What are you doing in my seat?"

I turn my attention up to the gentle voice. A young woman with short red hair stares down at me, one eyebrow cocked, a coffee cup between her fine fingers.

"Ah, sorry, was told to fill in." I slide off the chair and skirt around her.

Her navy uniform is tight on her pretty hourglass frame. She tilts her head and smiles. "You can stay if you need to finish anything."

I glance at the screen and hit send. Her face is unreadable.

"No, all done." With a forced smile, stumbling backward, I turn and walk along the wall toward the stairwell door. And hope nobody takes issue with my bright blue in the sea of navy. The door gives way easy under hand as I spill into the stairwell, spluttering through a nervous laugh before jumping down the stairs three at a time. Elated, I fly through the foyer and out the glass door. I steady myself with a hand on the silver rail and jog down the steps.

More of the city is lit up now, some of the power must have been restored. I walk home at a slow pace, taking in everything around me. I wish Clara could see it. I mean, as elitist as the people may be here, it's a stunning place. Then again, I guess anything would look good after growing up in the Provinces. Where the only thing that held any wealth was family and smarts. The first because family is essential to survival. The second, essential to escaping a life of poverty and hard labor.

I reach my building and to my delight, the power is back on. Entering the silver doors, the doorman greets me with a crooked smile and raised eyebrow. He has never seen me out at night, unlike some of my peers who regularly test curfew.

"Evening, Miss Tessa," he says.

"Evening, Joe."

"Everything alright?"

"It is now." Gifting him a bright smile I hit the button for the lift.

The elevator slows at the last floor, and I step out and walk to my door. I swipe at my hip to open it but my hand comes up empty. No access card.

Where the?

Gut churning, my heart skips a beat.

It's still on the desk in comms.

With my stupid damn face, my department and officer number, all over it. Something is touching my ear. I raise a hand, fingers meeting plastic. I pull it away, letting it rest in my palm.

Bile claws its way up my throat at the sight and I swallow it back down.

The earpiece.

6

CLARA

SHUFFLES PULL me from restless sleep. I crack an eye open. The girl beside me is surrounded by Medicos. I jolt up on the bunk. A small gathering of roommates huddles by the showers, whispering, eyes wide. The Medico closest to her pulls a sheet over her face. I swing my legs over the bed and hit the floor.

"What happened?" I ask one of the guys who's consoling a girl tucked into his side under one arm.

"Izzy tried to wake her up so she wouldn't be late for mess hall duty. And didn't, obviously." He nods to the stretcher now carting the girl's body out the door.

"Does anyone know how she died?"

He throws me an impatient glance. But before I can ask another question Johnson walks over, and the smirk on his face sends bile rising. What did he do?

"You have something to do with this?" I spit. Each word laced with something deadly.

"Of course not!"

"You were right there, right next to her, Bendall. You had access, and motive."

"What the hell? Why would I want to kill one of my roommates?"

"Why would you not? First it was Trina," he waves a hand at the bunk to my right, "now her." His hand flings to the bunk at my left. "You're not exactly on solid footing at the moment. You could be off to Sector Three or even Four, any day now."

I cross my arms and close the distance between us. "As could you. How do we know it wasn't *you* who snuffed her out?"

He huffs an indignant laugh as if that's the most absurd thing he has ever heard. Honestly, I wouldn't put it past him. Ever.

"Nobody said she was murdered. You two cool your jets. She probably caught that disease Trina got. I heard it works fast on some blood types." The voice breaks us apart.

We both turn and stare at Michels. Even Johnson is stunned to silence. How does this guy know that kind of detail about the disease? Why are we being left to fend for ourselves and not being quarantined at the first sign of sickness?

"What else do you know that the rest of us don't Michels?" Johnson growls.

"Nothing much, that's it. Only what I overheard the

Medicos talking about in the infirmary last week when I was getting stitches taken out."

Johnson's gaze drops to the guy's arm. Sure enough, a rectangle bandage still covers the side of his wrist. An incident with a machine no doubt.

I turn my focus back to him. "Right, if the disease is contagious as you say, we should probably keep our distance. Anyone could have it."

The rest of our dorm moves out heading for breakfast; like one of our own didn't just turn stiff and get carted away. No ceremony or passing thought spared as they chat amongst one another and head out the door.

"Whatever, let's head to breakfast before the good stuff's all gone." The girl under his arm says with a sniff.

Despite being her closest roommate for the past two weeks I didn't really interact with her. Not getting attached to people is my number one strategy for surviving this place. Guilt for not getting to know her gnaws my gut over not talking to her when she had tried to strike up conversation the few times we were in close proximity.

"You coming?" Johnson waits by the door, his gaze sweeps over my singlet and sleep shorts.

"In a bit."

Ignoring the chill that slithers up my spine, grabbing up my uniform, I track to the nearest shower stall to change. Once I'm ready for the day's shift I pull on one boot, the other dangling between my fingers, and head for the door. Someone is blocking the exit with a bag, his back to me.

Nate.

"What are you doing in my dorm, Prendergast?"

He turns back, and his brows drop as I jump on one foot to shove the last boot on.

"*Our* dorm."

Seriously?

They say keep your enemies close. Mine are in my dorm. Close enough.

I slip past him. The corridor is quiet, and I make my way to the mess hall. A moment later, familiar footsteps come up behind me.

Remmins.

"Morning, Bendall."

Clean shaven and in his uniform, he could definitely pass for something to take up my time. I offer him a smile. "Morning, Remmins."

"Asher."

"Okay, morning Ash. And please, it's Clara."

He tilts his head giving me an incredulous look. What? I ran with it. "Ash suits you better."

"I guess it's better than Ashley or Ashie."

"Who calls you Ashie?" A stupid grin stretches my face, and he shakes his head.

"Nobody. Ever." His gaze turns steely, but a smile plucks up on one side of his face.

I throw my hands up as if defending my life. "Alright, you have my word. It will be Asher, but most likely Ash."

"Fine," he drawls, and turns into the hall. With a glance between us we go our separate ways.

Even though nothing has happened between us since that time in the corridor after the infirmary, I can't afford to be seen to have any advantage. Sabotage is not uncommon in the Sectors, especially in these proving weeks after recruitment.

To keep my spot here would be ideal. I have no intentions of slipping further away from the city. If there's any chance that I'll make it to the city, it will be by moving up in rank. Not plummeting to the slums by screwing this up. I wander along the buffet with a tray, and something like stewed oats slops into my bowl. Smothering it with sugar, I grab a mug of coffee before plopping at the table with my roommates.

"Where'd you go to Clara? You weren't affected by the disease, were you?" the girl to my right says, shuffling away on the bench seat, with a solid dose of side-eye.

"No, I wasn't. How does it spread anyhow? Does anyone actually know?"

Nobody has an answer, so I dig into my oats. The heat sears my tongue, and I swallow it quickly. At least the coffee is half decent today. Having had my fill of breakfast I decide to head to the factory floor early.

The floor is empty when I wander around, running a hand over the smooth, cold metal of the machines. And even though this is not where I had intended to end up, I can't help but appreciate the giant machines for what they are.

Efficient.

Tireless.

Robust.

Like every soul I know from the Province. The doors to the factory swing open, and Ash strides in.

"You're a bit early, Clara." He hugs a clipboard and walks to the desk on the back wall. Dumping it onto the desk he flips through a logbook before turning back and leaning on the desk. When his eyes meet mine, I frown. "What do you know about the disease?"

He breaks his focus and searches the enormous room as if hunting for the right thing to say. Or he could be contemplating what he should tell me and what he's allowed to. But people are dropping like flies around us, and all we get from the supervisors is hush.

"Ash," I say and walk to where he leans on the desk. His hands clamped on the edge of the table behind him uncouple and fold over his chest.

"Should I be worried?" I ask.

He huffs a small, listless laugh and shakes his head. "There's nothing you can do about it, Clara."

"What do you know?"

"As much as you do."

What isn't he telling me?

"Seriously, you know more than we do. You're a supervisor, Ash, not a pleb like the rest of us here."

"I promise you. I don't know any more than you do. We have no idea what causes it; how it is transferred from one person to the next; or why nobody is able to cure it. Or," he pushes off the desk, letting his hands fall by his sides, "how it chooses one person over another. So, drop it. For your own good, drop it, Bendall."

I sigh and make distance between us. Fine. If he won't tell me, I will find out by myself. "Sure, I'll forget it. Maybe it'll find me next, and you won't have to worry about me asking too many questions. Or have to bother feeling bad when I don't make the cut at the end of the week."

"Clara." He steps forward, and his hand brushes my arm.

Retreating a step I force a smile. "You don't owe me anything, Remmins." I turn and walk away, but his hand catches my wrist. I spin back as he closes the distance between us.

"It's not the best idea for us to start anything. The other recruits will," he glances at the door, "they'll think I've fudged your quotas. It's one thing to do so under the radar. Another thing entirely to get caught for it."

"But filling my quota for half a shift was okay?"

"Nobody but you and I know that shift went toward your quota."

Not true. Somehow Johnson is onto us. He's keeping our dirty little secret. For now.

"Why?" I say.

His gaze drops to my mouth.

"Oh, I see. Payment up front for something in return."

"No, I—"

I pull my hand from his grip. The memory of his warm, large hand is like fire on my skin.

"You what? Thought I'd owe you, and you could collect whenever it suited you? How many recruits do you black-mail with full quotas to lure into your bed, Asher?"

"Stop it, Clara. That's not what this is."

His face turns to stone as hurt flashes through his eyes.

I can't do this.

I can't *feel* like this.

Not now.

"Don't bother going easy on me Remmins, I don't need your pity."

As I turn and stalk toward my machine the doors open, and recruits file in. Johnson glances between me, now halfway across the floor and heading from the wrong direction of the room, and Remmins. He scoffs. His face pulls into something like distaste as he shakes his head and slams a hand onto the big red start button of his machine.

Oh great, just freaking great.

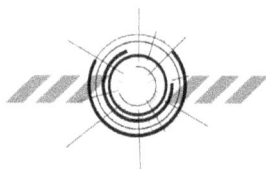

REMMINS HAS BEEN RIDING my ass all day. Can't he hound some other poor soul about quotas. I mean, I understand he cares about his factory output—we all do. Nobody wants to land themselves a one-way ticket to the Wastelands. But for Jimny's sake back off buddy.

"Another one!" He grabs up another bolt as the last one runs dangerously close to the last of its material.

"Yeah, I'm on it. Calm down, Remmins."

His eyes narrow as he glances between me and the machine. In all fairness, this is what I asked from him. The man knows how to deliver.

I snatch the bolt from his hands and drag it out of the crate. It's been a long day, and we are into our ninth hour of manhandling these oversized rolls. My hands ache from stretching around the girth of each one. It slips between my palms, and they cramp up.

"Shit!"

The bolt drops to the floor and unravels.

Damn!

"Accept some help, Clara. Everyone else has been helping each other. You are the only stubborn ass not working as a team today."

"Screw you, Remmins."

Johnson walks past, running a hand through his smug hair. "Lovers quarrel already?"

"Bugger off, Johnson," I snap.

He sniggers and walks back to his machine. How many breaks is that asshole going to have, he's walked past like five times in the last two hours.

Remmins ignores him and loads the bolt into the metal cradles. Sinking my hands onto my hips I raise my face to the ceiling and close my eyes. The last thing I need is for every last Engineer on this floor thinking I'm the teacher's pet.

Heavens above.

Remmins is gone. He's back to the center of the floor, glancing at me.

Why can't he simply stand there and leave me alone? It's literally his job. Our quotas are not that bad, surely. What happens to him if our quotas suck?

Probably nothing.

I wander back to the machine and check everything is running smoothly. Finding nothing amiss I slip next door to Vivi. She's strung out.

"Hey, you okay?"

"Yeah, but—" she sighs, sagging against the machine. "Today is so hard."

"Tell me about it." I turn my aching hands over in front of me. They shake and I slide them into my pockets.

"I don't—" Vivi lurches to one side and blood drips from her mouth.

"Vi!"

I grab her under the arms and lower her to the floor by the side of the whirring machine. Remmins strides to where I am crouched by her side. "What's going on?"

"She's sick. She needs the infirmary."

He nods toward the door. But when I try to pull Vi to her

feet she groans. Remmins is under her other arm in a heartbeat. He helps me walk her to the door then plucks his radio off his hip and spits out an order. "Wait here. Someone will be along for her in a minute."

"Sure," I turn to Vi, "hey, how you doing?"

She closes her eyes, and her breaths steady. "I'll live. I hope." A small smile pulls up on one side of her mouth. The stone that lodged in my throat moments ago when Remmins swooped down to help slides all the way to the pit of my stomach.

She's pale.

She looks like death.

And she's the only person here that I care about.

The door opens, and two Medicos file in around Vi. They wave me off, and I wander back to my machine to finish the last hour of my shift. I pray to whatever deity is left, wherever they exist, that Vivi doesn't have the disease. Her symptoms are not like the others. Just the same, I hold my breath.

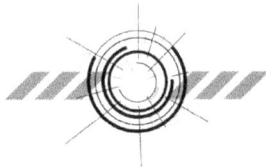

THE MESS HALL IS PACKED. And when Remmins drops into the seat beside me I raise an eyebrow at him. He forces a smile. Great—pity company. He can go back to the cool kids table and leave me the hell alone.

"Don't you have an officer's table to sit at, Ashie?"

His fork pauses halfway to his mouth, and his brows lower. Oh yes, I did. Maybe now he'll leave?

"Nope." He snaps the foods from the fork with his teeth.

I cant my head with the best sarcastic expression I can muster. "Really? You sure you wouldn't like to talk shop and quotas for another half an hour with Evans, Ashley?"

He turns in his seat and drops his fork. I can't pull back the smile that splits my face. This is too easy. I love it.

"You gonna eat that?" He stabs the meat on my plate and takes a bite.

I feign a manic chuckle and pluck my plate and cutlery from the table and move to the next table over. A moment later, he drops beside me and stares. Doesn't he realize every single person in the mess hall can see him?

Can see me.

Us.

"Stay where you are. I have something for you." His words are quiet. Strained.

"Yeah right." I grab my plate up again but his hand stops me.

"Stop, Clara." Desperation lines his eyes. "Please?"

What the hell? "Fine, what is it?"

"I can give it to you later, not here."

"If you're talking about—"

His hand squeezes mine before returning to his side. I close my mouth. He tracks his attention to his food and eats it in silence. When I can drag my eyes from his face, I stab my potatoes as if they are Nate Prendergast.

If only.

After a few mouthfuls I'm not hungry anymore. I leave the table, put my plate onto the collection trolley, and stalk back toward my dorm. Halfway down the hall a warm hand closes around my wrist and pulls me into a small passage off the main corridor.

Ash's familiar scent wraps around me. But what catches my gaze and steals my breath is what he is holding. A comms. With my name on it in his handwriting. He glares at me, shoulders heaving.

Staring at the paper in Ash's hand, I raise a hand to take it but hesitate. The only person who would write me is Tessa. How could she have got this through without getting caught? Why hasn't Remmin's handed this into his superiors?

"Take it, Clara."

His jaw is set hard. I snatch it from his hand. His fingers brush across mine. I ignore the shallow flop of a heartbeat that follows with the slightest touch from him. He steps closer as I unfold the paper.

It's a printed transmission.

It's short.

The words my sister has crafted, that no one else in this forsaken ring would ever be able to decipher, make me chuckle.

C.B.

Uncle Bernard is doing his usual thing,

blacking out every few days. All glittery one minute, out the next.

Mom and Dad don't know why, possibly he likes to be a rebel?

Defying the Medicos, perhaps?

At any rate, you will be happy to know that Rita flew the coupe this week. She looked blue but was darker when she flew higher; talking with the other birds. None of them could hear her. At least, that's what it looked like.

Will she find Georgie and fly off together? Maybe, maybe not—smash.

T.B

Dazed, I gawk at the paper for a moment before I remember Remmins is still glaring at me. But there's no anger in his face, as I track my gaze back to his, just one eyebrow cocked. Curiosity. He must have read this ridiculous comms. Poor guy. He's probably thoroughly confused.

Good.

"How did you know it was for me?" I ask.

"You're the only *C B* under my watch, Clara."

"Really? Your loss I suppose."

"Indeed."

He clasps his hands behind his back and pivots on his heels and strides for the main corridor. This is the second time he has covered for me. And he's starting to grow on me. Making my stupid heart crack open a sliver . . . Urgh.

No Clara. Absolutely not. But . . . Then again. "Wait!"

He stalls, pausing, before turning back.

"Ash, I need to reply."

He nods and walks away.

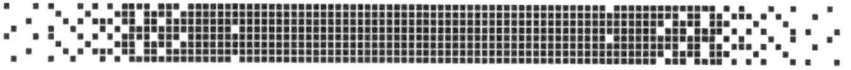

7

TESSA

The coded message from my sister brings tears to my eyes. I slap a hand over my mouth. Not only was my message transferred but it was also delivered and I received a response. Thank you A Remmins whoever you are. Right now, he or she are the lifeline between my sister and me. The girl with my access card found me and slipped the message under my door along with my card. She signed a small note, Amber. Does this mean she is willing to help me?

I reread the message. The contents make my gut sink, the same way it did the first time I read it. A disease is spreading in the Sectors. Well at least in Sector Two, for sure.

Clara wants me to see if I can find out anything about the disease. With access to the HQ mainframe, I could hunt for information about it. A memory hits me like a tonne of bricks. The comms I saw about the disease and the rebels.

Are the two related? Why have only the Sectors been hit with the disease. Surely the city would have cases of it too . . .

I slide down the door that has been supporting me since I swiped the message from under it five minutes ago. My butt hits the carpet, and I stare blankly at the wall on the opposite side of the room. There is no talk of this in Sontaria.

Why?

How?

Bolting from the floor I slide into my desk chair with renewed vigour. I tap the Visi-Screen and swipe until I come to the comms for my unit. How do I access other departments comms? I flip the paper over in my hand. A watermark shimmers on the bottom right corner as I hold it up to the light. A bundle of letters and numbers are embossed into it. I tap on the mainframe access icon, and it asks for a password.

I enter the string of hidden numbers and letters and tap the green icon to the right. The same screen I saw in HQ on Amber's comms desk flips up.

Holy hell!

Thank you, Amber.

I scroll through comms after comms about quotas from the various Sectors. Each is signed by the area's supervisor, not the officer in charge. A line of them is from sector Two with A Remmins signing off, over and over. The tallies increase with every week. Is he Clara's supervisor?

The alarm on my wrist gadget beeps. My shift starts in twenty minutes, and I can't be late. It's our first day in real aircrafts. Jumping up out of the chair I grab my boots and make the hangar with two minutes to spare. My access card beeps as I press it to the blue panel. A large door slides open to an enormous structure housing a range of aircraft.

Elites in blue jumpsuits wander around, going about their pre-flights and missions no doubt. A tall woman stands in the center of the organised chaos, wielding a tablet-type screen I now know as a Visi-Tile, directing other trainees to their aircrafts.

When I reach her, she scans my card and points me toward the nearest aircraft. "Your trainer is already in the cockpit."

"Thanks."

I think.

Damn, am I late?

Stepping up into the aircraft, it's much bigger than I imagined. I've been studying the blueprints, the schematics, and looking at the displacement-powered Viper978 for weeks. But on the page is nothing like in real life.

My trainer, the one with the voice like melted caramel I assume, sits in his seat with his head down going over whatever it is that has him absorbed. I pad into the front of the craft and slide into the co-pilot seat.

"Hey, sorry, I didn't think I was late?" I offer.

His head snaps up. His gaze widens as he studies me for

a heartbeat. "You're not—" he drops his focus to the Visi-Tile. "Not late, that is. We should make a start."

"We should."

That voice.

Those hands.

Messy brown hair framing his square face. Dark eyes home into the Visi-Tile on his lap as his jaw works. The moment I realise I'm staring he looks back up at me. All he does is nod.

I open my mouth to say something; to apologise for staring.

"Buckle in, Bendall." He points to the harness with a small smile.

"Yep. Yes, harness. Right, got it."

I bumble to find the panel for the five-point harness and tap it with shaking fingers. It slides around me instantly but somehow this time it's too loose. He leans over to tighten it around my middle, and I freeze like prey in the line of sight of a predator. His scent crowds the small space. His after-shave. Woody and crisp. The vein in his neck bounds, and I pray to the heavens above my face is not as red as a damn tomato.

"All good?" he asks.

"Yes," I utter, training my attention back to the dash-board that's lit up in front of me.

"Today, I pilot so you can familiarise yourself with the craft. Next time, this will be your seat, and I will be assisting."

The thrill that washes over me at hearing there will be a next time is utterly ludicrous. My brain is mush, I swear.

"Sure, great," I breathe.

"Oh. You can call me Officer Matthews."

I nod. "Thanks."

"Right let's send this big girl into the clouds." He presses his Visi-Tile onto the side of his seat and it stays where he put it. Magnetic?

Matthews glances at me. "Preflight checks are all yours, go ahead."

I run through the checks he taught me via headset while I was closeted away in the dark sim. It is automatic now, having done it so many times. When we're ready to leave the hangar Matthews takes over. He flips me a small smile before pushing his finger up the control panel and we hover at a standstill before gliding out into the sunshine. He radios through for clearance, and we pause at the first large painted white X. He runs through a few more checks. "Right, ready?"

"Uh huh." Butterflies swarm in my belly. "I mean, yes sir."

Me and heights are not friends. Never have been. Our relationship is more like bully and victim. With me getting the wedgie only high heights knows how to deal out. The undies over your head type. I close my eyes as the ground slips out from beneath us.

My stomach flips and sinks, and I grip the armrests of the seat. I can't see him but Matthew's dark eyes burn into me. It's like salt on a very new, open wound. I force each breath in and out of my lungs, I can do this.

I can do this.

"You alright there, Tessa?"

His voice is so soft, so ethereal, I can't help but open my eyes. And regret it a second later when behind him is open sky and no more buildings.

"We can go back down if you want. But—"

I shake my head furiously. No. Going down means I fall behind in my training. "Give me a second."

Bile rises in my throat.

"Hey, tell me what you can hear."

Hear? Why does he want me to do that? Listening for a moment, I make a running tally in my head. "Your breathing. My breathing. My heartbeat. The disrupters. Your fingers sliding over the panel, only just though."

"Good, what can you feel?"

Oh, now I know what he is doing.

Grounding technique.

"The seat under me. The cool reverse air of the ca—" The craft shudders with a gust. My fingers dig into the armrests. "Ahhh. The wind outside," I huff out on a whimper.

"Now. Open your eyes and read the gauges please."

What? No way.

"That's an order, Officer Bendall."

I crack an eye open. The altimeter reads ten thousand feet. Already? We're still pitched upward. The fuel monitor reads full. "Fuel full. Altitude is ten thousand feet. Heading is—"

"Next time your gut gets the better of you, override it with your brain. The quicker the better, okay?"

My breath stutters out again as our eyes meet. This time I release the armrests and offer back a smile with a nod. "Okay."

"We are over the Sectors in the northern training area if you want to see below."

"No," I utter.

"Next time then."

Sectors? "Which Sector?"

"Over the border of Sectors One and Two, actually."

"Yes, please I want to see Sector Two."

"I can only show you this small part. We're in the northern training air space. The main airspace over the Sectors is restricted . . ." He taps a button and the floor below us disappears, sliding out so we can see through a large viewing panel. Hands firmly around my harness straps, I search the land below us. It's nothing to see really. Acres of farming like the edges of every other Sector and the Provinces.

"You know people in Sector Two?" he asks.

"You could say that."

"Right, well our thirty minutes airtime will be up soon, we better head back." He slides a finger right and the craft banks around in the same direction. The disrupters either side of us whir, the left louder as the right peters to a dull hum. The seat all but sucks me into it, and I track my gaze to the gauges on the screen.

"It will become easier, I promise," he says quietly.

"Sure hope so."

He chuckles and takes us back to base. Every movement he makes is smooth and controlled. I can't help watching his hands. Like they play a fine instrument. We finally make ground, and Matthews taxis the craft back into the hangar. The second he kills the engines I'm up and out of my seat fast. He gives me a quizzical look before following me out. We walk back into the building, and he leads me into a small meeting room.

"Let's debrief." Matthews sits in a chair at a small white table, resting his Visi-Tile on top. "So, you were in the northern training area airspace. You made a good start on handling your fear of heights. Do you have any questions for me?"

"I—" I can't think of anything. "How long do I have before you make me do that by myself?"

He chuckles but smiles. "After about ten hours of flight time, twenty take off and landings, then you go out to the training area by yourself and back. No overbearing trainer required."

"Oh crap."

He is schooling his face as he leans over the table. "Tessa, you can do this."

"How do you know that? I mean academics is one thing. Up in the air with no way down is another."

He frowns, confused. "No way down?"

"What if I get up there but freeze and can't make it back down?"

"Then I guess you crash into Sector Two."

His stare is all fire. But it's not annoyance that lines it. Something like a hint.

Or a warning.

8

AS IF MY miserable existence couldn't be any worse, I glare at the newest recruit to our factory floor. Bundled up in a cast, and limping between crate and machine is none other than Nathanial Prendergast. Urgh. It's bad enough he's even in my Sector, my dorm, but now he's on the same factory floor as me?

Said it before, will say it again . . . Screw my life.

All six foot, two inches of him. Dark skin, tight knit brows and a mouth that makes me angry. His eyes darken as they find mine, matching his current mood. He's frowning, and his lips are pursed tight.

He struggles with the bolt, his arms flexing as he hauls it up and drags his injured leg behind him. Shuffling to the machine that was Vivi's he lifts the bolt. It slips into the first saddle as he turns trying to hoist it up to the second.

The bolt slips and tumbles to the floor with a thundering ruckus. I sigh, slamming a hand over the stop button on my machine, and stride over to him. With a face of stone, he glares at me as I lift the bolt and secure it into the holders. I smooth out the material and feed it into the mouth of the steel beast before hitting the button on the side. The machine roars back to life.

"What the hell are you doing?" he growls.

I turn back and step into his space.

"You're welcome, Prendergast."

"Get out of my workspace, Bendall." His face is twisted with hate. That mouth again, curled with a snarl.

Heavens above.

"As you wish, good luck with your quota, *Nathanial.*"

He rolls his eyes and turns back to the machine. I make a face behind his back and stalk back to my machine. The second I fire it up, the tension in my gut unravels a little. Stupid, ungrateful idiot. Why the hell I thought it was a good idea to help Nate of all people is beyond me. Muttering to myself I focus on my work. Head down, tail up.

The buzzer rings in the last minute of our shift and I let the last of the current bolt feed through before running some routine maintenance; a quick top up of the thin, yellow oil in a few places; clearing out the stray threads that gather around the base of my machine. Stilted footsteps track behind me, and I spin back. Nate's eyes wander over my frame before he snaps it to the door as he walks out.

Remmins appears by my machine, clipboard in hand. "Big day, Clara?"

Not making eye contact, I brush away fabric lint from the

large rollers that are now stationary. "Huh. Would have been better if Prendergast didn't take up my time."

"A hard man to help. If he doesn't keep up, our quotas will slip behind too far, we won't be able to catch back up. Not even with both of us helping him."

"Doubt that ass will let me anywhere near his machine. We're not exactly friends."

"You know each other?"

"Yup. From the same area in the Province. Nate has been tormenting me since we were kids. Five minutes with the two of us in the same space has both of us riled up. So, I guess you can thank him for my sweet disposition, Remmins."

He surveys the floor, like he wants to say something but won't.

"Spit it out, Ash. You can tell me I'm not sweet, I'm not delusional." I chuckle, but it comes out forced.

"It's not that, at all, actually. If our quotas don't improve, I may be reassigned."

"What the hell?"

"To a less demanding department of Textiles, if I'm lucky."

"I didn't know they could do that. What do you mean lucky?"

"They can and they do."

"How far behind are we?"

"About a week's worth at the moment."

"Shit, Ash. Why didn't you tell me sooner?"

He huffs a laugh and runs a hand through his hair. "Would you have cared?"

"What's that supposed to mean?"

His eyes find mine, and heat rushes to my face.

Oh. That.

It's not that I don't find him attractive because I most definitely do. I didn't think he was interested, and after Tessa's message I have kind of been lost in my head. I walk to where he stands leaning against my machine and lean on it beside him. He looks down at me.

Those brown eyes study my face, and my stomach flips like the hot cakes Mama used to make Tessa and me when we were little girls.

"Clara," he utters.

"You think this is a good idea, Remmins?"

He rolls off the machine and crowds me against it. I take in the shape of his jaw. His ruffled dark hair, and crooked smile. His knuckles brush under my chin, raising my face higher, his gaze dipping to my lips. "I have no idea."

I press my hands against his chest and release a shaky breath. "Me either. Maybe—"

He tilts his head.

"No strings?"

Life in Ring 2 is unpredictable. The last thing either of us needs is to become attached.

"No strings," he breathes.

His fingers brush the stray hair that has slipped from my bun off my neck. Sucking in a ragged lungful of air I push off the machine, so I'm mere inches from him. Our breath mingles. My heart races, but in the best way possible. I dip my chin and give him a coy smile. "Your place or mine?"

He chuckles and takes my face with both hands, briefly kissing my lips. "Mine."

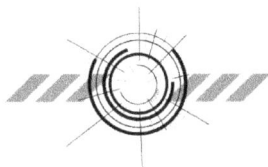

ASH REMMINS IS A NEAT FREAK. Figures, I guess. His room is minimal and screams control freak. I huff a laugh as I take in the room. A large bunk. A metal cabinet that I assume is for clothes. Uniforms. A desk with two neat piles of papers.

Even in his bathroom items are lined up on a single small, light-green shelf. I study my reflection in the slim rectangle mirror, buying myself a minute, to make sure I'm not about to make a mistake.

This is Remmins, the man who has put his position in the Sector at risk to help me meet my quotas.

He's a good man.

I slip out of the small bathroom space. He sits on his bed, elbows on his knees, hands clasped with his chin resting on them. His eyes are closed. It's possible he's contemplating this as much as I am.

Kicking off my shoes by the door, I pad to where he sits and let my hands wander through his dark hair. It's like the silks we work on for the city sliding between my fingers.

He opens his eyes and looks up at me, and I smile down at him.

"You sure?" he asks.

I nod. His head hits my stomach, his hands grip my hips. Heat pools low in my core with his firm hold on my body. It has been so long since I've done this. And being around this man for weeks makes everything so much more intense. As if what's between us has taken on a life of its own.

I work the buttons of my shirt and when the last one pops open, I let it fall away. He presses a kiss to my stomach. Fire surges in my veins. His hands move up my ribs to my cotton bra. He shuffles back on the bunk and pulls me onto his lap. I straddle him, taking his face in my hands. "Ash."

His mouth is on mine a heartbeat later.

Oh Heavens.

He's warm and soft—in ways. All hard ridge and strong legs underneath me. I wriggle out of my shirt, and he brushes it from my shoulders and onto the floor. His lips wander over the soft flesh at the top of my bra. My fingers scramble for the hem of his shirt. He still has far too many clothes on.

His smile moves against my skin as I tug his shirt upwards. He loosens the top two buttons and lifts his arms up. I rip it from his chest and toss it with mine. Staring, I take in the ridges, muscle and the scars. A light dusting of hair covers toned pecs, the same hue as that gorgeous dark hair on his head. My breath shallows out.

"Hey," brown eyes lock onto me. "You alright?"

"It's—" I swallow. "It's been a while since . . ."

"We can take it slow, Clara."

I smile. I don't need to take it slow, but I will take a moment to catalogue every angle and plane of him. I trace a finger over his jaw and down his neck as his Adam's apple bobs. Letting my finger slip, I brush it over his collar bone and between the contours of his chest. Mine heaving with every breath. My bra wringing the air from my lungs with each forced inhale.

As if reading my mind, he reaches around and releases the clasp. Pulling the unwanted confinement from my body, I let it join the clothes on the floor. Deft fingers pluck the band from my tight bun, then the ponytail under it, and my strawberry blonde curls spill over my shoulders. Ash groans, his eyes darkening.

"Tell me where you want me." His words are gravel.

"Everywhere, Ash."

His lips skim my nipple, and I try to reign in my ragged breaths.

The small radio that usually hangs on his hip squawks. He hesitates but goes back to dotting kisses over my breast, mumbling, "Ignore it."

"If you say so."

Hands in his hair, I trail my nails over his scalp and down the back of his neck. The radio crackles again, and I distinctly hear his name. He groans but doesn't stop.

"Are they looking for you, Ash?"

He growls and shakes his head as his fingers slide behind

my pants, brushing over my hip bones. At this rate, I will have barely touched him before he's travelled every inch of the top half of my body. "You have way too many clothes on, Remmins."

The radio squeals. This time, they try thrice. His head hits my stomach with a long, heady groan. His hands slide up and around my neck. "Of all the times for someone to need something."

"Did you want to answer it?"

"Maybe they'll go away if I don't?"

"Or—"

Bang. Bang. Bang.

A fist thunders onto the other side of his door.

"Damn," he breathes.

I push off his lap and swipe up my shirt and bra. He takes his and shrugs it on. "You can't be here, Clara." The words are barely a whisper.

I pick up what he means and duck into his bathroom, closing the door silently. A second later, his door opens. My boots are on the floor by the desk. I slam my eyes shut and pray whoever it is doesn't notice.

"What couldn't wait until tomorrow?" Ash snaps.

Yes, what? I would like to know what could be more important than Asher Remmins all over me. Wrangling back a smile at my lame joke, I dress.

"There has been a development with the latest Engineer with the disease, Vivian. And she won't stop screaming for Clara someone," a man says.

I don't recognise his voice. But I sure as hell recognise who he's talking about.

Vivi needs me.

"This involves me how?" Ash asks.

"We have been to her dorm, she's not there. None of the other Engineers on her side have seen her. She's your responsibility."

"Fine. I'll track her down and send her to the infirmary ASAP."

"See that you do. Find out why she wasn't in her dorm while you're at it, Remmins."

"Yes, sir."

The door closes and Ash tracks toward the bathroom. I slide the door open.

His face is stone. "Come on, let's get you to the infirmary."

I shove my boots on, and he gathers his radio and access card.

Ash holds the door open, and I slip out.

"Did you want to reply to that comms, after we see Vivian?" His expression is stone melted to concern, lined with a little mirth. Did Ash Remmins suggest rebellious activity?

"Yep. Then we can pick up where we left off."

"We can," he says with a crooked smile.

How can I let this one get shipped out. All because of our lousy quotas. "Ash," I lift my eyes to his face, and he glances down as we walk along, "how do we make up the quota?"

"You want me to stick around, Bendall?"

"Don't flatter yourself," I roll my eyes, "I don't want to be kicked to no man's land with your sorry ass."

"No, that would be a *terrible* idea."

He tussles my hair with his hand. My gut sinks. Neither of us can afford to be sent to the Wastelands. That would mean any chance of getting to Tessa would be lost forever.

9

TESSA

EVERY COMMS I scroll through is the same as the last. If I never see another written word in my life, it will be too soon. I have been at this for four hours. The second I made it home from training, around eighteen hundred hours, my butt has been glued to this chair. And I have found approximately . . . nothing.

Big fat whopping nada.

Urgh. Surely, there is some mention of the disease, it's infiltrating the Sectors as we speak. The Sectors are responsible for supplying the city. How is nobody talking about this?

My wrist gadget pings. Someone is at my door. At this hour?

Springing from the chair, I pad to the door. Red hair fills the space through the small viewing panel.

Amber.

What on earth?

Finger pressed to the access button; my door slides open with a small hiss. She looks around the hall before walking inside without a word. The door closes behind her a second later.

"What are you doing here, so late? Or at all?" I ask.

She smiles a little, scanning my room. "Always wondered what the top level looked like. It's a bit less than I imagined. Very minimal."

"All this way to see what my room is like?" I raise an eyebrow, crossing my arms.

"No, Tessa."

She wanders around, running a hand over the screen of the food dispenser, before ducking her head into the shower room briefly. "Nice, better than the Comms quarters at least."

"What floor are you on?"

"Third."

"Why are you here?"

"To help. But I need something from you first." In her hand is a slip of paper, similar to the last one I received from Clara. My stomach flips and I move toward her, eyes trained on that small piece of paper. She retracts her hand and takes a step back. "Ah ah. First you need to give me something. Promise that you will never share with anyone how you came about these messages."

"I promise." I absolutely do. I would never rat her out. That would be sibling comms suicide.

"What are you doing with my access information anyhow?" Amber tracks to the desk.

"Just trying to see if there's anything on my sister."

She turns back and watches me, hands gripping the desk either side of her as she sinks onto it. "Really?"

"Yes?"

"You're not convincing me, Tessa."

"I—"

She shoots off the desk and moves to where I stand. Her brows pinch as she folds her arms. "Whatever you find, make sure when you find it, you keep it to yourself."

I open my mouth to reply, but I have no idea with what. Do I want to find more than I am looking for? Am I supposed to be?

Amber's gaze tracks to my food dispenser. "We don't have one of those either. Must be nice to be the city's favourite."

"I can't even work it properly," I huff out with a laugh. She relaxes and pads to the screen and small cut out where the food deck sits. Brushing a finger over the screen, she hesitates before tapping on it. It changes from the blue backlit lighting to white.

How the?

"What did you do?"

"If something happens and you feel unsafe, tap the power button three times quick. It's a beacon, like an SOS. If you don't shut it off within the minute, someone will arrive at your door."

She taps the power button, and the dispenser screen flicks back to blue. "Why would I need help? Why would I feel unsafe?"

She turns to face me square on and glances to my desk where the Visi-Screen is still lit up, the gold city emblem spinning. "Not everything in the system is meant to be found. You might need this button. Remember it, please."

Thoroughly confused, I step back. "Fine. If I need it."

She peruses the room before turning back and heading to the door. With a quick motion, she diverts to the right and drops the small piece of paper on my desk.

The door to my quarters swooshes and thuds shut. A moment later, I am at the desk with the paper in hand, heart thundering. I flip the paper and scan the other side. It's not from Clara. It's handwritten, not typed. My stomach plummets.

Bendall,
Main training hangar.
2200 hrs – tonight.
Matthews.

Wide eyed, I let the paper drop back to the desk. What the hell?

I glance at the time.

21:38

I need to leave. Now.

Grabbing up the standard issue jacket from the hook by the door, that's been unnecessary thus far, I wave a hand over my access panel. I use the elevator to get down as fast as possible.

Then something occurs to me—why did Amber bring a note from my trainer? Why didn't he page using my gadget? Something's off.

The elevator door jerks open, snapping me back to reality. I step out and make my way past Joe. His head tilts as he watches me fold my collar up and head in the direction of the training building.

Every so often, I glance behind me. I have never felt unsafe in the city. This random, unorthodox message delivery has my nerve up and I walk fast, eyes darting everywhere as I go. The streets aren't abandoned by any means, but they are quieter than usual.

When I arrive at the training center, I walk straight through to the back of the building until I am at the door to the hangar. I hover for a moment, trying to decide if this is a good idea.

Why would Matthews need to see me after training? Why so late at night? The only other people around will be Elites working on their night vision flying.

Finally, I swipe my access card and push through the door. The aircraft I usually take is docked in the first space as it always is, the cockpit lit up. I wander past a few Elites discussing flight path alternatives and reach the door of my aircraft.

"Hello?"

A shuffle comes from inside. "Bendall. In here please."

Right aircraft then.

I make it to the cockpit and Matthews is in the pilot's seat, chewing on what must be a very late supper. "Take a seat."

"Okay . . ."

I drop into the copilot seat, and he hits the door button. The aircraft doors shut, the locking mechanism hissing closed. The dash is alive. The white and blue light accentuates the angle of his jaw and makes his messy brown hair much darker.

"Did I need to make up for something?" I ask, still unsure as to why he brought me here. Why the note via Amber?

He studies me for a moment before clearing his throat. "How do you feel about stars?"

"How do I *feel* about them?"

His brown eyes burn into mine. Is this some kind of attempt at getting closer to me? Is that even allowed? I mean, I can't say I'm not attracted to him. Or that he's not my type. But he is my *trainer*. "Stars are fine."

"Fine, hey?" Matthews starts the aircraft, and I slide my harness over and secure it. We taxi out to the tarmac at a low hover, and he radios for clearance as the craft lifts into the air a second later.

My stomach flips, the way it always does when I leave the ground. He stares ahead, taking in the screen ahead of us. High up and clear of the city, he sets the autopilot and undoes his harness.

The next thing I know, he's out of the seat and walking toward the back of the plane.

"What the hell?" I disengage mine and follow him. The plane is long and wide, enough space for cargo or three rows of seated officers. The back ends in a tailgate. Matthews taps the panel by the side of the rear and the gate lowers with a low whine.

Is he going to toss me out of the plane? Some kind of culling technique for Aeronautical Elites that don't make the cut? Gripping a hand strap that dangles above my head, I wait for what comes next.

To my surprise, he slides down the wall of the plane, by the opening and rests his head back. The wind whips the strands of hair that have escaped my bun over my face. I dip my chin and bend my head to the side, trying to see what he is staring at.

Stars.

Millions of them.

I shuffle closer to the edge of the plane. Sliding down the opposite wall on shaky legs, I grip the metal handle above my head. He is staring at me again, and I huff a wobbly breath.

"Is this some kind of tough love technique to cure my fear of heights?" I shout over the noise of the wind outside.

The open air between me and the ground starts inches from my seat.

Matthews shakes his head and closes his eyes. "What are you looking for, Tessa?"

"Aren't we looking at stars?"

He inhales, deep and slow. "On your Visi-Screen. On the comms?"

"What?" The word is too soft for him to hear. My expression must have given me away because he releases his grip and stands, closing the space between us. As I look up at him, and fear lances through my veins. Is this it? Is this what happens to Elites who don't toe the line. To ones who don't stay in their lane? Who snoop and break the rules.

His hand drops down. "Up."

"No!" I shake my head furiously.

"Bendall, stand up."

"Uh uh. I wasn't hurting anyone. I only wanted to talk to her. To make sure she's alright." Tears burn behind my eyes. My entire body shakes with fear, humiliation, anger and disbelief. They would really take out an Elite, over a few comms?

Matthews tugs me to my feet, his hands under my arms. Half limp from fear, I collapse against him. My cheeks redden with embarrassment. He smells like my days spent in this place training. Like the nights I can't fall asleep and he's in my mind—in the fire that floods my body with every thought of him. That woodsy smell with a hint of caramel, as if his voice matches his scent. A ground out cry slips through my lips. My hands turn to fists and slam into his chest.

"Let me go! Please, I won't touch the comms ever again! Please." When he doesn't move, forcing my fear back down, I drop my hands to my sides. His face is almost amused, mouth tilted up on one side. Eyes narrowed a little, darkened they burn into mine, like he is seeing something else entirely.

"Where is she?" he asks. The wind almost steals his words, but I catch them before they disappear.

"Sector Two."

"Why didn't you simply ask?"

"I—" I fold my arms, hugging my body tight. "You would have helped me?"

"Digging around the comms from your private terminal is a very *very* bad idea, Tessa."

"How di—" I shut my mouth.

Amber. Of course.

His focus leaves my face, glancing the blanket of stars that hang above us. A moment later he looks back to me and worry laces those dark eyes. His hands come to rest on my arms, and I breathe him in.

"Stay in your lane, Bendall. Those who stray from it, don't always fare well."

"What are you talking about, Matthews?"

"Stop digging for information you're not supposed to have."

I brush his hands from my arms and step a little closer. "Or what?"

A small smile pops over his lips before he schools it away. "Or you will end up a Wastelander. And that would be a crying shame."

"Huh, I'm sure you wouldn't miss me, Matthews." I drag his name out. Because I like the way his eyes flicker when I say it. His finger touches my chin and lifts my face up as he searches my gaze, as if trying to discover the meaning to my sudden sass.

"You sure about that, Tess?"

10

CLARA

NATE'S limp deepens as the shift wears on. Serves him damn right. Snarly prick. He hobbles to his crate, the machine behind him clunking with an empty intake. My first instinct is to ignore him, but when he drops the bolt and swears through gritted teeth I sigh and slam a hand on the stop button of my machine.

His scowl finds me before I'm even halfway to where he stands, his weight on his good leg. How on earth they expected him to work in Textiles with an injury like that, I will never know. I grab up the bolt and lift it onto the cradle above my head.

"I can do it, Bendall," he spits from where he stands, face reddened, hands shaking and scowl thoroughly etched in.

I bite my tongue to stem the first thing that springs to mind. I don't care how much he hates me. We have a quota and over my rotting carcass is he stuffing that up for the entire floor.

His hand swallows my own, his body presses into my side as he reaches for the end of the bolt. "I said leave it!"

Turning back, I flick his hand off. "Get over yourself, Nate. Quotas in this Sector affect everyone. Not just you."

With both hands he grabs the bolt and snaps the strap over the end, securing it tight. When I go to pull the fabric down and slide it into the wide mouth of his machine he crowds me against the large metal side. "Leave it, Clara."

His dark eyes search my face, hands by his sides. Shoulders rising and falling rapidly, like he's had to outrun the Control officers in the Province, he brushes against me. A strand of hair falls over my face from my bun and I sweep it aside. His head tilts and his Adam's apple bobs. He growls, ragged and heady. If I didn't hate every fibre of his stinking being, I would say this is intense.

But I do, and he absolutely reciprocates.

Always has.

"Bendall? You good?" Remmins snaps from beside us. I didn't see him come over.

"Fine." I say through clenched teeth. "If you don't mind, Prendergast. I have a machine to attend to."

His face slackens and he steps back, taking most of his weight on his good leg. I glance back as I walk away. How can someone I loathe have that effect on me? I shake it off and clear my throat.

I make it back to my machine and slam a shaking hand onto the start button. I dip my head and drag in a breath. Air that I am sure was always there, rushes back into my lungs.

The grunting sound of a jammed machine sees me snap my head up.

Shit.

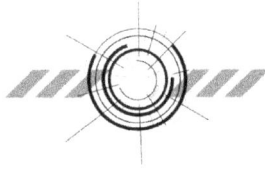

IT'S BEEN three days since Vivi asked for me. The infirmary was full when I went to her. A few of the bunks occupied by injured Engineers, but most are filled with those in the early stages of the mysterious disease that nobody will tell us a damn thing about. And from what I can see, no supervisors have contracted it as yet.

Hovering outside the infirmary, I wait for the change of shift when they do their twenty-minute handover. If I can slip in and talk to Vivi, she may have heard something. Anything. Three infirmary officers wander toward me in the corridor, chatting.

I pull out the document I swiped off Remmin's impossibly neat desk and pretend to be studying it intensely, leaning on the wall a few feet away from the door to the infirmary. The officers ignore me, walking inside for their shift.

A moment later, I slip in behind them head down making a b-line for Vivi's bunk. The curtain is pulled around and I disappear inside her cubicle. Instead of her pretty brown eyes and infectious smile, a middle-aged man stares back at me, his face blank.

Where the hell is V?

"Sorry, I must be in the wrong room—"

"No, please," he begs as a cough steals the last of the word. His hands reach to cover his mouth. Purple and green bruises line his arms. Holy hell.

Despite self-preservation, I step closer.

"How long have you had these?" I nod to the bruises, and he closes his eyes.

Once recovered, he sighs. "Two weeks after I contracted the virus."

I stumble backward, slamming into a metal trolley. A tin cup and kidney tray with clean swabs crashes to the ground.

Murmurs rise and footsteps quicken. I back through the curtain and steal away into the next cubicle, hands holding the material closed. Medicos file in, checking in on the man who apologises for the mess but doesn't rat me out. I say a little prayer for him.

"Clara?"

I move toward her voice. Vivi is on the bunk, dressed in a white infirmary gown, her face viciously pale. The starts of bruising over her arms as well. I don't understand, she only got sick a week ago.

Now, I am sure she has the virus. My heart flings in my ribs, the air that was in my lungs a second ago is nowhere to be found. My heart aches a little for my first and only friend in Sector Two.

"Viv," I utter.

She forces a smile. "It's okay, Clara. Honestly." She coughs. "Decades of service in the Sectors is worse, really."

I try to huff a laugh but fail.

"Heavens above." I pull my bottom lip through my teeth. Tears burn the bridge of my nose, but I refuse to let them fall.

"Hey, can I tell you something?" she whispers.

"Sure."

I rest a hand over my heart and move closer to her. She stifles a cough and holds a hand up, as if to say stay back. Hesitating, I stay grounded where I am. She grips the side of the bed lifting herself up a little.

"Something is off about this disease, Clara. It's too selective. I'm not saying that because it's me. It's targeting Engineers, not Supervisors. Not one superior has been in here sick. Not one. You have to find out what they're doing."

So, I'm not the only one to put two and two together.

Smart girl our Vivi.

"I will find out what's going on. How to help you, I swear."

She tries to sit up. Automatically I move to help her, and her hand shoots up between us again. "You are no good to us sick. Go on." She waves toward the door.

I promise to come back tomorrow, or the day after. Waiting until the rounds start, I slip out of the infirmary unseen. Before the door, a small desk sits to the right against the wall. Papers and files are stacked on top. Names of patients. Numbers. Reports titled by month. I pluck up last month's file and slink out the door. Shoving it up my shirt and tucking it in, I hunch over a little to hide the bulky rectangle.

The second I'm back in the dorm, I slide it under my mattress. Making myself appear busy, I go about getting ready for a shower. People mill about doing the same. And when the last person leaves for supper, I wander into a cubicle.

Stripping down to bare skin, I flip the lever and wait for the steam to rise. It thoroughly engulfs the small space as I step into the water and let my eyes drift shut. My back to the water, I roll my head on my shoulders and stretch aching muscles.

I hate showering when others are in the room, and I have made a habit of taking long and slow ones when they all go to supper. Sometimes I miss out on the better food, but it's a sacrifice I'm willing to make for the luxury of a long, hot, uninterrupted shower.

The door to the dorm thuds closed. I snap my head up and eyes open. Boots. Footsteps drift toward the cubicle. I recognised the boots and the gait, my gut sinks like a stone in shallow water.

Johnson.

No.

The door opens. I grab for my towel but it disappears from the hook a second before my fingers reach it. I back up into the water, arms over my breasts. He steps into the space and closes the door behind him, fixing the lock. The one I forgot to turn when I came in here.

No.

No.

No.

Of all the people I would welcome into my shower; to touch me, he would never make the list. If he was the last man on earth, I would die celibate.

Now, trapped here with him, my breaths turn shallow and a stone lodges firm in my throat. There's no use in yelling for help. There's no one else here. I back up further, but he closes the distance. My back hits the shower wall. A lose a whimper and hate myself for it instantly.

Son of a bitch.

Johnson's leer roves over my naked skin, making it crawl, and bile rises up my insides. I throw a hand up. "Stop! Get the hell away from me!"

He chuckles and runs a hand through his greasy blond hair. The bulge in his pants confirms what I imagine he came into my space to do. The Sectors are rough. We have to be built tough enough to survive the things that happen here. But being forced wasn't on my list of expectations.

Ever.

I was naive.

"Back the hell up and out of my shower, Johnson!"

"Oh, come on Clara. Don't be like that. I promise you'll like it. Won't even take long." The smirk on his face sends chills down my spine.

Dammit.

Air chokes its way up, and anger coils in my core. Fire flares in my veins, and I take a swing at him. Catching my wrist, he ogles his way down then back up.

"Nice, Bendall. This really won't take long." His buckle clinks, his other hand working himself free. His hand slams around my neck and he pushes me backward until my back hits the wall. Standing in the stream of water, he fists himself.

A whimper slips past his grip against my windpipe. He tightens his hold and I scramble for air. Rallying, I make one last plea. "Leave me al—"

The stall door rattles. Something hits it hard, and it bursts open. My vision is fading in and out with Johnson's hold on my neck. I flail around, trying to hit him with whatever limb I can wield. My hair, matted to my face, shields my vision.

Johnson is ripped backward. "Hey! Get your—"

A fist smashes into his face.

Blood gushes from his nose. He crumples and bends over, grabbing at his face. The guy, I'm sure it's a guy—bigger, bulkier than Johnson, darker—grabs him by the scruff and slams him into the shower stall wall by the hook. A knee sinks into Johnson's gut. Another fist into his face. Upwards and hard. Johnson takes a swing and misses. He's thrown against the stall wall opposite.

Another fist into his face while he cowers on the floor. The guy, so familiar even through the blur of tears, drags him out of the shower stall and tosses him to the floor before turning back to me. Behind the guy now standing with a heaving chest and arms hanging by his sides, Johnson scrambles to his feet and runs from the dorm.

I rub my hands over my face, trying to coax my vision back.

My mouth drops open as I meet his dark eyes.

My heart thunders harder.

His jaw clenches, throat working. He shuts the shower door and walks out.

Nate.

11

TESSA

THE VISI-SCREEN IS A LIAR. It has to be. Nothing else would make more sense.

I reread the comms.

THREE LOCATIONS HAVE BEEN PINNED down for possible hideout for the rebellion. This information will not be actioned on until further notice. The last thing Sontaria needs is the Sectors or Province acquiring themselves a martyr.

Location 1 - transient, nomadic loca-tions that are only shared every few days.

Well, that is useless.

Location 2 - Boiler room, City Center Plaza.

Location 3 - Catacombs underneath the train station. Orders are not to engage.

DO NOT ENGAGE

Rebels in the city. Could they know something about the disease Clara is talking about? What about the cure? The city won't engage with them, yet. What does that mean? They'd have the resources, I would think. Unless . . . Unless the city is timing the rebel's exposure for their own benefit. The city is nothing, if not strategic. Elites are the top one percent of every last person in this ring.

Smart doesn't start to cover it.

If they are not engaging with a rebellion that could be growing in their own city, they have a reason. One the rebels are most likely not going to like. Nor come off best with. Is Amber part of the rebellion? She practically enabled me to contact Clara, which is prohibited. And she's somehow connected to Matthews.

I wipe the search history from my Visi-Screen. Grabbing my jacket and access card, I rush from my room. In the foyer on the ground floor, Elites are getting ready for their day. Some stand around chatting, others organising their satchels. Those must be in Academics. I have never seen an Aeronautic or Comms Elite carry a bag or have papers that they need to tote around either.

"Morning, Miss Tessa," Joe greets me as I walk outside.

"Morning, Joe. Busy day planned?"

"Absolutely," he responds as he always does. Standing on the front door for sixteen hours, busy isn't the right word for what he withstands every single day. More like tiresome, torturous, or stoic. All appropriate words for Joe in their own right.

Instead of heading to the training building, I take a gamble and make for Headquarters. It will be bustling at this hour, and I plan on slipping in unnoticed. I need to see Amber.

Now.

I climb the tens of wide steps to the revolving doors of Headquarters, Elites file inside in tight, collar-coded lines. A blue Aeronautic trainee is going to stick out like nothing else. I pull a slip of paper from my pocket and write out Amber's code and name, hoping it is enough to allow me through the door.

As I stop at the entrance, an officer with a gun sweeps his gaze up and down my uniform. A frown drops over his features.

"I'm here to see an officer in Comms. My trainer sent me over."

He tilts his head, so I flash the paper and Amber's name. He snatches it up.

Please don't open it. Please.

Deft fingers flip it over as he reads the name and number before pressing it back into my hand and nodding for me to enter. Once inside I release a quiet breath and head for

Comms level, reminding myself, this is for Clara. If I can get to the rebellion, I can find out what she needs to know. Or even better, help find a cure.

Moments later, Amber's heated stare pins me to the toilet wall. I shouldn't have come.

No, I need to help my sister.

I'm not leaving until I have information on the rebels. End of story.

The toilet cubicle is small. "This really isn't the best place for this conversation," she utters, fingers pinching the bridge of her nose.

"Would you rather we did it at your desk?"

"Fair point."

"So, what can you tell me?"

"Why do you want to find them? You're an Elite who just arrived in the city. The last thing you ought to be doing is getting tied up with trouble."

"So, you do know about them."

"Heard of them, but honestly, who hasn't?"

"I didn't know a thing about a rebellion until I stumbled across a comms. There was never any talk of rebels even in the Province. You would think, a place like that would have a by-product of some sort of rebels, but nope. Not a thing until I came here."

She frowns and sighs. "You should stop digging around before something or someone finds *you*."

She's the second person to tell me that this week, and I huff an indignant laugh. I mean, as far as snooping goes,

I've only read a few slightly questionable comms. The only thing of note was the one on the rebels. I was careful, I covered my tracks.

"If I show you one of the old hideouts, will you stop looking?"

Mouth agape, I snap my eyes to hers.

She continues. "Don't look at me like that, I was in the Provinces a few years before you were. I know what it's like to have family you care about." She stares at the screen before shaking her head. "My parents still live there. You have to promise to drop it, if I take you."

"Fine."

No person on this earth ever said the word fine and meant it. I most certainly have no intention of dropping it. Not until I have helped my sister in every way possible. Someone enters the bathroom and closes a stall door. We both freeze momentarily before locking eyes.

"Right then, meet me out front tonight around twenty-one hundred hours," she whispers.

I nod and she exits the stall. I wait another minute, just in case, before pushing out of the cubicle and heading for the front door.

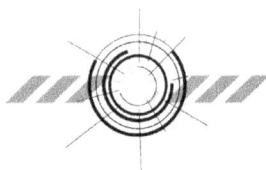

THE DOORS to Headquarters are locked tight. I sit on the steps and pull out a small Visi-Tile I was issued during induction to jot down any study notes. Now, I scribble out anything that ties to the rebellion or me asking about it. Anything I can remember from the comms and Amber's help. I glance at my wrist gadget.

21:04

She's late.

I go back to my Visi-Tile and slide the stylus across it to run a line through anything I think doesn't sound right. But my thoughts wander back to last night with Matthews. For a second, I thought there may have been something between us. I have always noticed him. Has he even noticed me? Or am I simply another trainee to fill his day and log hours alongside?

When I come to the end of my list, F Matthews sits on the bottom of it. I circle the F, wondering. I draw a double line under the initial F, as if it will help me figure out what it stands for.

"Finn."

Jerking my head up with a start, Amber stands over me, lopsided smile on her pretty face, eyes lit up. I clear my throat. "Um, pardon?"

"His first name, it's Finn."

"Oh," I utter as heat floods my neck and face and I pray she can't see it in the evening streetlight. The fact that she found me lingering on his name . . .

"We should be going, you ready?" Amber says, looking up and down the street.

"Sure." I stand and follow her. Two Elites out for a walk. "How do you know about the locations, you know, if they're abandoned?"

She shakes her head and gestures to a side street. Turning left, we walk in silence until the narrow space between the buildings swallows us whole.

"I was associated with someone who used to be part of the rebels. Back when I was a newb like you."

"What happened to them?"

She doesn't answer right away, and I don't push. Finally, she says, "they were in an accident and got sent to Sector Four. I heard, on the network, they didn't last."

"Where are they now?" I regret the words the second they leave my mouth.

"Wastelands." She forces a smile and picks up the pace.

We are heading toward the City Center Plaza, a huge array of shops all bundled together across four blocks. We reach the dirty back alley behind the large complex, and Amber wanders to a cellar door and pulls it open. It's rusted with age and whines something fierce as she lays it back, waving me through the opening.

Without hesitation, I climb downstairs. It's dark, and the tang of damp and mould fills the cold space. A light bursts to life behind me as she treads her way down. Her wrist gadget. Why didn't I think of that? Whispering, "light," mine illuminates the space around me.

At the bottom of the extensive stairwell, the huge empty room around us is lined with metal filing cabinets, wooden desks and odd chairs. It's like a poor version of the Comms room, but with one difference.

No tech.

No screens.

No cables or wireless desk top machines.

Just desks, knocked over seats, and papers that litter almost every surface, as if they left in a hurry, fill the space. They were obviously not worried about whatever the papers contain. I step across to the nearest desk and pluck up a sheet. It is covered in names and numbers. Similar to the one the officer held on her clipboard at selection. Very similar.

"Well, this is it. Nothing much to see. Now, can we go?"

"Wait a sec."

At the next desk, the metal drawer pulls out easy. Nothing. Only an old pen type implement, and a small, round metal object. I pick it up and the front of it falls open, exposing a white face with N, E, S & W. The letters are spaced evenly around it, connected to the center by lines and an arrow that spins when I move the piece. Inside the lid a flame is etched into the brass metal.

Curious. I shove it in my pocket for examination later.

"We should leave, Tessa. The last thing we need is to be caught out after curfew."

She shifts on her feet, glancing up the stairs every few seconds, as if the security officers are going to thunder down them at any moment. "There's nothing left here. You have your proof they exist, now let's get out of here."

"Fine."

I follow her up the stairs and into the alley way. It's darker than a few moments ago. Another partial blackout? I scan the skyline. Most of the buildings are lit up as normal. Nothing appears out of place. Amber strides ahead of me. If we are caught out after curfew, what will we even say?

"Amber, wait up!"

She throws a look over her shoulders as if to tell me to be quiet, and I hurry after her. She glances at me again, her face pulled into a frown. "Promise me you'll leave this alone now."

She holds up a hand with a pinkie sticking out. Is she serious? Stifling a chuckle, I link mine with hers. "I promise to leave this alley alone."

She tilts her head giving me an incredulous look. We round the corner into the main street.

"This is where we part ways. If you need comms again, send word first. Security has been pickier lately. I'm not sure they aren't monitoring every single Comms Elite now."

"I will. Thank you for tonight," I say softly as we approach our building.

She gives me a small smile and veers off when we enter the lobby of trainee quarters. I swipe my access code and the doors swing open. I step in and tap the icon for the fortieth floor and the elevator rises, floor after floor. The doors open with a soft ping, and I step into the corridor.

It's dim. Not lit by the usual blue and white lights. I march toward my door, desperate to get inside. Something doesn't seem right. Fear trickles down my spine. Every breath rattles like thunder and sounds even louder. I swipe my access panel and wait as the door slowly swooshes open.

Taking a step into my room, I release a wobbly breath.

A hand grabs my wrist, spinning me back.

Shit!

My gut flips. Lightning, like erratic buzzing, flies through my veins.

A guy in a dark hoodie crowds me against the wall, just inside my room. I swallow past the terror that has closed over my airway. It's the same guy I passed in the alley that first night. His hand tightens around my wrist. The other slams against the wall by my head as he leans down and tilts his.

My door swooshes shut. He pushes the hood from his head as his gaze finds mine.

My mouth gapes on a sharp inhale.

12

CLARA

BY NORMAL STANDARDS, I should be grateful to Nate. Hell, maybe I am. But the disgust that lines his face as his glare eats into my skin, has me so far from gratitude I need binoculars. Even from across the mess hall this morning, his expression sends my gut plummeting.

Urgh. Whatever.

"You look happy this morning," Ash says plonking onto the bench beside me. Nate's focus snaps back to his food. I narrow my eyes, as if it's my only play for revenge against the dirty scowl he's been throwing my way for the last ten minutes. "I'm fine."

Ash sips his coffee and plucks a slice of toast from his plate. "You want to come over tonight? There was a surplus of rations and Supervisors got the pick of the lot. I have *contraband*." He winks at me. The last time I was in his room we had decided on a no strings arrangement and lost half our clothes to the floor.

Now, I could really use a way to blow off some steam—along with Nate's stupid glare. "Sure. What time?"

"Seven good for you?"

"Yup." I throw down the last of the coffee in my mug, it's cold. I don't even care. Snatching up my tray I dump it on the service trolley on the way out, before pushing through the double swinging doors. Footsteps march up behind me, and I hurry, heading straight for the factory floor.

When I stop at the doors, they're still locked. Dammit.

Spinning back, Nate is inches from where I stand, my back hits the door. Heat flushes my face as anger rises in my veins, like fire crackling to a steady roar the longer those dark eyes scrutinise every part of my face. "Get out of my space, Nathanial."

He huffs a breath, not moving. Hands clenched by his sides. His throat works but after a moment he makes space between us. "You shouldn't be alone in the dorm, Bendall."

"Don't tell me you actually care," I hiss.

His eyes widen a little. "I don't. Don't flatter yourself."

Voices float toward us from down the hall. I slide away from him, my back still to the door. He steps back, but falters on his bad leg. My gaze drops to it, and he catches the movement. His mouth puckers for a second before he schools it to a thin line framed by a stony face. The door behind me buzzes and I push on it, slipping through before his mouth can run at me with whatever is going through that head of his.

Head down and hands busy, I keep to myself throughout

the shift. Only glancing in Nate's direction when his grunts are audible over the machines. The days are too long for someone with an injury like his. Not that he would ever admit that the stupid ass. I finish up and tally my quota before handing the final number to Remmins. The small smile that lights his face when I turn and walk toward the door reminds me of our plans.

I wander past Nate as he struggles with his last bolt. Fabric secured, he hunches over and grips his knees, catching his breath. "Stop slacking off Prendergast, we have quotas to fill, you lazy prick."

Standing tall, his hate-laced eyes track me as I saunter toward the doors, letting my hips sway. Hesitating at the exit, one hand on the metal push panel, I turn back. Remmins's eyes narrow as I snap a glare to Nate and blow him a kiss with a smirk. His mouth moves, as if saying screw you. But I can't hear it over the machines and it's nothing new coming from him.

The door swings closed behind me, and I walk to the infirmary. Maybe Vivi will have some news for me today. I file in with the rest of the visitors, Vivi's bunk is empty.

So is the man's bunk next to hers.

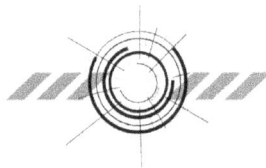

AT NINETEEN HUNDRED HOURS, I knock on Ash's door. It swings open.

"Hey Clara."

His hair is ruffled like his hands were just in it. Messy hair is cute on him.

"Hi," I say, a little coy. After Nate's incinerating glowers today, and the fright Vivi gave me being moved to another bunk, a little fun with Ash is entirely what I need. He wanders to his small table and drops into the chair.

Something amber swirls in the glass gripped tight in his hand. This is new. I kick off my shoes and take my hair out of the bun that has been pulling my scalp tight all day. Strawberry blonde waves settle over my shoulders. Ash's eyes peer over his glass, taking in every move I make.

I pluck up the bottle on his table, pulling out the cork, and raise it to my nose. The tang and burn has my face twisted up. How can he drink this stuff? "Damn Ash, you expect me to kiss you with this on your lips?"

"No . . . yes."

"What do you mean?"

"Are you sure you want to be here, Clara?"

"Yes, I'm sure."

"It's only—"

"What, Ash?"

"You seem to have a relationship of sorts with Prendergast."

"Are you kidding me? The guy hates my guts. We do *not* have a relationship."

"Mhmmm."

I sit on the table in front of him and he shuffles backward, chair and all.

"This is how much I don't have a relationship with Nate Prendergast, Ash Remmins." I work on the buttons of my shirt. Flipping them loose, one by one. His eyes follow my hands, roving over the places where the shirt falls away. Reaching the last button, I wriggle it from my shoulders and toss it on the floor. Next, I slide off the table and push the standard issue pants over my hips.

Ash downs the last of his drink and leans to place it on the table. On his way back, his hands land on my hips. Hungry, strong hands travel over my stomach, skimming across ribs and around my back. My bra pops open a heartbeat later. I chuckle and he sinks his head between my breasts. This is as far as we got last time. Here's hoping there are no interruptions this time round.

"Ash?"

"Mhmmm," he rumbles against my stomach, as my hands play through his hair and down the back of his neck.

Heat pools low and fast as his thumb glides over my skin and into my panties. They're the only thing between Ash and my naked body and I take his head in my hands, tilting his face up. "Yours have to come off too."

He chuckles softly but stands. Now, his gaze falls on me while I make quick work of his buttons and toss his shirt to the floor. I trace my fingertips over his toned chest. He closes his eyes, breaths deepening further with every inch my fingers travel lower.

"Clara," he whispers.

"Yeah?"

"We should slow down."

"If you think so, Remmins."

"Please don't call me that, not here. Not like this."

"Okay, Ash."

He opens his eyes and something like hurt flashes through them ever so quick. I grab his face and drag his mouth to mine. His hands cup my breasts. It takes everything I have not to moan into his mouth, like a schoolgirl. Every inch of him is warm and hard and overwhelming.

"Tell me what you want, Clara."

For a handful of heartbeats, I stare at him. It's been a long time since I was with someone who asked what *I* want. Who even cared. It's entirely possible that he's different because he's ten years older than me.

"I want your mouth, your hands on me. I want you inside me. But only after you have touched every part of me with your mouth and hands first."

A small smile pulls up on his face. His dark eyes are lit with delight. His voice is raw when he says, "lay back."

With a soft giggle, I lay on his table. Now I'm glad I had a long shower. I was careful to make sure the rest of the dorm was milling about this time. Ash is between my legs a second later. His hands grip my ass, and he moves closer to the edge of the table before pulling his seat over. He's hell bent on taking his time.

Oh damn.

"The day you arrived here, I couldn't stop thinking about you." He steadies himself above me with one hand and cradles my breast with the other as he crowds me. "These beautiful things, I wanted them in my mouth." His head dips. Tongue swirling around my left nipple, and then my right, I arch into him. His smile moves against the soft side of my right breast.

Heavens he's good.

"Every time I even glance at your pretty face, I'm rock hard, Clara."

"*Every* time?"

He rolls my nipples between his fingers. "Every. Damn. Time."

"Well, you have them now, let's play."

"If that's what you want? To just play?"

"Uh huh. That's what I want."

His face slackens a little as I press my lips to his and he nudges me open. We are a tangle of teeth, lips and tongue. Heat and pleasure. Desire and hunger. How long has Ash Remmins been without this? I can't imagine many Engineers file through these doors. He's not the type. Too quiet. Too stoic and respectful.

Finally coming up for air, his hands are gripped around my thighs. "Need more?"

"Yes, Ash."

His thumb finds my apex, circling it in a torturous wide circle that misses the point with every frustrating revolution. I groan and he gives me a cheeky smile. There is no doubt he is playing with me.

"You know I can torture you just as much, Asher."

"I am very aware of all the ways in which you torture me." His mouth is hot and hungry. His finger finds the spot I have been needing it to, and I whimper against his mouth as he pushes my legs wider.

"Ash," I rasp.

"Clara," he utters lowering his head to my breast, teeth plucking at my peak before tangling his tongue around it and sucking it. My hands crawl through his hair, and he groans into my chest. He likes that. I want to touch him. He isn't close enough.

"I want to touch you. See you."

He releases my nipple with a wet pop and straightens, removing his pants and boxers. His hard, thick length springs out, with a slap against his stomach. I slide off the table and circle my fingers around the tip. He shudders and a breath catches in his working throat.

"Back on the table." His words are gravel.

I do as I'm told.

He drops into the chair and widens my legs with warm, firm hands. Pressing kisses up each thigh, he runs his tongue through my wetness. I grip the edges of the table with both hands.

"A—Ash," I stutter.

His fingers find my entrance. "You want more?"

"Please."

He leans over, grabbing up the bottle of contraband. He spins the lid off its thread and tips the bottle, wetting his fingers. It's cold on my nipples. He licks and sucks, sliding two fingers into my wet heat. I buck off the table. The tang of the liquid fills my senses and a heady, dizziness hangs out of reach.

His thumb runs circles around my apex, sending me higher and higher.

"You like that, Clara?"

His voice is strung out when I open my eyes to find his hooded. His gaze burns into mine. Those dark eyes are going to haunt my days, I just know it. "Yes, please don't stop."

His free hand grabs the bottle. He drips a little liquid onto my throbbing apex before sinking back onto his chair and lapping it up with his tongue. I explode around his fingers. Hands frantically pushing through his hair. "Oh my go—Ash."

He chuckles against my electrified center, sending me higher again.

13

TESSA

CARAMEL, woodsy.

Finn.

Matthews, I mean.

Finn Matthews crowds me against the door. My heart putting forward its best effort to punch a hole through the metal behind me.

"What were you doing?" he growls.

I raise my chin to meet his now dark and fiery eyes. Something in my core bursts to life and flutters upwards crashing into my lungs. A moment is all it takes for my breaths to peter to less than bearable swift burns.

"Where were you, Bendall?"

"Are you asking as my trainer?"

His jaw feathers, eyes widening the tiniest bit. "Yes."

"Well, in that case, none of your business, Matthews."

"You were out after curf—"

"I'm aware, thank you." The curtness of my tone sends him reeling back as if slapped.

"What? You can tell me what to do but I can't be unhappy about it?"

"That's not—"

"Not what, Finn?"

His mouth opens, then closes. Finally, he says, "stop looking, Tessa. Stop, it's not worth it."

"Says you."

He pierces me with an incredulous stare.

"You should probably leave. After curfew and all." I wave a hand at the door.

He stalks out into the corridor. I wait for the swoosh and clunk before sliding down the wall to my seat. The rawness of everything I felt in the last few moments comes crashing down. The realisation that the rebellion is real. They exist and may know about the cure for whatever is plaguing the Sectors and endangering my sister.

I flip my access card over in my hand, letting the thin plastic scrape against my palm each time.

Amber and Finn.

The rebels.

The comms instructing the authorities to not engage.

The training airspace that borders Sectors One and Two.

So many puzzle pieces. Now, I need to figure out how they fit.

I need to see the whole picture.

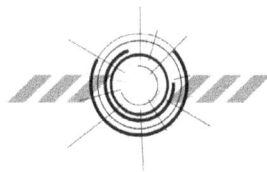

I LIED. I said I would drop it, and I lied.

Sorry, Amber.

Finn . . . not as sorry about that to be honest.

I slide between the shadows after curfew, tracking my way toward the second possible location for the rebel hideout. I half expect Finn to appear from the shadows, in his black hoody and moody as hell, to escort me back to my quarters.

The hour is late, almost midnight, and I'm farther from my quarters than I have ever been since I arrived in the city. It's freeing and terrifying all at once. There isn't supposed to be crime in the wondrous city of glass, but not everyone who lives here is an Elite, at least, not all the time.

My destination is the catacombs beneath the train station. Heavens knows where the entry door would be for such a place. The train station building is long and old. Most likely one of the original structures when the city was founded. The long historic building is framed by wide steps on the city side, and a long, wide cement platform on the train side. The green and grey trim, which I didn't pick up on last time I was here, is immaculate—like it could've been painted yesterday.

At a run, skirting the building, I hunt for any sign of an entrance. When I have been around twice, my legs ache with exertion. Breathless I bend over, scanning the underside of the platform. No trains after curfew.

Electricity flings along my veins as I jump down onto the tracks. There are tens of three-foot vault-type doors. I spin the wheel on the first one and tug it open. A short space, filled with cables, is all I find. I move to the next.

Another cable-filled vault.

Next.

This one has fuses, and lever switches. Power for the main track I assume.

Next.

No luck.

Opening the last one of this side of the tracks, my heart sinks. Another useless small space. I turn back. The opposite side of the tracks is lined with as many doors. It's well after zero one hundred hours now. I hesitate before the long metal length that encases the electro-rail strip.

Not active, it is a dull grey thin line. During the day, when this place is teeming with life, they would be blue, turning white as the train sails over them, fading back to blue as is it disappears.

I could jump over and start the other side. But I have training in six hours, and I need sleep. Can't have Matthews thinking I'm slacking off, or worse, too absorbed by finding the rebellion to concentrate on my training.

A surveillance light swings over the tracks.

Dammit!

I duck under the platform and jog hunched over back to

the start of the building. Voices of a few officers out on patrol, drift down from above.

Footsteps march toward me on the platform. If they realise I'm here, I'm done.

Rounding the corner where the platform ends, four officers stand talking.

Carefully, I slink backward. There's nowhere to hide.

Unless . . .

I turn the wheel on the first vault and slip in, pulling the door shut as much as possible. The small space is warm, and I hug my legs to my body. I will wait them out. Maybe they will be gone in a moment. My eyelids are heavy. It's been a long, eventful day. Resting my head on my knees I let them fall shut. Only for a few minutes.

Just a tiny nap.

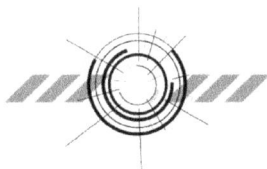

THE ROAR of the train right beside me jerks me awake with the start of a lifetime. My heart flings into my throat as I take in the small, cramped space I am folded up in. I fell asleep. Daylight splinters in through the crack where the door has fallen open an inch.

I turn my wrist gadget and tap the screen.

06:00

Crap. I have to be at training in twenty minutes. An early

start to claim our air space this morning. I wait until the train swooshes to a stop and tentatively push the vault door open. Above me people rush around, departing or arriving.

I slip out and run around the side of the building. Nobody sees a dishevelled Elite in Aeronautics blue. I stretch my legs, taking off at a sprint. The much needed pull on each muscle loosens the tension in my weary body, and I relax a little about the fact I slept in a cable vault last night.

I make the training hangar with three minutes to spare. Matthews is standing by our aircraft, Visi-Tile in hand, as he no doubt does his own preflight check. Snatching up a Visi-Tile on the table beside the craft, I move in beside him. His gaze runs over my hair. No neat bun today. Heavens, I didn't even eat breakfast or do my teeth. Heat floods my neck and face, as he turns on his heel and walks into the aircraft.

"Rough night?" Finn says, as I drop into the pilot seat.

"Something like that."

He raises an eyebrow before letting his attention drift back to his Visi-Tile. "None of my business," he mutters.

His tone is flat, like he's completely uninterested. Like he doesn't care.

"What are we working on today?" I ask, trying to shift the focus.

"Forced landings." He snaps his head up; his eyes burn into mine.

Right. Where we cut the disrupters and plummet to the ground, priming the engines to restart in an effort to save ourselves from being compressed into the ground with this tin can as our coffin. Super.

Forced landings were the one piloting skill I scored the poorest on in the sim. Agility, manoeuvring, tandem flight were all ninety percenters for me. Forced landings, not so much. Nerves start in my gut, sending my hands into a tremble as I fumble with the harness. Finn leans over and taps the side panel and the harness slides around my torso, securing me in tight. No escape now.

I run through the pre-flight checklist and start the engines.

Finn swipes through screens on his Visi-Tile, as if uninterested. Fine by me.

He radios ahead for clearance, as I taxi to the launch pad. As we leave the ground, he doesn't look up. He either trusts me to not screw this up or he is lost in his head somewhere. I choose the first one.

Once in the northern training area I set the craft into a pattern before leaning back in my chair and crossing my arms over my chest. I stare at him, waiting for him to acknowledge where we are. To acknowledge me. Any contact at this point would be something.

He doesn't respond.

"Finn?"

No response. He's engrossed in whatever is on his screen.

"Should I cut the engines, Matthews?"

He flinches but doesn't shift his gaze.

Should I shut down the disrupters? Would that pull him out of his head?

"Killing the front engines now." I move my hand over the controls.

"Hey, sorry, what?" Dragging his eyes from the Visi-Tile to my own his mouth gapes.

I reach for the control panel and slide the bar for the front engines down. His hand lands over mine. "Stop."

"Why? Aren't we here for a forced landing?"

His chest works through deep cycles as he slides the Visi-Tile onto the side of his seat, waving his hand over the panel dock. His panel slides out to his lap.

"What's got into you?" I ask. Where is the guy that was in my space demanding answers two nights ago.

"Nothing, I—" His hands fall away. "Forced landings are an essential skill for all pilots. Engine failure. Sabotage. Attack. All could require you to guide the craft down safely."

"Sabotage or attack? In the magnificent city of glass?"

Catching my mocking tone, he swipes through a set of screens and taps a red panel before looking back at me.

"Recording paused," a robotic woman says.

"You remember the flight sessions recorded? For further training purposes."

Shit.

I knew, I forgot.

"Sorry," I whisper, knots tie in rapid succession in my gut. How could I forget that? How could I be so stupid?

"Don't be sorry, Tess. Be smart. Stay an Elite. Stay safe."

For what seems like forever, all I can do is stare at him. His gaze has turned dark, and he runs a hand through his hair, messing it up. My heart rate kicks.

"Why?"

"What do you mean, why?"

"Why do you care what happens to me, Finn?"

We sit, mere inches apart, suspended ten thousand feet in the air. The electricity that hangs between us is ridiculous. But as he said, these trainings are recorded. We can't afford a lengthy gap in the recording, lest we are hauled into Headquarters for an explanation. As if reading my mind, he slides the bar back to green.

"Recording in progress," the robotic woman drones.

He clears his throat and darts his focus to the dashboard screen. "I will run you through the first forced landing. In real time they can be stressful."

"Okay."

My whole body vibrates with something addictive that has nothing to do with the fact we are about to plummet toward the ground.

"Harness check," Finn breathes.

I tug on both straps. "Check."

The air all of a sudden is far too thin up here.

Finn's fingers drag downwards on the panel and the aircraft goes quiet.

My breath stops.

"You're okay, Tess."

We hover for a moment and then the weight of the craft

drags us toward the earth, gaining speed as we descend. I grip the chair with white knuckles. Unable to garner control over my breathing, my vision blurs. Finn is counting softly.

When he gets to ten Mississippi, whatever that metric is, he slides four fingers over the panel, firing up all four engines at once. The craft pitches upwards and Finn's eyes shutter closed. If he's praying, I'm going to kill him, right here.

The roar of the engine subdues the rising panic that claws its way up my insides.

Heavens above.

How am I supposed to pull that off on my own? We level out and the engines drone back to the normal steady hum, and I release a ragged breath. A brilliant smile splits Finn's face. He damn well enjoyed that.

"Nothing to it," he says with a chuckle.

I roll my eyes at him. I don't even care if he writes me up for it.

Go ahead.

"Your turn," he says, searching my face.

"Uh uh, no way. I couldn't even breathe just then, how am I supposed to think straight?"

"I'll talk you through it, you will be fine. I promise, Tess."

Every time he calls me that, it's almost as if he . . .

When we rise to fourteen thousand feet again, his fingers slide the four bars down. Silence fills the cockpit.

Shit, shit, shit.

The craft drops, sending my stomach into my mouth.

"Breathe, and count. One Mississippi, two Mississippi, three etc," Finn orders.

I reach ten missis-whoever and slide the bars back up on all four disrupters, forcing air in and out of my lungs like it's the only thing that can save me. Maybe it is.

"Pitch up," Finn says.

I pitch the craft up and we climb back up, every thousand feet we gain, the knot in my gut loosens a little.

At ten thousand feet, Finn takes over and sets the auto pilot. "Great, you did better than most of your intake on the first go. You are much more capable than you give yourself credit for."

Heat floods my neck, setting my face on fire. Adrenaline peaking, it thunders through my veins. "Thanks," I breathe.

The most gorgeous smile lights up his face. What I wouldn't do to kiss that mouth, those cheek bones, that jaw.

His Adam's apple bobs.

"Take us home, Officer Bendall."

The words are formal, but they are pure gravel. Like his words are at war with what they are and what they actually mean. The expression on his face is twisting between desire and neutrality.

Banking the craft, I set the heading south.

All of a sudden, this oversized hunk of metal is far too small.

"Tess, what were you doing at the train station last night?"

I freeze.

Taking my hands off the panel, hovering them an inch above. Like a naughty kid caught taking extra rations.

"I wasn't—"

"I saw you."

"Out after curfew Finn Matthew, how very un-Elite of you."

The recording is paused again. If he wanted to land me in trouble he wouldn't keep pausing it. He's protecting me. Like he was two nights ago when he warned me to drop my obsession with the rebels. "Not your business, I guess."

If he thinks I was there to hook up, he'll leave it alone.

"All by yourself?"

"Maybe, maybe not. Are you following me?"

"You are playing with fire. And they're no ordinary flames, they're not what you think."

"How do you know so much about this?" Setting us down on the launching pad, I turn to meet his gaze.

His hand moves. "Recording in progress," the robotic woman drones.

"I've been here much longer than you have. I pick up on things."

"What else are you picking up?" I say as the harness retracts and engines turn silent.

"That you really, really need a shower." His face lights up with cheekiness I haven't seen before. It's stunning.

And now, I need a cold shower.

14

CLARA

NATE'S ASS is in my face. Literally. Hate the man, love his form. He is bending down to gather up the sheets for the industrial-sized washing machine. The giant metal auto-wash machine drones at a low hum, waiting on its next meal of cotton. I happily oblige, tossing in armfuls of sheets, pillowcases and light-knit blankets.

Heavens above, I can only imagine the cooties on this lot. Nate and I are assigned laundry duty this week. I'm grateful it's not kitchen duty. Much hotter and much less room to move. The last thing I want is to be rubbing up against a sweaty Nate Prendergast. Don't get me wrong, the guy is cut and that face— I toss in more linens. It's only his entire personality I can't stand.

He shoves a load into the machine in front of him and slams the door shut. I'm surprised the metal doesn't warp under the wrath of his outright loathing for being on any type of duty. Guess Sector One Engineers had staff. How lovely for them.

"You almost done?" he snaps.

Bugger off, Nate.

"Yup."

"How long do these things run before we have to come back?"

"About an hour, then we load the wet stuff into the driers."

"Fine. I'll be back in an hour." He stalks out of the room, limp nowhere to be found. Urgh, how can one man be so damn hot and such an ass at the same time.

For a Saturday morning, this is actually not a bad way to spend our free time. Everyone else is out in the training yard. Because hauling bolts and walking five miles a day back and forth across the factory floor apparently isn't exercise enough.

Begrudgingly, I follow Nate to the training grounds. I hit the ground running and join the passing joggers pounding their way around the yard. It takes me a few laps before the burn in my legs settles and I fall into a comfortable pace.

Nate is doing strength exercises in the center with a group of guys. Bending to lift a weighted bar, he snatches it up but falters before rising and it falls from his grip. Pushing up he rubs his thigh, studying the bar and weights over, as if deciding which ones he can handle.

His leg is obviously hindering his capabilities.

He tries again. The guys around him have stopped and

watch as he struggles. A smirk spreads over Johnson's face. Asshole would be eating this up after what Nate did in the shower cubicle. If it wasn't for Prendergast, who knows how far Johnson would have gone. I loathe to give that thought airtime.

We jog past the strength area, and I snag Nate's attention. Tossing my head to the side, I gesture for him to come and run. He may not be my favourite person, but I'll be damned if I'll give Johnson an inch with this. "Think you can beat me round the yard, Prendergast?"

I know for a fact he's faster than me. As kids he was always the one to catch me in games of Red Rover in the school yard.

"You must like losing, Bendall," he shouts back tilting his head to a spot in front of me. The pack of joggers I was with has left me behind. I pick up the pace. He jogs over and gives me the side eye, before taking off at a run. I lengthen my stride and match his fast gait.

"You can't let Johnson under your skin." I puff through deep breaths.

"Wasn't going to."

"Yeah right," I huff.

He picks up speed, but his bad leg lags a little. I match his pace, pressing my hand into my side. I don't have a stitch, but Johnson doesn't know that. Nate's limp deepens, and I drift closer. "Keep going."

His face is twisted with pain. The basic training is six laps. We have done four together. His breaths are heavy. The pain in his leg must be intense. I fall back a little and he glances over his shoulder.

"Go," I rasp.

We are on the last lap and he's back to a slow jog.

"Not much better than a girl, Prendergast!" Johnson has gathered a small crowd of guys, who now stand with their arms over their chests and smirks smothering their faces. What I wouldn't give for the chance to shut that asshole up. I catch up to Nate and meet his sideways glance with my own. "Don't let him win, Nate."

He powers ahead, pumping his arms. I take off after him and we fly around the training yard. Nate's face is stone, his mouth curled into something vicious. His leg must be on fire right now. Hands sinking into my sides as we near the starting point and go the sixth lap, I slow down with a stagger.

Nate keeps going. He's a quarter a way round the seventh lap when he falters a little. Johnson's leer, however, is directed at me. He misses the second it takes Nate to right his stride. I stalk to where Johnson stands and fold my arms over my chest. "Still think he's no better than a girl?"

Johnson scoffs and throws his head back before stepping into my space. "Move those tits out of my face, Bendall, or I will take what I want. And your damaged boyfriend won't be around to save you next time."

Damaged.

The blood in my veins turns to lava and my hands ball to fists.

"One. Nate's not my boyfriend. Two. You will never lay a finger on me."

His eyes run up and down my sweaty body, snagging on my breasts. A smirk grows over his ugly face, and I let my hands fall to my sides. I'm not afraid of this tosser.

Not one bit.

"It won't be my fingers you'll be getting, Bendall."

I slam my fist into his nose, so hard my knuckles scream with the sting that follows. I land another and another.

Firm hands grab my arms from behind, and I fall backward, hitting a hard, sweaty wall. Probably one of Johnson's posse. Typical. The M-O fits.

"Let go of me!" I struggle but his grip tightens.

"Stop, Clara." The words are calm, solid, and *familiar.*

I throw my heel back and connect with a shin before the voice registers. He groans and his grip loosens. I spin back as I realise who's holding me.

Hell.

The amusement on Johnson's now bloody face confirms it, as he holds the back of his hand to his nose.

Nate.

"You two are something else, you know. Fighting like you hate each other every minute. We all know it's a facade." Johnson waves a hand at Nate and me before walking back inside the building.

I tug out of Nate's hold and step back. He bends down and rubs his shin through his pants. It's his bad leg too.

Dammit.

I hold out a hand. "Nate, I'm sor—"

"Don't, Bendall." He turns back and limps inside. I stand in the now deserted training yard. Heavens above . . . I was honestly trying to help.

With a sigh, I pad back inside. The laundry should be ready for the dryers now. As if I haven't spent enough time with Nathanial today.

Inside is quiet. The weekends are always much more relaxed than during the week with officers and Engineers hurrying around to make quotas, fill orders and the like. I wander through the corridor heading for the laundry. It's below the main floor, so I push through the door to the stairwell and descend the stairs lost in thought. Voices drift down, echoing around me, pulling me from my daydream.

"The injury is slowing him down. This Sector is too much for him. No other Sector will want him, not with a busted leg."

"You're probably right. The lower Sectors are harder labour than One and Two. He's going to end up in the Wastelands if he doesn't start making the minimum quota."

"Shame to lose a strapping lad like that. Unfortunate that Sector One didn't follow protocol with the maintenance. If they had, the accident wouldn't have happened."

The air in my lungs stalls out.

Nate.

"Regardless of what happened, his options are limited now. Either he pulls his weight here or he's going to find himself in a bad position."

Their voices fade and the door on the level above me whispers shut, and I take off down the stairs, two at a time. I burst through the last door at the end of the stairwell and into the laundry room. Nate stands by one of the dryers, stuffing it with wet sheets and what not.

Hovering inside the door, chest heaving, I hesitate. A little from my rapid descent down the stairs, but mostly for the guy in the room. I realise in this moment; he is the last connection I have with home. The last part of home that exists here. A little piece of the Provinces, that reminds me of my parents, and the life we had. Of Tessa.

"You gonna stand there, Bendall? Or do your job."

He's still hauling wet laundry into the machine. I shake my head and swallow before walking to my washer and pulling the oversized door open. The load of heavy, wet linen tumbles out toward me, and I stumble back a little. Damn it's heavy.

Something folds in behind me. No, someone. His arm reaches over my shoulder, large hand pushing the wet sheets off me and back into the machine.

I slip away from him and grab a large trolley, pushing it up against the mouth of the washer. From the side, I pull the sheets and towels into the trolley. Nate stands on the opposite side of the trolley, watching me. His face is unreadable.

Finally, the last of the wet linen is out of the machine, and I push it over to the dryer. So heavy. It always is. Slowly, I put it into the dryer, and shut the door after the last of it makes it in. I slam a hand over the button, and it hums to life, tossing the sheets around the barrel as it turns. Spinning back to return the trolley, Nate's hands are gripped firm around the side of it, as he stares at me.

"What?" I breathe.

"Thank you, Clara."

"What for?"

His jaw feathers. "The training yard."

I tilt my head to the washer. "Guess we're even then. Thanks for not letting the washing eat me."

A half smile breaks on the side of his face, and he schools it back. "Have no intention of doing this job by myself."

With that, he pushes off the trolley and stalks out the door. Back to his old self. Stone cold, arrogant Nate.

Great.

Who likes change anyway?

15

TESSA

I FOUND IT.

Well, I found the only door that doesn't end in countless cables or a trillion fuses. I slip inside and pull it almost all the way shut.

"Light," I whisper.

White light pours from my wrist gadget, illuminating the narrow tunnel ahead of me. It pitches downward before turning the corner. The underground space is deadly quiet.

I take a step. It echoes through the tunnel.

Sucking in a sharp breath, I hold it.

Trying to make myself lighter, my steps delicate, I push forward toward the spot where the tunnel turns. Every few hundred feet, I pause and listen. Leaning against the cold cement wall, I let my eyes drift shut as if that will help me hear better. Every so often, small gaps are set into the otherwise plain wall. Like a doorway should exist there but doesn't. Deep enough for a body to fit.

When I hear nothing, I keep going. The light on my gadget flickers. Damn. If it goes out, I'll be stranded in the dark. Could I grope my way back to the door? Lost in a mild panic, I almost miss the voices and heavy footsteps that bounce through the tunnel toward me.

I hurry toward the closest gap and slide around the hard corner, flattening against the back wall in the darkened space. "Light, out."

Darkness folds in around me, as my breath stops.

Two people walk closer, they're in no hurry. Chatting about new recruits that must be under them.

Huh.

So, *not* civilians then. Curious.

They amble past my dark hideout, and I wait until their footsteps fade out completely before slipping into the tunnel. "Light."

The tunnel bursts with light and I hurry, making certain to keep my footsteps feather soft. When I come to another corner that veers to the left this time, I pause and listen again. Chatter further down the tunnel—many voices—the sound fades before disappearing altogether. Like they were shut behind a door.

I strain to hear steps coming my way. If the door opened, was someone leaving?

Slipping around the corner, I roll my wrist into my side to mostly douse the light. A door sits ten feet from where I stand. No light spills out from under it. It's soundproof. If I am going to find out about the disease, I need to get closer.

Inside would be better but that won't happen without blowing my cover.

The door jerks and I stagger backward and fumble over my feet to rush back the way I came. "Light," I whisper as soft as I can. The gadget dims and my right shoulder slams into the wall. I stifle a grunt and still, flattening against the wall, as footsteps close in fast. There's no time to find a gap to disappear into now.

One set of boots thunders toward me. I hold my breath, letting my eyes slide shut as I count the seconds that pass.

Rough hands grip my arms.

No!

The overwhelming smell of woodsy caramel shrouds my senses. What the hell?

Snapping my eyes open, I squint against the darkness. The familiar angles of his face take shape as a hint of caramel hits me, and my mouth gapes.

"Finn?"

His finger presses over my lips. I didn't even see him raise his hand. His brows are pressed down, mouth a thin line. What is *he* doing here?

Before I can say a word, he's guiding me back the way I came. My heart flings in my rib cage like a trapped bird. I run through every interaction we have had and try to piece together why he would be down here. He's a trainer, one of the more senior officers, running around in dark tunnels after curfew.

As we reach the exit door by the tracks, he shoves me

through it, and I spin back to protest. At the sight of his distraught face, I clam my mouth shut.

"What are you doing out after curfew? Why the *hell* are you wandering around in dark tunnels that are out of bounds?"

"I—"

"No," he shoots a hand between us, "you shouldn't answer that, Tessa. Back to your quarters. Don't get caught out."

Tessa, not Tess.

Annoyance and embarrassment twist in my gut, sending heat to my cheeks. His jaw feathers. He's a damn liar.

"Right," I huff. Anything that I thought was between us after our last training session has evaporated. I fold my arms over my chest. If he thinks I am going back to my quarters, he has another think coming.

"Yeah, I'm not going anyway, Matthews. Not until you tell me why you're hanging out with the rebellion."

His eyes widen and he tilts his head back a little before his face sets to stone. "No idea what you're talking about. This is an after-hours card game. We bet, gamble. It's not exactly legal. Hence the hour and the location."

I don't believe a single word he is saying. "Sure, where's your currency then?"

"I lost it all on the last game."

"Do you suck at gambling as much as you do at lying?"

He steps close, hands by his side, briefly looking off into the distance. "Go home."

"What if I don't want to? What if I told you I have been looking for the rebellion for weeks. What if I told you I have been sending comms to Sector Two. To my sister."

His eyes lock onto me. "You think this is a game?"

"No! I do not. My sister is in trouble and the only way I can help her is via the rebellion. So, if you don't mind—" I push past him and walk back to the vault door. His hand grabs my arm and I hesitate before turning back. I close the distance between us, and look up into those dark eyes, as he searches my gaze.

"Siblings don't exist, Tessa."

He thinks I'm making this up? Maybe he thinks I've lost my mind. Did he not read my file? He could have assumed it was fraudulent. Finn Matthews is a mystery to me most days.

Hot and cold.

Interested, then not.

Trainer and friend, never both at the same time.

"I can assure you Clara is real. She is in Textiles, dodging some vile disease that conveniently has never made it to Sontaria. So, you can take your hand off me and let me protect my family the only way I know how," I spit.

His grip loosens but then he walks forward, forcing me backward to the wall beside the door. His hands land on the wall either side of my head as he dips his, eyes burning into mine.

"You don't want to walk in there unannounced. You have to be invited. Otherwise, they offer you up as a red herring to the officials. It's there way of keeping a low profile while appeasing the powers at be, letting them think they have the rebellion under control." He shakes his head, his dark hair flopping in his face. "What a ridiculous notion."

He's . . . proud.

A member of the rebellion. It's written all over his gorgeous face.

"So, invite me in, Finn."

He just stares at me. A moment has passed, and his brows furrow as he says, "It's not me you have to convince, Tess."

"Oh." I have nothing else to add. Mind reeling with everything that has unfolded in the last ten minutes.

He pushes off the wall and takes my hand, walking down the tracks. "Where are we going?"

"Somewhere we can talk without people hearing."

Throwing his black hood over his face he takes off at a jog, not letting me go.

I don't think I want him to.

Five minutes later, we are deep in the heart of the city, turning down a back alley before the training center. Rain has started drizzling, my shirt is wet and drops run off Finn's hoody. My hair has come loose and is matted to my cheeks and neck—hand still clutched inside his. He pushes through a door that is framed in padlocks. I raise a brow before glimpsing behind us.

Nobody is out at this hour. Not that I can see in the shadows at least. We walk down a narrow corridor with minimal orange strip lighting. Something thumps below our feet, vibrating its way through my body. Finn lets my hand go and stops where a tall, built guy stands beside a heavy looking door. The big guy studies me before returning to Finn. "Not flying solo tonight chief?" the guy says to Finn.

"Tessa, this is Max." Finn forces a smile, as I take in the muscled door guy dressed in black, military-style clothes. His wide-set blue eyes glitter over a crooked half smile. Tattoos cover his bulky arms and neck.

Okay, what's that about? What is this place? Does he usually come here alone? Max pushes the door open, and the thumping noise is only overpowered by the random flickering coloured light in the large space inside. We step inside and the door thuds shut behind me. The noise rattles my bones. Its thumping beat rises through my body like an accompaniment to my frantic heartbeat.

Finn turns back and says something, pushing his hoody off. I can't hear his words, and I shake my head, hoping he understands I didn't hear. His hand wraps around mine and he leads me to a quieter corner. People mill around, some moving to the beat, some cuddled together. Some are some are kissing, hands everywhere.

"What is this place?"

"Cavum Nigram," Finn shouts.

Latin for *black hole*. My studies in the old language and many other things were extensive for the last two decades. He moves closer and drops his mouth to my ear. "Do you want something to drink?"

"I'm fine, thank you."

He disappears into the swarming crowd, and I lean against the wall. It steadies my vibrating body a little. Here in this hidden electrified room, people are unhinged. Nothing like this exists on the top side of the streets of the city. Elites wouldn't dare to waste time or mental focus on such frivolous activities.

Apparently, some do. I huff a small laugh. Finn appears, drink in hand and a bottle of water, which he places into my palms. Hand on the small of my back, he guides me to a booth. His warmth wraps around me. Despite the packed room the cool underground ventilation pulses around us as we move.

We drop into the booth, and Finn slides along the seat until his back hits the wall and he's facing me. I sit in the booth and place the water on the table. I had so many things to say to him—to ask. Now, this close, in this overstimulating place every last word has dried up.

"Tell me about Clara."

A little stunned a turn my body to face him. "Why?"

"I want to know. How come she ended up in the Sectors?"

"We—" I remember her face as she was sent from the building to the group of Engineers. The moment my hand slipped out of hers when I was sent to the Elites. "She's my twin sister. If you wanted to know how we came to exist."

"I'm not pulling information from you to hand you over to the authorities. You caught me outside Order of the

Flame headquarters for Heaven's sake. If anyone's going to the Wastelands, or the gassing chambers, it's me." His eyes drop to where he has taken my hands in his.

Air leaves my lungs and doesn't return.

He's right, the Wastelands would be a mercy for a caught rebel. No wonder they keep their doors closed and their numbers curated. The price any one of them would pay, would be inconceivable. The image of Finn being executed sends my throat thick, and my stomach into knots. I swallow and suck in a ragged breath.

"I need to help her, Finn."

"I know, Tess."

Everything goes black.

Silence folds in around us.

The echo of the bass beat rings through my ears before drowning in a tide of white noise. Finn's grip tightens on my hands. "Hell, not now!"

16

CLARA

LAST ONE READY for breakfast as usual, I pull on my boots.
The shower on the men's side starts. Okay, not the last one
then. I wander to my small metal drawers and fling open the
top section. I pluck up a hair tie and pull my long hair into a
ponytail before grabbing another and rounding the long
length into a bun.

Something thumps in the shower. The smell of soap
drifts around the dorm. Someone is using up their rations.
Idiot. You run out of soap; you run out of mealtime buddies.
Nobody wants to sit with walking body odour. Not even in
the Sectors. Basic hygiene has been drummed into us since
we were little kids, and for good reason.

You let yourself go in the Provinces, disease is quick to
find you. There is a place for those who were too lazy or too
poor to maintain proper health. A mass grave on the
outskirts on the southern side, not too far from where Nate
and I grew up. You don't forget a place like that.

Another thump.

A strangled curse.

Bubbles crawl along the floor, out from under the shower door on the men's side of the dorm. What the?

I step around the traveling, wobbly suds and make my way to the closed door.

"Hey! Your soap is bubbling up the dorm, ease up!"

He groans.

Whoever is inside slips and hits the floor with a sickening thwack. Urgh. Was that my fault?

"Crap, are you okay?"

A grunt is followed by a long, pain-filled moan.

Oh great.

"Should I go find one of the guys to give you a hand?"

"No!"

Nate.

I step toward the shower door cautiously. "Nate, it's Clara," I say softly, the way you would a wounded animal.

"I know it's you, Clara."

A little stunned, I hesitate outside the door with a hand raised to the lever. "Do you—"

Shaking my head, I try to calm my racing heart. Desperately trying to force images of Nate from my mind. Angry Nate. Annoyed Nate. Obnoxious Nate. Naked . . . Nate.

I clear my throat. "Do you need some help?"

"Go to breakfast Clara, I'll be fine."

I drop my hand and step back. My boots are covered in

suds, and I have to steady myself from slipping. "See you at breakfast, then."

I walk to the door. He groans and I hover for a second. Thinking better of it, I make my way to the mess hall.

One rehydrated serving of eggs and a half slice of toast and Nate still hasn't walked in. I throw down my coffee and take my tray to the service trolley. Instead of heading for the factory floor I go back to the dorm. When I step inside, the shower is off, but the door is still closed.

I wander over to it, trying to not slip in the clouds of bubbles lining the floor. "Nate?"

Breathy curses spill out under the door.

I slam my hand on the lever and shove the door open. His annoyed, angry stare lands. Slumped in the corner at the back of the shower, his leg lays at a weird angle. He's shivering. Teeth chattering.

Stubborn ass, he should've let me help. I pick my way through the sudsy mounds to where he is. Grabbing his towel on the way, I drop it into his lap where his hands are currently protecting me from something I may or may not want to see.

"Come on, let's get you up."

"You don't have to Bendall, I can manage." Heat rises in his cheeks.

"Sure, you can." I roll my eyes at him. "Don't be stubborn. You can be annoyed at me later, when you're on your feet."

He tries to push off the floor and slips again. His feet and hands too soapy to make purchase on anything. I drop my hands and nod. "Come on, I'll pull you up."

His face is stone, chest heaving. After a moment, he raises his hands and I slip mine inside. His hands affirm around my own and I tug. He lurches forward . . . and collapses.

"Ahh! Stop! This is no good."

"What about on all fours. Then you can crawl out and push up on your bunk?"

He gives me an incredulous look.

"What? I promise I won't gawk. Won't even ride you like a horse."

The pain on his face melts as he bursts out laughing. I can't help but laugh. He is so damn fine when he smiles. Pity he never shows that side of himself.

I cluck my tongue, tilting my head toward the shower door. "Giddy up, Prendergast."

He chuckles again and the towel slips down a little. Hating that I can't pull my stupid stare from his body, Nate finds me frozen with eyes locked on him. I snap my gaze back up and swallow past the stone lodged in my airway. "You're freezing, Nate. We need to get you up or something."

He raises a brow.

Urgh! Word choice Clara. I stifle a groan as my stomach flips. Ignoring it, I step over him and grab his hands. Enough of this, whatever it is, because the fire that's currently lancing through my veins is pooling low in my belly, fast.

"Now, Nate."

He pulls up, his legs scramble for purchase on the sudsy floor, as he gets to his knees. His breathing is heavy, he must be in pain. Instinctually, I run a hand through his hair. Stilling with realisation when he looks up at me. "Sorry, I— you . . ."

"It's okay, Clara."

His head drops to my stomach.

I freeze.

He's catching his breath. That's all.

He reaffirms his grip around my hands, and I help him to his feet. Even with his busted leg, he stands taller than me. His eyes dip down to mine, before dropping lower still to my lips, then my neck, to my chest. Taking a tentative step backward, I rub the heel of my palm over my airless, aching lungs. "You good?"

He adjusts the towel around his hips. Remnants of suds and drops of water run down his toned torso as he clears his throat and nods.

"See you in a bit, then." I spin on the spot. Realising a second too late, it was a mistake. My feet slip out from under me, and I fall backward and slam onto the floor. Air rushes from my lungs, replacing the space with a burn that smarts.

Mouth gaping, I gasp for breath, tears springing into my eyes. Hands flailing across the floor, I stare vacantly at the ceiling before the notion to roll over hits. As I turn in the suds, Nate kneels next to me. A stupid shit-eating grin is plastered on his face.

"You really should watch your step, Bendall. You wouldn't want to be caught out flat on your back, little honeybee."

Honey-what, now?

I groan, feeling every inch of me that met the hard floor. Pushing to my seat, his hands drop down. I slap mine into them, and a second later I'm propelled up and onto my feet. I slam into the bare, warm wet wall that is Nate. My neck and face flush like they have the right to. He smiles softly but releases me.

"Thanks," I utter.

"I think we can call it even, Clara."

"What? No honeybee?"

His eyes rove up and down my form, taking his time, like it's something he has always wanted to do but never let himself. I hold his gaze when it drags slowly back up. "Don't go getting any ideas, Prendergast."

"Wouldn't dream of it, Bendall."

Of course not.

This time with grace and poise, I turn and leave. With a glance behind me as I reach the door, I find Nate by his bunk. Pants on as he shrugs his work shirt over his shoulders. Said it before, I'll say it again. Love the form, hate the man.

At least, I *think* that's still true.

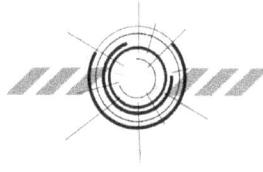

NATE'S QUOTAS are so shitty, they make Johnson look good. Dammit.

He is going to have his lame ass transferred or worse if he's not careful. Remmins has been distant since Nate's been around more. I don't know what is going on there, but I intend to find out. My no strings attached arrangement with Ash is starting to be a no anything deal.

I miss our fun. I miss Ash. Calm and grounded, he's comfortable. Being around him is easy. We haven't managed to consummate our no strings deal, which leaves me wondering a little. He is brilliant at getting me off but never takes it any further. Do I want the whole deal? All the strings?

Honestly, I don't know.

I turn from my machine to see Nate watching me adjust the bolt in the cradle overhead, and he offers a small smile. Every shift, he starts out strong only to fade, his limp slowing him down more and more as the hours pass. I set my machine up and jog to Nate's. He's down the far end of it trying to adjust something with a wrench. The bolt he fed in thirty minutes ago runs dry. The machine clunks.

I shoulder up another bolt and walk it to the intake end. With the empty one on the ground, I push the next one into place. Remmins walks over, his face unreadable. "Where's Prendergast?"

"Down the end, trying to sort some issue."

He walks past. I feed the material into the mouth of the giant machine, careful to keep my hands clear of the grabbing teeth that snag the fabric and feed it into the guts of it. A minute later, I'm checking the maintenance panel to make sure nothing is amiss, and Nate appears at my side.

"Leave it, Bendall."

Well, there's thanks for you.

"Pick up the pace, Prendergast, or the whole floor pays for your laziness." I don't break eye contact as his face pulls into something akin to a sneer. Before he has a chance to retaliate, I wander back to my machine and check the through feed at the back before double checking the bolt and intake. Everything is lined up and feeding through perfectly. Ash runs a hand over the steel as I lean on it, my eyes wandering back to Nate.

"You don't have to help him, Clara."

I shift my focus to Ash. "Yes, I do. Kind of gotten used to having you around Ash Remmins." All I can think about is him crowding me against this noisy steel beast to put his hands all over me.

He huffs with a small smile, and I swear his cheeks blush. "Well, with such abysmal quotas, our no strings arrangement is looking sketchy at best." Now, sadness fills his eyes but he recovers quickly as one of the other Engineers walks over asking for help.

Johnson.

Awesome.

Like I need him starting rumors about Ash and me. The rankings come out tomorrow. Would the officers take it into consideration if rumors flew? I don't plan on finding out.

The shift ends, and we all file our weary bodies from the factory floor. Nate limps from the room, trailing behind the first group of Engineers to clock off. How much pain does a limp like that cause? I make a mental note to visit Vivi and score some painkillers while I'm there.

I wait until there is only Remmins and me left on the floor. I push off the machine where I have been half leaning and pad to his small desk that's central to the enormous room. His head is down, his hands working fast as he flips through papers, tallying quotas and punching figures into the old plastic calculator.

"How is it looking?" I ask.

Not answering, he flips the papers back to the start. He clears the calculator and begins again. He adds up the totals from each machine and each day for the last week. When he gets the same number as the first time he closes his eyes, and leans back, running a hand through his hair.

I angle the papers on the desk so I can see the numbers. Each Engineer's name and daily tallies fill the pages, with weekly totals on the bottom. The calculator flashes.

−4962

We are four thousand, nine hundred and sixty-two feet behind?

That's almost a day's worth for an entire floor. To anyone else that would mean nothing. To Ash, it could mean being removed from his post.

My stomach plummets, breaths shortening.

Hell.

"Ash . . . "

He doesn't open his eyes, sucking in a long slow breath.

"Ash, talk to me."

"I can't make up that much, not in the next twenty-four hours."

"You can't. *We* can."

His eyes open, and I give him my best smile. He chuckles and hooks an arm around my waist, pulling me onto his lap. I stifle a squeal and dot a kiss to his forehead. Gosh, I have missed this. How can I let him suffer for our shortcomings?

I can't.

I won't.

"Come on Ashie, we have work to do."

I pop up from his lap, and he grabs my hand. I turn back and lean down, finding his mouth with my own, my free hand on his jaw. It feathers against my palm. I break from his hold, and I scruff up his hair with a hand. He's just so damn delicious with his hair all messy. Like I can imagine him undone.

"Four thousand, nine hundred and sixty-two feet ain't waiting for no man, Remmins. Let's make it happen."

We set to work, running eight machines. Or should I say, they run us. Ragged. By midnight I am exhausted, and we've only finished one thousand, eight hundred feet. We are close to halfway. By dawn, if my calculations are correct, we should make it.

The door, the one I'm certain Ash locked, rattles.

"Ignore it," Ash says jogging past.

The door rattles again.

I turn back to my machine, checking the intake before reloading my next machine with a fresh bolt. The door rattles, relentlessly. Whoever it is will have us busted with their persistence. I stalk to the door. A familiar scent seeps through. Images of the soapy floor and naked man flood into my mind.

Nate.

Unlocking the doors, I crack one open slowly.

Brows lowered, his arms fold over his chest. "What's going on?"

"Nothing."

"You didn't come home, I mean the dorm, after shift. Or mess."

"Don't tell me you're worried about me," I scoff and go to shut the door.

His hand slams around the edge, stopping it from closing. "Let me in, Clara."

"No. Go back to the dorm, Nate."

"You're making up for my quota aren't you." It's not a question. He's figured out why we're here. What he doesn't know, is that Ash will pay for his low numbers if we can't catch them up.

"Whatever, go back to bed."

"No." He pushes through the door and takes in the eight running machines, four of which I am currently neglecting by standing here talking to him.

"I'm helping." He pushes through the door.

"Nate," I protest.

He moves into my space. "Wasn't asking, Clara. I'm helping you."

"I— we don—"

Nate strides to a dormant machine and fires it up, doing the same with the next one along. Ash tracks Nate's movements before offering him a nod and a smile and going back to his work. For a moment, I take in the two of them. One man I adore and am so comfortable with. One, I loathe, well at least I thought I did.

Now, I'm really, really not sure. They are so different.

Day and night.

Love and hate.

No, not hate. Not anymore.

17

TESSA

FINN'S HAND finds mine in the dark. People are hustling around, and murmurs turn to yelling. Darkness blinds us all, and I slap my palm to the wall behind me. The other in Finn's hold still, I lace my fingers with his. No way am I getting lost in this power outage.

"Tess, we have to leave. The city will go into lock down in three minutes. You have to be back at your quarters, or someone is going to notice you're not."

"That never happened last time! How do we get out?"

"Light, half," he whispers.

His wrist gadget glows ever so softly, illuminating his face.

Of course.

"Don't let go, okay?"

"I won't."

We weave our way through the throng of sweaty bodies, heading for the bottlenecked doorway. Finn pushes past a group of guys in shorts, tattered singlets, and some have their chests bared with t-shirts tucked into the back of their shorts. Their sweaty skin rubs up against me, and I tighten my grip on Finn's hand.

Somehow, he slips past the push and shove. We run down the corridor toward the alley entrance. Clear of the hidden door, Finn drags me to one side. A group rushes past, disappearing into the shadows quickly.

"What's—" I start.

His finger presses against my lips, and he shakes his head. "Not until we are back in your room. Stay close, stay in the shadows. No noise," he whispers.

I nod, and he releases my hand.

Instantly, I wish he hadn't.

Finn takes off at a lope, somewhat stooped, his head turning side to side as we go. He's scanning our surroundings every ten seconds. We make the tall, silver building in no time, bursting through the back door and up the stairwell. Out of breath and on heavier footsteps than I would like, we reach the fortieth level. Everything is dark. As it is outside and in the stairwell.

"How do we make it inside with no power?" I ask.

Finn turns his head looking around the corridor for anything to slide between the door and jamb. A cleaning trolley, with mop and broom sits on the corner by the last door. I walk over to it and handle the broom. "This do?"

"Anything flatter?"

A small brush with a long, flat metal handle for cleaning

the air vents hangs from the top of the trolley. Perfect. I pluck it from its hook and jog back to the door. Sliding the handle end in, I put my weight behind pushing it sideways. The door splits open wide enough for Finn's hand. I keep the long, thin brush for next time, and slip into my room. The door thuds behind me, and I spin back.

Finn stands with his hands by his sides, eyes roaming my room. Despite being here once before, he still seems curious.

"You should go before the lock down," I utter.

His gaze flicks back to me. "I should."

But he doesn't move.

If he isn't quick, he'll be stuck here. He takes a step closer. Sweeping his hoody off his head, he opens his mouth to say something but slams it shut.

"What is it?"

"I don't *want* to leave, Tess."

Oh.

Butterflies, like the type I only saw in my old biology textbooks, big and beautiful, take flight in my core. I run a hand through my hair, but it dislodges more strands from my now messy bun.

Finn's eyes track the movement, his throat working. He closes the last of the space between us, and I raise my head to meet his brown eyes.

"We could both use a shower, Matthews."

A small smile plays on his lips and his brows lower slightly, as he searches my face for a moment.

"Go ahead." His words are gravel. He pulls his hoody

from his back, the muscles in his arms and back flex, and tosses it on the bed. He paces by the bed, a tight black t-shirt hugs his toned torso, his uniform pants still topping his standard issue Elite boots.

Blood rushes through my veins at an alarming rate of knots. Heat surges in my belly with proximity to him.

"Sure, I won't be long. Make yourself at home."

He smiles and wanders to the window, lacing his hands behind his neck as he stares out. His shoulders rise and fall in deep cycles. I pad to the shower room and shove the door closed along its tracks. It hits the end, bouncing open a little way. Undressed, steam filling the small space, I pluck the band from my hair and let it fall around my shoulders.

Stepping into the steaming water, I moan a little with the instant relaxation it brings. I can't even help it. What a day. What a day and night, to be honest. That underground club was something else. By the strained gazes we got when we entered, it's highly illegal. The lock down alarm starts up. It lasts for two minutes. Then newly installed auto bolts inside every door in the glass city lock—in one synchronous movement. Clunk.

My door is locked tight.

Finn isn't going anywhere tonight.

The thought sends a thrill through me. A second later, guilt churns where butterflies once were. He's my trainer. Who will be marking me off and giving me a ranking in a few weeks. Nothing should happen between us.

Should.

Just like he should have gone home.

I guess I'm not the only one in what I thought was just my imagination running wild. The door to the bathroom is cracked open. Finn walks past, eyes forward as he heads for my desk. The Visi-Screen is useless, maybe he wants to write something down?

He sits in my chair. I hold a hand under the shampoo dispenser. Sparkling gold liquid drops into my palm, and I lather it before running it through my hair. Peach and vanilla scents penetrate the curling steam. It's heavenly.

Finn glances back as I place my hand under the auto-soaper and collect a portion of shower gel. With his gaze on me, I rub the soap over my arms and belly and lastly my chest. A breast in each hand I massage the soap around them. His focus jerks to the papers on the desk.

A heartbeat later, Finn peers back and this time he doesn't look away. My breath shallows out as heat swells and a throbbing starts up in my center. I've had a total of one boyfriend before. A nice enough guy, but we never went all the way. I never felt the need to with him. Now with the mandatory contraception all Elites are given in the Medi bay in our first week. . .

Now, simply looking at Finn Matthews has my body on fire.

Now, I feel the need.

Heavens save me.

The chair falls back as he pushes away from the desk to stand. A moment later, standing in the doorway of the bathroom, he pushes the door open slowly. I step back into the water stream and let its hot piercing droplets wash the soap from my body. Tilting my head back, mouth open, I catch some.

Parched.

From watching Finn, watch me.

"Tess," he rasps.

He lowers his head as I move out of the stream, sweeping the water from my eyes with both hands. "Finn?"

I should be self-conscious standing naked in front of him. The deep, ragged cycle of his breath has me—

I don't.

"Tell me to leave," he utters.

"You can't."

"Tell me anyway, please, Tess."

I pad to where he is. The absence of the water's heat sends my skin to gooseflesh and my nipples to stiff peaks. I pull the zip down on his hoody and push it from his shoulders. He tracks my hands, one after the other. Wet palms on his shirt, I leave handprints, his darkened eyes run over my body.

"I don't want you to leave, Finn, even if you could."

His hand is behind my neck, his mouth covering mine a second later. He tastes as good as he smells, all caramel with a hint of spice, and I groan against his mouth. His fingers grip my jaw as he breaks from the kiss.

All heat and breathlessness, I study at him, the burn in my lungs floods to every part of me.

"I haven't—" I can't even finish the sentence. In this small moment, I'm embarrassed to be basically untouched at twenty-five. Nobody has ever caught my interest after my one and only boyfriend. Although many tried.

His forehead rests against my own, his thumb travels softly across my bottom lip. "We only do whatever you want."

The fault in his plan is that I want *all* of Finn Matthews.

Whatever I want is a hell of a lot of things. A smile kicks up on my lips with that thought, and I tug his uniform shirt out from the waistband of his pants. "I want these clothes off."

Finn chuckles, pulling the shirt from his shoulders and tossing it to the ground. Now it's my turn to explore, and I let my fingertips wander over his chest. Between the valley that lies in the center and downwards to his navel. I dip it farther to the dark line of hair that tracks south before disappearing into his pants, flanked by a defined V.

He closes his eyes and releases a huffy breath with my touch.

"Is this okay, Finn?"

Nodding, his Adam's apple bobs before he opens his eyes. "Anything else you would like, Tess?"

I run my hands through his hair and drag his mouth down until it is a whisper from my lips. "A little more, please," I breathe.

"Anything you want, you can have." His voice is like boots over ground glass.

I fumble with the clasp on his pants, as he covers my hands with his and flips it open easily. I push his pants over his hips and down, until he stands in standard issue jocks and socks. He must have taken his shoes off before he sat down. By the bed?

The bulge in his underwear steals the last of my breath. I trace a finger down the rigid line and his breathing shatters.

"Tessa." My name is barely audible.

I dot kisses over his shoulders before tracking my way up his neck and across his jaw. This man. I could literally eat him up. His hands land on my hips and he claims my mouth with his the second I lift my head up. I open, and he sweeps inside. My hands gravitate to his hair.

Breath hitching, he is completely riled up. I slip a finger behind the waist band of his jocks and slide them down. They fall past his knees, he kicks the pants and jocks out from under us and sweeps me up onto his hips. My center is soaked. It rubs against his stomach in achingly delicious small movements as he steps us back toward the shower.

"Finn." I wrangle enough breath to string together a few words. "I want everything you have, please."

"You have it, Tess."

The water pelts down around us as he walks through it and my back meets the wall. His hand slams beside my head, and I wriggle out of his hold. My feet meet the warm, wet shower floor as his fingers run circles around one nipple. Any rational thought leaves my mind. But I want him to be my first, and I want him to enjoy it too.

"What do *you* want?" I ask.

"I want to taste you, Tessa. Then I want to see that beautiful face fall apart as you come with me buried inside you."

Heat flushes my neck as I huff a laugh. Tell it how it is Finn. I like that he is direct and honest. Similar thoughts have consumed my mind about him, more times than appropriate. I wrap a hand around his hard length and brush my thumb over the tip briefly. He shudders, and his lips part, eyes tightening.

"More?" I whisper.

"You have no idea how much I have thought about these sweet hips, those gorgeous breasts, what it would feel like to have you wrapped around me, Tess."

Heat rises to flood my face with the fact that Finn Matthews has been fantasizing about me. It's utterly flattering. I track his hand as it traces circles around my stomach before dipping lower. I widen my stance, hungry for more, as his fingertips dance around my throbbing apex, the place I am desperate for him to find.

His mouth finds my peaks. Teeth grazing over one stiff peak before hunting down the other, and I writhe against the wall. Wriggling my hips I moan; I need him there. He chuckles, and the sound vibrates through my body.

I love it.

His fingers sweep over my apex, and I can't help the whimper that slips from my mouth.

"Finn . . . Please, don't stop."

"Wouldn't dream of it, Tessie."

A strained laugh tumbles up my throat. Tessie. That's new.

Then he slips a finger inside me, and I melt against the wall. Whimpers pouring from my lips like damn birdsong at sundown.

"More?"

Gripping his arms as he finds my gaze, I nod, unable to form words any longer. A second finger pushes inside me and his thumb swirls over my apex. "You like that?"

"Uh ha—I," the syllables are gibberish. But by the smile splitting over his face, he got it. "Good."

As something heavy and warm starts to build in my core, he drops to his knees. "W—what are you doing?"

"I said I wanted to taste you, Tess."

"You did," I huff.

"Can I replace my thumb with my mouth?"

"Oh, um okay. Will that feel better?"

Cheek lights up his eyes, as he smiles. "You can tell me when we're done."

I nod.

He moves his mouth to my center, replacing his thumb as he said. The second his hot tongue glides over my apex, and his fingers curl inside me, my legs start to tremble.

Oh. My. Heavens.

Wetness rushes to the center as if it wasn't already there, and I need to hold onto something. Anything. I run my hands through his hair. His tongue flickers over my apex.

My hands curl to fists around his messy brown locks, as I arch off the tile, whimpers turning to cries.

I spiral out of control. Legs shaking, I snap a hand from his hair and massage my breast. Letting the nipple roll between two fingers. Finn grabs my hand pushing it back into his hair, as he takes up the task of fondling my breast and teasing my nipples with his free hand.

Something electric surges in my center, flooding my body.

"Finn!"

I buck, arching from the wall. Waves of bliss course through me. My breath is gone. He works me over, inside and out, until the last wave recedes, and I am limp against the shower wall.

"What the hell was that?" I rasp.

He stands and pops his fingers now covered in my wetness into his mouth. As he pulls them out again, his darkened gaze burns through mine. "That was your first orgasm, Tessie?"

"I guess. I've never had *that* before."

"We are going to have to remedy that." He slides his arms under my butt and hoists me onto his hips.

"Where are we going?"

He gives me a smile that would melt hearts. "To give you whatever you want, the right way. As many times as you like."

His contagious smile blooms over my face. "I think I need that."

"Lucky we have all night then."

Reaching the bed, he lays me down on it and crawls in beside me. With the blanket pulled up, he holds me until the shivers that rose en route to the bed fade. His hard length digs into my back. I roll over and find his mouth briefly before breaking away.

"Show me what to do, Finn."

18

CLARA

YOU COULD HEAR A THREAD SNAP. Every single Engineer sits in the mess hall. Waiting. The silence is pure torture. Ash stands rigid beside the other senior officers, clipboard in hand. He's been distant the last few days. The panic that has been slowly building deep in my core is now a raging eruption, burning through my body.

"Listen up. This the make or break for some of you. The quotas for the last month are in. The reports on each of you tallied against your productivity and overall performance, including," he coughs and shakes his head, "including any behavioral issues off the factory floor." His eyes burn into Johnson.

My gut eases a little as I look to Nate. He's tense. Jaw slammed shut tight. Any second now we'll hear his molars shatter.

"The following Engineer's will stay in this Sector and this factory; Stevens, Howard, Collins . . ." I tune out as he rattles through twenty Engineer's I only know by name. I track my focus to Remmins. His dark gaze burns into me. What's with him?

The drone of the speaking officer fades back in. "Bendall, and finally Prendergast, by the skin of his teeth." Evans's focus flickers to Remmins. Does he not believe the reports Ash submitted? "Everyone else, is to be transferred to Sector Three by end of day. If you are leaving, you have the rest of the day to sort out your affairs and pack your bags. If you heard your name, you're on shift in five minutes!"

Two Engineers sit rigid at their tables on either side of the room. One very familiar, the other not so much. Evans missed them. They weren't called.

"The following Engineers are immediately removed from the Engineer program and will be evicted to the Wastelands in three days for immoral conduct. Johnson. Baker."

Nobody dares to move. Johnson stares at the officer. Pure hatred laces his eyes. One of the girls who didn't make the cut sobs into her hands. Baker stands and slams a hand on the table before stalking out. Johnson follows him. They won't get far. The officers manning the doors and hallways will have them in moments.

Evans starts coughing. It's hacking. Wet. He doubles over and before steadying himself on the table closest. Not even supervisors and senior offices are immune to this disease. Nobody helps and when he straightens, he pushes out his shoulders back, hugging the clipboard, and clears his throat, loudly.

"There is one other matter. This factory will be getting a new supervisor. Factory output has been suffering for the past few months. A change of blood will shake things up."

What?

I stop breathing.

Hands clutching the side of the bench seat. I try to meet Ash's gaze, but he stares off into the distance somewhere above my head. I don't understand. What happened that he's getting a transfer? His jaw feathers. Hands balled to fists. What are they doing to him? My breaths burn up to nothing more than choppy gasps.

The crowd files through the doors and into the corridor. I push against the flow to where Ash stands with the other officers. Why is he being shipped off? We fixed the quotas. He's still working in his supervisor capacity. He hands his clipboard to Evans and stalks toward the side door of the mess hall that leads outside.

Two steps behind him when he bursts through the door and into the sunshine. I grab his arm and he startles, spinning back.

"Ash!"

He clenches his jaw, standing inches from me. "Go back inside, Clara."

"No! What is going on?"

"You heard. I'm leaving."

"It's not leaving when you're being chased out."

"Fine. I'm being sent away." He throws his hands up.

I stand, rooted to the spot as shallow breaths swallow my lungs too fast. "Why?"

"My quotas are too slim. My methods not harsh enough, or something."

"We caught up on the shortfall! What the hell happened?"

"Johnson reported our after-hours activity to Evans. All the hours we worked off shift, including the ones I helped you with, they were scratched from our records."

"So, that means my quotas and Nates, were all too low?"

"Yes."

"So why are they sending you to Sector Three and not Nate and me?"

"I'm not goin—" He closes his eyes and hangs his head. "I took the losses to make sure you stayed here. Nate too."

He's a supervisor, why didn't they ship Nate and me to Sector Three? Hold up, did he say he's not going?

"Ash." I step closer, he raises his head and opens his eyes but his face isn't stoic or remorseful, it's devastated. "What do you mean you're not going? Not going where, Ash?"

"To another Sector."

"You have to report to the city?"

He shakes his head.

Something flips in my stomach, pushing bile upwards.

I can't breathe.

"Clara." His hands are around my arms. "It's okay, really. I knew I was on thin ice before you ever got here."

I rest my hands on his chest, and he folds me into his arms. Tears streak down my cheeks, soaking into his shirt. A stone has wedged its way into my windpipe. His head lowers to my hair. "I will miss you though, Bendall."

I choke through a sob.

We never even got to . . .

Dammit! I am so sick of this. So sick of other people controlling every single, tiny thing we do. Every aspect of our lives. So those spoilt rotten city brats can live a life of luxury.

In our humanities classes as kids, we learnt the Sectors outnumber the city population ten to one. With the top one to two percent only ever making it the glorious city of glass. Those odds work in our favor. They may have the funds, the technology and the authorities tucked under their high-brand belts, but we have the people, the heart and nothing to lose.

Almost.

Ash releases me, and something snaps. His mouth dips for a long, slow kiss, and I melt for him. His hands are in my hair as I grip his shirt. I have no intention of going to the factory today, not if this is his last day here. I jump up onto his hips. His grip slides around my waist a heartbeat later.

"We can't go back to my quarters, Clara," Ash whispers, forehead resting on mine. "Supply shed?"

"Anywhere with you is good with me, Ashie."

He nips my neck and I release a tortured giggle. Tears flow again. They were right, those people that say you don't know what you have until you lose it. Because my heart, right now, is breaking clean in half with the thought of being here without Ash. He's a good man.

He doesn't deserve this.

"And me you, Clara Bendall. But I don't want you following me alright?"

"I—"

His finger pressed over my lips. "I mean it. Stay here, stay safe. Make your quotas. Keep clear of this disease. Please."

I nod and tears dislodge, slipping over my jaw, as my chin wobbles.

"Hey," he breathes, a hand wiping away the wetness on my cheeks.

"Hey," I whisper back.

"Can I give you something before I go?"

His eyes are dark as my breaths plummet in deep, rapid cycles. "Of course."

He walks us to the supply shed as I pepper him with kisses, legs wrapped around his waist tight. The long domed, corrugated iron tunnel with double doors is halfway between the front gates and the factory. He swipes his access card over the small panel on the left door and pushes it open.

It's warm inside. Like a hothouse for non-perishables. Ash deposits me on a large bag of flour as the door closes. His mouth trails kisses down the column of my neck. I fumble with his buttons, trying to remove his shirt as fast as possible. His hands wrap around my fingers as he chuckles. "We can take our time, Clara. I *want* to take the time."

Since this is our last moment, he means. I'm catching what he is not saying. Our time together just got shortened to hours. "Sure, Ash. Tell me what you like. Your turn this time." Eyes searching his face as my chin wobbles.

Ash Remmins was the only person in this lousy Sector who has stood by me, even through my more stupid decisions. Vivi was my first friend here but Ash proved his loyalty time and time again. If I'm honest with myself, he's the first guy that hasn't felt like hard work. Like being around me is second nature, a place he wants to be.

Nothing like Nate, who hardly tolerates me when there's no mental goal at stake, and even that's a new development.

"Hey, where'd you go, beautiful?" Ash tilts my chin up with his hand.

"Sorry, I was thinking about this. Us."

"We'll make it count, Clara."

With a nod, trying to stem the burning behind my eyes, I swallow. "Anything you want, Ash Remmins, is all yours."

"The only thing I want is you." His mouth covers my own, and I slide my hands behind his neck. He moves closer, pressing in between my legs. I want him there. I want him everywhere. His hands tug at the hem of my shirt, and I raise my arms. Dotting kisses down my neck his hands slide around my back, releasing my bra. Every inch of my skin is laced with electricity.

"Hey," I rasp.

He pops my nipple in his mouth. The arch of my back, offering up more of what he has, is automatic. I moan as his hands return to my hips with a firm grip.

"Ash, this is—" I stifle a whimper as he grazes his teeth over the other nipple. "This is supposed to be about you."

His deep throaty chuckle echoes through me. Emotion squeezes my heart tight. This is the last time we will ever . . . Anything.

I take his head in my hands. "Stop, please stop."

When his worried gaze finds me, it takes everything I have to rein in the splintering in my chest. This man. Urgh. Life is a horrid bundle of bullshit. His hands wander over my face. "What's wrong?"

"Everything," I breathe. "I don't want you to go."

"I don't want to go, Clara. But this was my last probation assignment. I haven't exactly been accommodating to the authorities. The Sectors were better for me than the city but—"

"You were an Elite?"

My hands fall from him. Stunned, all I can do is stare at him as I wait for him to answer.

"City planning division. Only lasted three months before I was found lacking. Then Sector One which was a repeat of the city. So, I ended up here. Now—"

"And now, you can't stay in the Sectors either."

"Ring Two has no place for defective Elites or Engineers."

"Why didn't they put you back on the labor, the machines?"

"I started on the machines here Clara and I'm simply out of chances."

"Oh." Every tiny glimmer of hope I had with every new angle I come up with dies in an extravagant ball of flame. I've got nothing. No idea how to save Ash from being tossed like rancid scraps to the Wastelands. He's not half as upset about this as I am. He must have known it was coming, or at least on the table. If it wasn't for Tessa, I would go with him.

In a heartbeat.

I kiss him, hard then soft. Before he has a chance to object or distract me with one of his loving on Clara moves, I slide two fingers inside his waistband at either hip. He dips his head, hooded eyes burning straight through me.

"Let me adore you for a minute, please?" I whisper.

"I'm not complaining, beautiful."

The smile that stretches my face is so wide it hurts. Lord, when he calls me pretty little names, I melt to a puddle. I push his pants from his hips. They hit the floor and I run a hand over the fabric of his underwear. He's hard and big. I sink to my knees, and he groans.

Pulling down his briefs, his hard length springs free. The tip glistens. The head, soft and huge. My mouth waters as I run a thumb over the tip, and he grips the bench behind me. Good man. With slow, drawn-out movement, I slide the tip into my mouth.

His hands are around my face a second later. I take him

as deep as I can until he trembles, leaning against the flour sacks.

"Clara," Ash rasps, hands hunting for my arms, "up here."

I release him, running my tongue around the tip one last time. Rough hands haul me to my feet, and I giggle. His mouth smashes onto my lips. Hungry, all tongue and teeth. I can't get enough. It's like the first time I have had the raw, unrestrained, *real* Ash Remmins.

He's everything.

And . . . As of this afternoon he is lost to me.

Shuddering breaths give way to sobs.

The gorgeous face that leans back from me blurs. "Hey, hey," he whispers, hands on my face. "Please don't worry about me."

"I—" I haul air into my lungs like I've been underwater for far too long. "I'm not worried about you. I know you can take care of yourself. What I can't handle is being here without you."

"I could never ask you to come with me. I need you to be safe, Clara. It's the only peace of mind I have left that matters. But—"

He's as torn over this as I am.

And I can't abandon my sister.

I won't.

I make a promise to myself, in this very moment, I *will* see Ash Remmins again.

He dots kisses to my forehead, cheeks and on my lips.

Strong hands sweep me up and deposit me back on the flour bags. "Let me watch you unravel, beautiful."

He sinks two fingers into my wet core and finds my nipples with his teeth. I arch into him, and he rubs his thumb over my apex. "Ash, don't make me wait."

His hands slip from my heat, pumping his hard length with one hand before nudging against my soaked entrance. "You sure, Clara?"

"Yes," I breathe as tears burn behind my eyes.

Slowly, he nudges inside. My breathing shatters and I take his face in my hands and drag his mouth to mine. This time our kiss is slow and deep as he sinks inside me up to the hilt. The stretch is delicious. He feels amazing.

Damn you, Ash Remmins.

He pulls almost all the way out and slams back in. Air falls from my lungs. My heart cracks knowing this thing we have, so perfect, is about to be lost.

I spiral higher and higher, as he leans back a little. "Clara, look at you." His voice is raw, the last word strangled by emotion. With the next thrust I explode around him. Every wave of electricity sending me higher, dragging Ash with me, as his face twists with sweet agony.

He pulls me into his embrace, and I breathe him all the way in.

"Ash?"

"Yeah, beautiful?"

"We will see each other again, I promise."

"I hope so, Clara."

A boulder the size of the moon wedges in my airway.

"Do me favor, hey?" Ash rasps.

"Anything."

"Sit with Vivi when you can."

I nod, the bridge of my nose prickles with the burn of tears. To hell with the Engineers, the Elites. Nothing about this life is fair.

Nor is it good.

Someone has to ignite change.

19

TESSA

FINN HASN'T LOOKED at me since I stepped into the aircraft. Mid-air, I'm currently telling myself he's tired or stressed. Because the option of him being upset over what almost happened in my quarters makes me nauseous.

Especially when I really wanted it to happen. If Amber hadn't tracked the two of us down so efficiently after the power outage, I would have let him take whatever he wanted. Urgh, I hate myself right now.

The aircraft lurches to the left and I correct automatically, altering the thrusters until the heading returns to its original setting. Today we are doing a terrain landing, somewhere in the middle of nowhere.

Just what I need, to be stuck in a confined space in the middle of nowhere with a man who won't look at me. He's quiet, keeping to direct orders. No chit chat today. No side glances.

No Tess and Finn.

After an hour flight that is so uneventful, sleep would feel like a party, Finn indicates that we are to land. I start the landing pre-check and start the descent. He taps the panel above his lap, and the heavy metal shield underneath retracts revealing thick plate glass. And there's the ground.

It's barren. Red dirt and hardly a living thing for miles. No-one would want to be stuck out here. Almost ready to touch down, I tap the screen. Something is not right. The right fuel cell has been ejected. What the hell?

I snap my gaze to Finn, he's undisturbed.

"Matthews, our left fuel cell has disappeared."

"What?" Tapping his Visi-Tile, he slides the screen around, checking it over. "Huh."

"Recording paused," the robotic woman's voice chimes.

"Huh? Is that all you can say? How are we supposed to take off again without it?"

Finn shrugs, keeping his focus on the screen. The back left disrupter splutters out and we swing on our axis a little before I hold the Viper steady.

"What is going on?" I increase the thrust on the remaining three engines to keep us from hitting the ground prematurely.

A handful of heartbeats later, he turns to me. "We need to be out of the city tonight, Tessa."

"What? Why?"

"Things are going down. The Order, they—"

"The Order sent us away?"

"Not exactly."

"What aren't you telling me?" Remembering my current task, as we hang minimum range from a full landing, I set the Viper down.

He doesn't answer.

I slam a hand on the screen and kill the engines. Smashing the harness panel, I wait for the restraints to retract. It only beeps at me, holding me prisoner in its grip. Inhaling, I press my palm over the panel again, and the harness retracts. I jolt up and stalk out of the aircraft and into the red, hot dirt.

Searing gusts whip my hair from my bun and into my face.

I scream and kick a reddish rock. It bites, denting the steel tip of my boot. So much for protection. A thin sapling sways violently in the wind's torrent. I stalk toward it, needing to be away from Finn. Away from the aircraft, the training, the city, the Order.

"Tessa!" Finn's voice is hardly audible over the gusts.

I keep walking, picking up the pace. The heat turns my immaculate uniform sweaty in moments. The red dirt that swirls with the wind sticks to it. I don't even care.

"Tessa, stop!" His voice is closer but I stalk through the shrieking winds, stomping boots hard into the dusty ground.

Go away, Finn Matthews. Leave me to my humiliation, shame and confusion. For once, why can't my life go the way I want it to and resemble something like what I have dreamt of. But no, not for you Tessa. You don't get to have the things you want.

A rough hand snaps around my arm, and I am hauled backward. I stumble over the smaller rocks and uneven ground. Seconds later, Finn hoists me over his shoulder. Every scream is promptly whipped away the second they leave my lips as I throw punches into his back. He groans as we move closer to the aircraft, and I am still pummelling on his toned, sweaty back.

"Stop it!" he growls.

"Screw you! Put me down!"

"No damn way!"

I thrash wildly and he falters, hitting the ground with his knees. I flail backward onto hard ground and scramble away from him.

"What are you doing?" A snarl curls my lips.

He stays on his knees as I push to my feet. "Helping you, believe it or not."

"Why should I believe a thing you say? You brought me all the way out here, for what? You had the opportunity to have everything I can give, and you didn't stay. Amber turned up and you high tailed it out of my quarters like it was on fire, Finn!"

His jaw feathers, eyes falling shut. "You think I want any of this? The sneaking around, the distance I have to put between you and me?"

He opens his eyes, hurt lancing through them as they find my face. The heat pumping through my veins dies out.

"What are we here for? Tell me."

"You need to be out of the city. The authorities found

unauthorised comms. Yours amongst them. The Order is trying to make anything of importance disappear, but in case they can't make them all disappear in time . . ." He stands and closes the space between us. "Tess, anyone caught via the comms they find, was to be imprisoned for execution."

The air leaves my lungs. What happens to Clara when they find our messages?

"No," I breathe.

"One of the officers, Remmins, was going to try to minimise the damage on Clara's end. But Tess, she could still face demotion or worse, the Wastelands if they don't buy his story."

"Why is he helping you? Us."

"I have a few contacts amongst the Engineers. So does Amber. Remmin's is her brother."

I stare at him. Mouth agape.

"Oh. Wow. What— I mean, how? Amber's last name is Lang. Siblings aren't—" I pad a small circle, hands running over my messy hair, before stopping to face him again. "But you weren't convinced when I told you about Clara."

His eyebrow raises with a coy smile. "Amber was born a few years after her brother. Their parents hid her during the days after her birth. And when a woman died in childbirth a few short days later, they staged it so authorities thought the baby survived. It didn't but that act of treason allowed Amber to live. Her biological parents became her 'adoptive parents'. Ash and Amber were inseparable as kids. But Ash was not settled like his little sister and didn't last long in the

Elite core. Luckily for us at least, he's in the Sectors, because we are going to need him there if he is to keep your sister safe."

All I can do is stare at him.

Things are so much more complicated than I thought. Sending a comms to my sister never felt as dangerous or stupid as it does right now. Dammit. What was I thinking? I knew comms between Sectors and the city was prohibited. Yet, I did it anyway. I am the world's biggest fool.

In a daze, I pad back inside the aircraft. I reach the cargo bay and slam a hand over the red tail button. The old bird whines and lowers her tail onto the burnt ground. I sink to my seat and shove my head in my hands atop my knees. When we were kids, everything seemed straight forward. The path was simple. Score excellent grades, with Clara. Make it into the Elites, with Clara. Live a great life, with Clara.

"If there's anything I know to be true, Tess, it's that we only have one shot at being an Elite. One shot at staying out of the Wastelands. And with this disease spreading through every Sector—"

I pop my head up. "How far has it spread?"

"All five Sectors now."

"What's the rate of infection?"

"The number of those infected doubles every week."

"Heavens above. What is the survival rate, Finn?"

He swallows now. "Ten percent."

A breathy cry slips from my lips. My sister is a sitting

duck. The people she works with, those she calls her friends by now, all at risk. Yet, the city is clean. Not one case reported.

"Why is it only in the Sectors?"

"We, the Order, found documents related to the disease. It has only infiltrated the Sectors. The city either knows about it and are taking precautions to prevent it from spreading to Sontaria, or something else entirely."

"The power outages, how do they relate to the Order of the Flame?"

He tilts his head a small smile pulls up on one side of his lips. "You figured that out, hey?"

Hands on my hips I raise my brows as if saying *well*?

"The power outages were our way of getting into the system. The firewalls were intense, but when the backup generator was on, it was only half protected. It bought us time to get in and find out what they're up to. Unfortunately, what we found was far worse than anything we had suspected. The Order is pure chaos at the moment. With the comms exposé, things are tense. Real tense. So, we stay here. We bide our time, Tess. We stay safe for as long as we can."

"What about Amber?"

His brows lower now. "Amber is fine."

"No, I used her comms terminal to send my message to Clara." I grip my hair with my hands, turning in tight circles.

"She wiped that after you did it, I doubt they will find a trace now. Unless you—"

"Unless I sent others."

"Did you?"

Fear snakes up my spine and I push to my feet. "Yes." I barely hear my own word.

Finn holds my gaze for what feels like an eternity. He must have suspected as much, hence the escape plan. I clear my throat, hoping my voice will return. "So, we're supposed to camp here overnight in the cold and what? Huddle for warmth?"

A small smile peaks over his lips. "Nope, I radioed in after you so graciously left the cockpit before. Told them we lost an engine and transponder was fried and we're fixing it. They will expect us back by noon tomorrow. So, seeing they know what we're doing, we can stay here, and we can have a fire. No one is going to see us in millions of miles of nothing."

"If they know where we are, then what's the point of fleeing the city?"

"I said they know *what* we're doing, not where we are with a dead transponder."

"What about the alternate tracking system?"

"Disabled when the engine went down. These old machines you know." He's almost smiling.

I'm glad someone is happy here. I shake my head at him. I'm thankful he's trying to keep me safe and am grateful to not be in the direct path of Elitism tonight.

"Tess?"

I turn back and Finn is close, he brushes a stray strand of hair behind my ear, and I drop my eyes to the floor. Shuffling on my feet, I wrap my arms around my body. "You don't have to pretend to like me, you know. Be honest."

"Who said I was pretending?"

When I glance up, he genuinely appears confused. "But you, when Amber came the other night, you took off like—"

His hands grip my face, he kisses me. I slide my hands up his toned body. He breaks away, not going too far. "I'm sorry about the other night. I didn't know if you wanted her to know. And both the Elites, and the Order, frown on inter-rebellion relations."

"What do *you* think about inter-rebellion relations, Finn?" My words are breathy.

"That you, Tess, are worth any price I could ever pay."

A small tense laugh, huffs from my tightening lungs. "Always with the right words, Matthews."

"You don't have to call me that, you know."

"What, the recording's not on?"

He throws his head back with a hearty laugh, and I smile. It is good to be out of the city. It feels like freedom.

Almost.

20

CLARA

HOW GODDAMN DARE *THEY!*

Ash stands in civilian clothes on bare feet. They're baggy on him. Like he was more built when he arrived, better nourished. This place has wasted him.

"Uniform, Remmins," Evans snaps. Ash hands over his uniforms, access card and boots. They have taken any chance he might have had to survive in the Wastelands. Did they have to do it in front of every single Engineer at this factory?

It's a harsh message.

Ten minutes ago, I was sitting with Vivi. Her condition is worse. She hasn't eaten for days. My heart was already fragile. Now, I shove my fists into my back pockets and force each raging breath—save I create a scene and make this even worse for Ash. Banished to the Wastelands is one thing, humiliated and left with no defense prior to banishment?

Un-freaking-acceptable. Fire floods my veins when Ash is told to kneel.

What the hell?

Buzzing pierces the almost silent training yard where we stand witness to the demolition of Ash Remmins. His gorgeous brown hair hits the ground. For hell's sake, what else can they take?

Ash's body jerks as another officer binds his wrists behind his back. I suck in a wobbly breath and will my feet to stay rooted to the ground. The logical part of me is one hundred percent aware this is a scare tactic aimed at the rest of us. The part of me that cares about Ash, more than I should, is livid. Irreparably devastated.

"Any last words before you board transport?" Evans asks.

Ash drags his attention from me, pushing back up to his feet. He squares his focus to Evans and his face changes to stone. "No."

"Very well," Evans waves a hand to the exit.

I can't stand still a second longer, pushing through the few rows of sweaty bodies between Ash and me.

"Move!" Slamming a shoulder into one of the guys, my hair whips in my face as I duck and weave, desperate get to Asher. People shift slightly as I near the front row, and I pass the last body in my way. Ash gives me a subtle head shake as a hand grips my wrist from behind.

Nodding to whoever is behind me with their tight grip on my skin, he looks over my shoulder. Some unspoken agreement. A small, sad smile pulls up on his lips. The officer shoves him in the back, and he stumbles forward, and disappears through the exit.

I spin back, focused on the hand still gripping my wrist too tight.

Nate.

Nate was who Ash was nodding to?

"Let me go, Prendergast!" I rip my wrist from his hold.

His head tilts to the side and brows lower. "Clara." Worry lines his voice, hands dropping by his sides. I suck in a burning lungful of air and spin away from him, stalking into the building toward the sounds of boots.

But the corridor is empty. I sprint down the hall to the left. When I find just more empty corridor I rush back the other way.

Nothing.

They were too fast.

I missed him.

Dammit.

I walk in a small circle before heading for the stairwell. The second the door closes behind me I release a scream, slamming both fists onto the wall. I turn my back to it and slide down. Frustration turns to anger, and I slam my eyes shut. The bell for end of day rings through the stairwell but I don't bother covering my ears. Nothing is as loud as the crack splintering my heart in two right now.

The bell fades out, and someone is standing in front of me. Over me. Whoever it is can take a hike. Something nudges my foot, and I keep my eyes closed. "Go away."

"No can do."

Nate.

Wish he would stop pretending to be nice to me. It's annoying.

"Stand up, Clara."

"Leave me alone, Nathanial."

He grunts, joints cracking as he moves.

Big hands are under my arms, and I'm on my feet. I snap my eyes open. But when I find his face, the string of nasty retorts I had ready to spit out at him dies in my throat. His jaw feathers as he steadies me on my feet. The second his hands leave my arms, he shoves them into his front pockets.

"Having trouble touching your arch nemesis, Nate?"

"Stop it, Clara."

"Stop what?"

He pulls a hand from his pocket and waves it between us. "This."

I huff a laugh and turn, opening the door. His hand covers mine and it slams shut, his other hand flat on the door above my head. He moves in behind me, crowding me into the door. "He asked me to keep you safe, Bendall. That's all. You don't have to take everything I do as a personal affront."

I turn back, wedged between him and the door I force my chin up. "And you're going to keep your word to Ash? I don't need your protection. Plus, you don't even like me, Nate."

His face twitches, as if flattening an amused response.

Typical, always mocking me. Same as it has always been since we were kids. He straightens a little and says, "Who told you I don't like you?"

I open my mouth to respond, to say something like it's so obvious. Nothing comes that sounds good enough. Or true enough. Apart from giving me the cold shoulder which he does to most people, and the teasing when we were growing up, he has mostly been indifferent. Save that one time at selection.

"Never mind," I utter and turn back and open the door. He backs away, hands dropping as he watches me leave.

I glance back as the door closes. Searching his eyes for something I can't identify. The air between Nathanial Prendergast and me has shifted, even if only a little.

Something is different.

I can't find a reason to hate him.

Not anymore.

Was my hating him always a one-way affair?

* * *

"Lock and load people. Quotas will be doubling from now on!"

Evans is our new floor supervisor. Just brilliant. Nate throws me a cautionary glance. The *don't do anything stupid Clara* look etched all over his stinking face. I will be the perfect Engineer. If only for the other Engineers that have to tolerate Evans. And to keep Nate from blowing a gasket, although that would be entertaining.

Nate is entertaining to watch.

His hands grip a fresh bolt, heavy with a thick fabric I'm sure would only be used for cold weather items. His forearms flex and his biceps bulge under his uniform as he loads it into the cradles. He's almost impressive. That limp of his is nowhere to be seen on his good days now.

On that note . . . Back to work Bendall.

The machine hums along. I swap out bolt after bolt, making sure to meet the faster speeds Evans set on every last machine. Like we didn't run ourselves ragged before. By the end of shift my legs ache and my hands and biceps are all but cramped up.

"Need a hand?" Nate asks from behind.

"Sure," I utter. Sighing, I tug the crate of empty bolt rolls toward the back of the factory. The double doors that lead to the loading bay swing open automatically when we close in on them.

"You okay, Clara?"

Exhausted, I simply nod and imagine a long, hot shower. The kind that melts your bones.

Nate takes my crate and his and rolls them to the out bay. I wait by the doors and when he walks back over, his limp is only just noticeable.

"Any slower Prendergast and I'll be able to take a nap."

He flips me off before lengthening his stride but I catch the grimace that he tries to hide. "Ready for supper, Bendall?"

"Starving, you?"

"I could officially eat a supervisor and his lacky."

I chuckle and he messes up my hair with his hand. His fingers in my hair is nice, and I lean into him a little as he walks beside me. "Nate?"

The thought slips from my mind when urgent boots thunder down the corridor toward us. Nate goes rigid, slowing down a little and I match his pace. My gut tells me those boots are heading for us. And for nothing good.

The door to the men's lavatory on this level is a few feet away. I steer him into it, and we tumble inside, rushing to a stall. Hand on his sternum, I push Nate inside the first one and lock the door. Other hand on the flimsy metal half door, I strain to hear.

The boots thunder past. Was I wrong? My gut rarely is.

Plastic creaks behind me as Nate moves. I turn back to find him sitting on the closed toilet, hands laced and supporting his chin, elbows on his knees. Those dark brown eyes bore into mine. Like a fish out of water my mouth opens and closes at the sight of him.

I was sure something bad was about to happen. Maybe I'm being paranoid. To be honest, the comms between Tessa and me have been weighing my conscious down for weeks. What happens to Engineers who disobey those kind of Ring-wide rules? Maybe I'll see Ash sooner than I think. Nate tilts his head, as asking for an explanation.

"Sorry, I thought—"

"Breathe, Clara." He unlaces his fingers and lets them fall to his thighs. "Remmins was afraid Evans wouldn't take his word for it about your messages to Tessa. He could've been right."

"Hell." I drag my hands over my face and stifle a groan. I should have ignored the comms. Tessa should've known better. I can't blame her, really. This whole situation is bogus. Separating humans like cattle. It's damn preposterous.

"Tessa will be fine. She's a smart girl. If she knew something would come of the comms, she wouldn't have sent them. Is it possible they allowed her to?"

He doesn't believe his own words. Of course they didn't allow her. Siblings aren't supposed to exist. We are tolerated, not celebrated. Urgh, I hate this. The not knowing. The sinking fear that any moment someone I've grown fond of will catch the virus. That any moment Evans will haul me into his office and declare I'm only fit for the Wastelands too.

"Don't think you're being paranoid, if that helps," Nate says softly.

"Great, thanks," I utter.

He grabs my hand and tugs me closer to him. I stand over him by a head's height and he looks up at me. "Not everybody in your life is the bad guy, Bendall."

His hand is still wrapped around my own.

"Then why does it feel that way?" The words almost choke me as heat floods to my neck and face. Nate stands and folds me into a firm hug, and I gasp. Me and Nate Prendergast friendly does not compute and I hesitate, hands suspended midair at his sides. Eventually I wrap them around his back, and he drops his face by my ear in my hair. "It will be okay, Clara. I promise."

Something raw in my gut stirs to life. Deep and searing. My breaths shallow out as I breathe him in. He is warmth and familiarity. He smells divine. Heady and too much. I push out of his hold, struggling to rein in my own reaction to him being so damn close. His stare snags on the deep cycles of my breathing, and his jaw feathers.

Dammit.

His hands are still on my ribs.

"Nate," I rasp.

He simply tilts his head and closes his eyes, like his name on my lips is something tantalizing.

My mind is still reeling with the ghost of Ash's touch.

"Prendergast, let me go." I can hear the borderline heartbreak in my own words.

He opens his eyes and swallows, his Adam's apple bobbing. "Why do you always do that?"

Furrowing my eyebrows, I lean back a little. "Do what?"

"That—this, put distance between us."

"Am I not supposed to?" My face twists with confusion and a hint of devastation.

"Is that what you want, Clara?"

"What I want is to survive Sector Two. To see my sister again, one day. To know that Ash is alright."

"There's nothing else on your list?"

Now his shoulders fall in deep, guttering cycles. Fire and hurt lance through his dark eyes as I pull out of his hold.

"No, Nate. Nothing else."

Hovering by the door for a second, I listen for any movement outside before heading back into the corridor. Leaving Nate in the toilet stall, I stalk toward my dorm.

Is there nothing else on your list?

I'm a damn liar.

21

TESSA

THE STARS HANG in the most magnificent blanket. It's like nothing I've ever seen before. Finn pokes at the fire we built with a long stick he broke off one of the few dismal looking saplings dotted around the red dirt plain we landed on. The night is dark with no moon, but it makes the shimmering points overhead that much brighter.

The cold rolls in from the north and I hug my arms around my body trying to keep warm. The fire is great, but the smoke is continuously shifting every time the breeze swings.

"You cold?" Finn asks.

"A little."

He pats the ground beside him, closer to the fire. I offer a small smile before getting up and moving to his side. It's much warmer. "Thanks."

"I can't have you getting cold, Tess."

"Oh, why not?"

"Guess it would give me an excuse to warm you up? Not sure that would be a great idea, I think I blew that last time."

"Why?"

With a sigh he stares into the fire. "I should have stayed. You wanted me to stay."

"I did."

He glances at me. "And now?"

I chuckle. "Where are you going to go Matthews? We're stuck here thanks to your little prank."

"Not a prank, I did what I had to do to keep you out of the city. If you had stayed—"

A take his jaw in my hand and turn him to face me. "You take care of all your trainees this well?"

I can't help the stupid grin that pulls up on my face. He smiles at me, dark hair flopping in his eyes as he dips his head. "Only the ones I can't live without."

The smile falls from my face, sending my breaths to a skimming burn. "You shouldn't say things you don't mean, Finn."

"What makes you think I don't mean it?"

I release his jaw, realizing I have been touching his face for way too long. With a long, deep inhale, I turn to stare into the flames. "Nobody ever really means things like that. People come and go. No-one has complete control over their lives. Not here."

"That's true. It doesn't change the way I feel about you."

"And when we go back, and things are back to normal?

Or worse, the comms issue blows up in my face. You going to follow me to the Wastelands, Finn?"

"I—"

"It's fine. It's my mistake to live with. I never . . ."

Never thought I would be caught. Isn't that what all criminals think? I'm a half-witted idiot. All I wanted was to know my sister was okay, to try and keep her safe. It was the least I could do after I left her in the Sectors. "I think I'll go to bed."

Pushing up from the ground, I traipse into the aircraft. The parachute that is meant for cargo landings lays spread out on the floor of the cargo bay. Another hangs above like a makeshift gazebo top. Eight-year-old Tessa would have squealed her heart out at a camping trip like this. Adventure. So romantic.

I sit on one side of the soft white parachute's and grab a first aid bag from under the bench seat to use for a pillow. With only old, moth-eaten grey cargo blankets for cover, I try my best to snuggle under their heavy weight. Unable to get comfortable, I sit up and untie the laces of my boots, slipping them off and setting them on the bench seat.

A little while later, when I have found a comfy position on the hard metal floor, Finn pads in from outside. He raises a hand to hit the tailgate mechanism's up and down toggle.

"Can we leave it open, a little longer?"

"Sure."

Kicking off his boots, he lays down by my side. His focus returns to the sky above us. The rectangle of stars wavers as we are mesmerized from where we lay on the makeshift bed. "I'm sorry about the other night. Not wanting to be there wasn't the problem, Tess."

I search the night sky and my mind for something that would ease the rift that has split between us since that night. Not really finding anything, I roll over and prop my head up on my hand with an elbow digging into the steel beneath the parachute silk. "We could always take up where we left off last time."

He turns and studies my face. "We could."

"Only if you still want to."

Finn sits up and shuffles closer. His hand cups my cheek before he slips a stray hand behind my ear. "I haven't been able to put you out of my mind since that night. I've—" he dips his head, swallowing. "I've never been that desperate for anyone in my life. Dammit Tess, I was so . . ."

Hearing him say those words has my heart racing, and warmth pooling in my belly. "I couldn't sleep at all that night. Not a minute." My confession is soft, and his knuckles brush over my lips.

"Can I make it up to you?"

Now, I push up to my seat. When I finish wrangling with the heavy blanket, I am inches from him. Heavens, that caramel scent has me all breathless. That jaw, those dark eyes. I can't drag my gaze from his lips. I want Finn Matthews to make it up to me all night, as many times as we can.

"Finn?"

"Yeah, Tess."

"Don't let me catch a moment of sleep tonight either, okay?"

He smiles, and my heart shatters at the sight.

"Me either, Tessie."

I love it when he calls me that. "Also, I haven't ever—"

Finn's kisses me, desperate but soft. But I pull back, I need to tell him this. At least, I think I do. "Finn, I haven't done this before."

"Never?"

"Never."

"The other night was your first everything?"

"Kind of, I've fooled around a little but never felt the need to go the whole way before. Until now."

The adoration that lights up his eyes steals my breath.

"We can take this as slow as you want, okay? Tell me if you want to slow down or stop."

Finn stares at me for a moment before running a finger over my jaw, down my neck and across the soft top of each breast just inside the open top half of my jumpsuit shirt. Goosebumps flood my skin. My heart flings around like a manic bird.

"Can I undress you?" he asks.

"Only if I can undress you too."

He chuckles and tugs his shirt off and gestures to his pants. "You can do the honors." He stands and I raise to my knees, the hard ridge of his swollen length fills the standard issue utility pants. Throbbing starts in my apex as I flip the button open and tug them down, leaving his underwear.

"Come up here so I can see all of you." Finn's voice is gravel.

I do as I'm told. His hands push the shirt from my shoulders and reach around my back releasing the clasp on my bra. The cotton piece hits the parachute fabric as Finn lowers his mouth to my neck, pulling me closer to him with both hands on my hips. My hands crawl through his hair a second later as his mouth finds my peaks. I arch into him, unable to stifle the little moan that slips past my lips.

"Mhmmm, these gorgeous girls keep my mind busy every single night, Tessie."

"Do they?" The throbbing in my apex turns to an ache. I need him everywhere. Releasing a hand, I slide it down my stomach to touch myself, and he bats it away with a breathy laugh. "Stop doing my job for me."

I shudder through a breath. His hands drop from my hips to my pants button and the clothing pools at my ankles. I trace a hand over his pecs and down his hard stomach, heading for the part of him I am desperate to touch. That thick swollen ridge, I want it free.

"Finn, take these things off, now."

"Yes, ma-am." He moves back a little and slides them off, stepping out and throwing them with my shirt. "Yours too, baby."

"Uh huh."

Tugging my panties off, I toss them over my shoulder.

Finn laughs, deep and hearty, returning his mouth to my breasts. His tongue swirls around each nipple, sending electricity coursing around every inch of me and fire to my core.

"Finn," I take his hand and push it down to my wet center. "Here, please."

"In a moment, patience."

I groan as he lifts his hand back up, grabbing my ass and hoisting me onto his waist. Gently, he sets me down on the bench seat before dropping to his knees between my legs. "First, I want to see you undone on my face. Then you can have me."

I grip the bench seat with both hands when he nudges my legs further apart. Air burns in and out of my lungs in rapid succession, as I lean back on the curved wall of the aircraft.

"Remember, tell me to stop if you need to."

"Uh huh," I utter.

Why is he still talking?

Hands gripping my legs he slides his tongue through my center.

"Oh, Finn."

"Slow, remember."

His tongue flicks over my bundle of nerves, and I squirm on the bench. He sucks it, sliding in two fingers and I melt against the wall.

Heavens above.

Mouth watering, I spiral higher and higher with every

long, languid pump of his fingers. His tongue flickers over my apex again and again.

"Finn!"

Pulling back, he stops as a half-smile cracks over his face. "You want me to stop?"

"Don't you dare."

He chuckles at my desperate plea. His tongue finds my apex again, turning circles around it before sucking hard, and I explode around his fingers. Bucking on the bench seat, against his mouth, I cry out. Hands weaving through his hair.

Each beautiful wave of blissful agony longer than the last. Finn works me through each one. Making them last. Making them count. This man. So perfect. I am all but limp and bent over hugging his shoulders, trying to steady my breaths. The intense feeling leaves me reeling and feeling very empty. I want all of him.

"It's not enough," I whisper.

"I know, Tessie. Breathe for a bit. You will need it for the next part."

"Okay," I rasp.

He pulls the jocks over his hips, letting them fall to the parachute. Once I'm recovered, Finn picks me up and turns us around, so he is sitting on the bench seat. "Straddle my hips, Tess. You have control. We only go as deep and as far as you want."

I step over and straddle his hips, kneeling on the bench. My breasts are right in his face. My soaked center rubs the length of his hard, warm length. I ache to know what he feels like. He positions the tip at my entrance and kisses my mouth. Opening for him, he sweeps his tongue in.

I lower a little, until only the tip is in. The stretch and burn steals my breath. "Oh."

"Just breathe, Tessie."

I nod, wanting this. Him. He returns his mouth to my peaks, sending me into an arch. He slides in a little further. The sting that follows catches me off guard.

I gasp.

He snaps is head up. "You're okay. So damn tight, so wet. You feel incredible."

A small smile stretches my strung-out face. He likes it. Good.

I want to feel all of him, and I want him to have all of me. Lowering a little more, the sting subsides. Now, it's better, it's delicious. The movement of him inside me is mind-blowing.

It's addictive.

I want more. I sink until our bodies are completely connected, with nothing left between us.

"Finn," I whimper.

"You're doing so good. Don't know how long this is going to last."

"You fill me up."

"You like that?"

"I don't think I could like anything more. It's incredible."

"You wait until we get moving a little."

"You want me to go back up?"

"Yeah. But real slow."

I rise, slowly. The sensation is too much, and I whimper. Finn flicks his tongue around my nipple, his thumb finds my apex. All at once I feel everything everywhere. "I need to move faster, please."

"Do it," he rasps.

I fall back down taking him all the way in with one swift stroke. "Oh!"

His head falls backward, and he slams his eyes shut. Heavens, did I hurt him?

"Finn? What happened?"

His breathing is erratic as I cup his face with both hands. The throbbing in my apex is so distracting. "Did I hurt you?"

"No. I'm so close."

"You liked that?"

"Tess. I loved it," he growls.

"You want me to do it again?"

His head lifts, and his dark gaze locks onto my eyes. "I want you to do that all damn night."

"Sure," I whisper through a smile and lower my mouth to his ear and nip the lobe. He groans as I wriggle my hips. His hands grip my waist. This time I rise a little faster.

"I want to come with you inside me, Finn Matthews. Like you promised me the first time we tried to do this."

His breath shallows out, and he swallows hard. I lower, slowly, watching his gorgeous face twist with ecstasy. Oh, I could definitely get used to this. I rise and lower with quick movement, and his grip tightens. "Come undone for me, Finn."

He huffs a strangled laugh and I cant my ass out and increase the rhythm. It just feels right. And . . .

Heavens above.

Heat pools, electricity floods my veins and my core shatters like glass. A thousand tiny glittering pieces as every wave contracts around Finn.

"Tessie," he gasps. His hands tug through my hair as he crashes his mouth to my neck, nipping and suckling upwards toward my ear. His hips thrust up into me. Rolling my hips into him hard as he comes undone, we unravel together.

I can't believe I waited this long to do this.

I *am* glad I waited for Finn Matthews.

But now, I have two people I am terrified to lose.

22

CLARA

VIVI CLINGS TO MY HAND, but her hold is clammy and weak. She is covered in a welt-type rash. The Medicos have tried to keep me from visiting. They can take a flying leap. Like hell I'm going to leave her now when she needs someone familiar the most. I pick up where I left off, on the paragraph halfway down the page. Vi's eyes are closed. She looks peaceful.

"The farther she ran, the freer she felt. The girl had long lost her shoes. She let the silky grass caress her feet with every joyful step. Feeling every tendril of the winds fleeting hold as it whipped her cheeks."

Vivi coughs, turning to her side.

Dammit.

I rub her back. The ridiculous gown and face shield they insist I wear makes comforting her awkward and I push it up, trying to calm her with soft words and small pats.

"Urgh, Clara," she gasps.

"It's okay. Save your energy, sweet."

"Would rather not." She forces a small, crooked smile. This long, slow, torturous process the disease puts its victims through is cruel. She wants it over, and I get it. Hell, I would do it for her, if it weren't for the hovering Medicos. I've never found fault in relieving another living being from pain if they are at the end stages.

"Yeah, well Ash would give me a proper railing if he knew I let you off easy," I joke. She tries to stifle her laugh, knowing it will only make her cough more.

"Do you miss him, Clara?"

I told her everything. And she was always more than eager to hear about each night Ash and I managed to steal. That last handful of moments I haven't told her about. It seems wrong to share that with anyone else.

"Not really," I lie.

Her brows drop and she tries to push up to sitting but gives up when her arms shake and give out. I rest a gloved hand on her forearm. "I'm so sorry, Vi."

"What for, you didn't make me sick."

That I know. Nonetheless, seeing her this way has me feeling a whole lot of things I would rather not. Guilt for being healthy. Regret for not spending more time with her before she got sick. For not being around when she was in the early stages of her fling with what's his name. I'm pretty sure he was demoted to Sector Three. I keep that to myself. "I wish I was a better friend to you."

She smiles and coughs, hands on the rail of the bed this time. Her rash flares every time she has a coughing fit.

"You did fine," she says, when she recovers.

"If I knew how to fix this, I would make it happen in a heartbeat, V."

"Forget it, C."

She hacks a laugh at her own joke. All humor has drained from me, as emotion clogs my throat and tears pool. I promised myself I wouldn't cry. Not wanting to make this any harder for her than it has to be. Right now, I need a minute.

I squeeze her hand and put the book down on the side table. "I'll be right back, my sweet."

Standing, I push through the curtain.

Far enough away that Vivi can't hear me I inhale, long and hard, tilting my head back. Someone, somewhere in the bay is crying. Another few patients coughing, their hack not as bad as Vi's. I should go back.

A fully gowned Medico stands in my way when I spin back to return to Vivi.

"Move," I snap.

"She only has hours left. You should stay. I'll send a comms to Evans."

"Do whatever, Evans can go screw himself, I'm not leaving her." I shove past. The guy dips his head, and sighs.

"Bendall?"

Pausing, I don't turn back. "Not all of us are worthy of your hatred."

With a cynical scoff, I snap the curtain to Vi's cubical back. Her eyes are closed. She's so still. Her breathing is noisy. Much more than before. The thin tubes that supply the oxygen that was flowing into her nostrils lays beside her on the mattress. The drip that was feeding into the vein on her left wrist hangs over the bedrail.

This was her choice.

Vivi . . .

I sit by her side and pick up the book.

Her brave, selfless damn choice.

I breathe past the grenade in my airway and wobble my way through her favorite page again. Sending her on her way with the imagery she has been asking for every time I visit, the scene of the girl skipping through the grass.

"And when the sun shone down on her smile, the girl knew the warmth that flushed her skin would forever keep her. Her days would always be happy. An easiness spread through her veins like beam-kissed honey. She turned her face to the sun, closing her eyes as she released her breath and let the winds take her home."

The rattle in Vi's throat fades out.

I stare at her chest.

It doesn't rise.

I choke on the sob that claws its way up my own. The statico that has been monitoring her built into the small bunk she lies on, starts beeping erratically. The Medico from before, dives through the curtain, stopping on the other side of where she lays. He does a set of vitals before hitting the panel by her headboard, quietening the machine.

Standing, numb, I wander from the cubicle. As I reach the door, a hand grabs my wrist.

I turn back in a daze. The Medico. The ache in my heart matches the expression on his face. Finally, a face that cares. "You can't leave with those on, sorry, Clara."

"Oh," I utter. Tears streak down my cheeks as I pull the face shield and gloves from my body, and lastly the gown. He scoops them up in a large biohazard bag and guides me to the quarantine room.

The door seals behind me, and I step back to the wall and hang my head. Ragged sobs pour from my lips, and I clutch my hands around my collar. Vi was the only friend I made here. She was a beautiful person, and now she's gone. Taken by some disease that is spreading through the Sectors that Sontaria keeps ignoring.

Like our lives aren't worth a damn thing.

I have news for them.

I scream, raw and hard and I turn, slamming my fist into the wall. Again, and again. The wall shakes under each blow. The whoosh of the quarantine room does its final sweep. I stand tall and brush my hair back. Letting my hands fall by my sides. They shake. My entire body shakes.

The door to the corridor clunks, unlocking.

I push through it and stalk toward the dorm. Halfway there, I change direction, I want nothing more than to vent this anger. I take off at a run. A few moments later, the empty training yard stares back at me. The punching bag swings in the gentle breeze and I am there seconds later, fists railing on the unsuspecting bag.

Fire rushes my veins. Anger, rage and desperation fuel every swing. Every hit. When my knuckles split and turn red with blood, I sink to the ground and wrap my arms around my body. Back and forth I rock chugging through screams and sobs. It started with losing Tessa. Then they took Ash from me, and now I have lost Vivi.

The ache in my chest turns to a lancing streak and I will each breath into my lungs not wanting to pass out. The pain eases, and I drop to the ground, my forehead on the grass. Breathing in the earthy tang, strands of hair fall around my face.

Sobs fading out, I roll onto my side and lay staring at the yard around me. The day is almost over. Nobody is going to miss me. So, I lay on the grass and let the world turn.

Spinning.

Spiraling.

Until it blurs and fades.

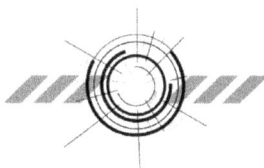

A HEAVY HAND rests on my shoulder. A familiar scent falls in. Whatever is underneath my right shoulder, hip and leg is cold and I shiver as I open my eyes. Darkness coats everything as I blink, trying to orientate myself.

The punching bag I flogged within an inch of its stuffing sways in the night breeze. The weight on my shoulder turns to a grip and I squint through puffy eyes at the figure over me.

Nate crouches by my side.

I have no idea why, but the sight of him has me in tears.

"Hey, it's okay."

His arms are underneath me.

The ground falls away and is replaced by his warm embrace. "Nate?"

"Shhhh."

He strides for the building. Inside, he doesn't walk toward the dorm but tracks for the stairwell. He turns, hitting the door with his back and shoving it open before walking down the stairs. I swallow past the emotion and take in his face. His mouth is a thin line and his jaw feathers. His breathing is heavy.

"Where are we going?" I ask.

"Somewhere no-one can witness your softer side, Bendall. Can't have them thinking you have a heart."

I strangled back the sob threatening to choke me and he glances down. Reaching the last door in the stairwell, Nate kicks it open. Somewhat recovered, I squirm, and he lets me down. I stand hugging myself, as he pulls linen from the clean trolleys onto the floor. He's creating a soft place for me to fall.

Literally.

My heart is not used to kindness from Nathanial Prendergast, and it splinters a little at the sight of him working. Another round of sobs cascade, sending tears dripping off my chin and onto the cold cement floor. Linen fluffed and pillows found, he walks behind me, hands cover my shoulders as he guides me onto the bed.

I should be suspicious.

It's Nate.

I should be angry at him for assuming he knows what I need.

Shouldn't I?

This is Nate we are talking about.

Nathanial Howard Prendergast. Arch-nemesis of Clara Ellen Bendall since the age of eight. Through the dirt wars of our first fight, thrashing each other around the school yard to the day we were Selected. Both Engineers.

Both caught off guard.

I saw how hard he worked to make the Elite cut. He more than earned it. Here he is, so close behind me. We pad into the middle of the ocean of soft white he set out. He lets my shoulders go and sinks into it, patting the space beside him.

I stare down at him, studying his face. The familiarity of it is like looking at myself in the mirror, I know every part of him so well. Even looking at someone with hatred in your heart, is still looking.

This close, with the two of us here, it's like I can see

parts of Nate I haven't seen before. Like the way his mouth kicks up on one side when he offers me a soft smile. Nothing but empathy lining his face.

Kindness.

Again, it feels strange.

He holds up a hand. "I promise I won't bite. Not this time, Clara."

With a wobbly laugh, I sink to my knees. He is wrapped around me an instant later, and I sob into his chest. Hard.

Warm hands rub my back. The air leaves my lungs and I struggle to pull more back in.

"Let it out. You've had a *hell* of a week, honeybee."

I grip his collar and scream. His breathing quickens. My forehead pushes into the ridges below his collar bone.

"I got you, Clara." His hands now track circles on my back.

A shattering pain rips through me, and I collapse into him. He swallows hard. I hear him groan between my breathy sobs and glance up to see his wrecked face.

Oh Heavens.

No, no more. No more pain. I cup his clenched jaw with my hands. "I'm sorry."

He shakes his head. "Don't you dare."

He hardens his face, dipping his head. "Not for me, not for anyone else. Don't ever be sorry for being who you are, Bendall."

I gape, torn between the status quo we have held our entire lives and this fierce defender of Clara Bendall before me, in this very moment. "You always this stoic, Prendergast?"

He laughs, but it's strained and fades out quick. "For the record, I never hated you, Clara. Not even for a minute."

"But, you—"

He tilts his head. "You are a colossal pain in the ass, your fuse is shorter than a toothpick and you are always right—"

"And you're a—"

"I wasn't finished, Clara."

He releases me and I rock back onto my heels, propping my hands on my hips. When I don't rebut, he continues. "You're also kind, loyal and . . ."

"And?" I shake my head, holding my palms up.

I swear his dark skin blushes, and I lower my brows. "What, Nate?"

He closes his eyes, chuckling as he drags a hand behind his neck. A heartbeat later they open, and I catch them straight away, as he sucks in a breath. "The only person I have ever wanted in my life. That day we met, my first day at that crappy little school, I couldn't believe someone like you existed. You take everything like a bull at a gate. You're like oxygen to a flame, you know—Strike that, you *are* the damn flame."

The shallow breaths that send my chest plummeting burn. I've spent the last thirteen years thinking this man hated me. The scowls he gave me, the smart-ass remarks. What the hell was that about then?

"So, you showed your adoration by being a complete ass?"

"Ah, yeah well, I'm not good at positive emotions. At least, I haven't been since my mother died."

Shit.

"Oh, I didn't know you lost her. How old were you?"

"Eight."

"What?"

"I was eight when she died."

Eyes widened and mouth agape, I press a hand over my mouth. Something like guilt-ridden devastation clawing at my insides. "How long—" I drop my gaze to my lap. "How long after you lost your mother was it when you came to the school?"

"Two weeks."

"Hell, Nate."

"Highly likely it was my grief, but you looked like you were a blessing made just for me." He holds a hand up as my mouth gapes further and my hand slips. "I know how ridiculous that sounds, Clara. As a grown man, I realize now that nobody can be that for anyone."

I move closer and trace a hand over his knuckles that are knitted together, whitened, in his lap.

"You never know, Nate. Don't count anyone out until they say so."

An hour later, and more words passed between us than our entire life spent together, we are lying on the linen. It's soft, and I'm exhausted. From today. From this preposterous life I have lived through where struggle lines every single day. I shiver from either the cold or the weariness, of which I can't be sure. Nate folds himself around me and sinks his face into my hair.

And I have never felt so safe in my entire life.

23

TESSA

THE ENTIRE ORDER of the Flame is gathered tonight. Men and women I've seen in passing around the city. Unsurprisingly, they are now all staring at me. Finn stands by my side as the members make a circle around an ancient looking, round stone table. In the center is, fittingly, a flame. My heart races as the iron rod that Finn holds disappears into it, as he rests the long handle on the edge of the small center fire pit.

After not having to run for my life after the comms incident last week, Finn met with the leader of the Order to see about getting me an invite. If I had known being burnt was part of the process, I'm not all that sure I'd be standing here. But there is no way in hell I am backing out now.

"Tessa Bendall, after considerable deliberation, we have made the decision to inaugurate you into the Order of the Flame," an older man says. His name is Hayward. The *order* of the rebellion I have studied up with Finn's help.

Inside the largest of the rooms in the catacombs below the train station, old looking pyres rest in brackets around the room, their flames at a low burn. Each member is dressed in some kind of ceremonial robe, like something out of old fashion fairy stories my mother told Clara and me as little girls. The kind where the damsel was always saved by a knight in shining armor.

Nowhere in those books was the heroine burned with an iron rod. And when I hesitate as they call me forward, Finn leans in. "It's okay, Tessie. It stings for a bit. Becoming part of the Order is more than worth it. We are fighting for our freedom and that includes your sister's."

I step forward.

For Clara, I would dance in the damn fire pit. She's my currency. Always has been, always will be. I hope Remmins is keeping her safe. Since we haven't heard from Sector Two for over a week, I can only assume he is, and that Clara is safe and healthy. I plant that thought at top of mind.

"Tessa Elise Bendall, you are hereby anointed into the Order of the Flame. In accepting this anointment, you are expected to carry out any duty assigned in the timeframe allotted. You will report to myself and Matthews weekly. Do you understand?"

I am eager to help in any way I can.

"I understand."

"Good. Your sponsor will give you the mark of the Flame. Every mark carried by a member of the Order is unique. Finn?"

Finn steps up to the pit and takes the iron rod, his now hand gloved. The end is a literal red-hot poker. The tip is so small. "Tell me what you want, Tessa."

"What do you have?"

He turns around, lifting his hair. A small, smudged burn line sits across the base of his skull.

"You may have whatever shape you desire. Note, that the more intricate the design, the longer it takes and the more pain it produces." Hayward nods to Finn.

"I want a flame."

"Very well," Hayward says.

Finn shuffles closer, rod in hand. The heat burns my neck long before the metal even touches my skin. A woman hands me a leather strap. I bite down and nod to Finn. He's quick. I groan through gritted teeth at the searing pain but it only lasts a few seconds.

"Done," Finn breathes.

The tang of charred flesh floods my senses and I ignore the bile that creeps up my throat. The skin around the area is tight. I skim a shaking hand behind my head, the tips of my fingers brush the stubby burnt hair above the mark. It will grow back.

I'll be able to help Clara now. Finn was right, it was so damn worth it.

With the ceremony done, we sit down to eat. Two long tables are carried in, food already sitting atop them. Folding chairs and wine come next. I haven't seen wine for years.

Nothing in Sontaria, the exception being the club we briefly visited before the last power outage.

"When are you taking your first solo flight?" Hayward asks, taking the seat next to me at the first long table.

"Next week, all things going well."

Finn smiles over his wine. Hayward studies the air between us for a sliver of a moment before digging into his food. Finishing his first mouthful, he stabs a piece of chicken and points his fork at Finn. "This one was a quivering mess at his anointment."

Finn laughs but nods. "I was literally terrified. Barely eighteen."

"How were you so young?"

"I grew up here, Tess."

Finn has never left the city?

"Wow, I didn't think . . ."

"You thought Elites didn't have children, Tessa?" Hayward asks.

When he says it, it sounds ridiculous. "I guess not. Obviously, they do." What happens to the Elite children that don't make the cut at the final testing and selection?

I fiddle with the stem on my wine glass, hoping the conversation will change to something less humiliating. Growing up in the Province, you are not privileged to the way of things in Sontaria. Just as well, or a revolution would have ensued long before I was born. Would that have been for the best? Briefly, I wonder what Ring 2 would be like if that had happened. What will it be like after the rebellion is done?

Hayward stands and taps a fork against his glass. The room goes deadly silent. "Tonight, we have much to celebrate. A successful raid with new information gathered to help the resistance move forward. Most of all, a new member! We do not take this lightly, Tessa Bendall, as I am sure you also will not. Welcome to the Order of the Flame. May your first mission prove your mettle and secure your place amongst your fellow rebels!"

A great cheer explodes around the room. People take up their glasses, some saluting me and others downing the contents as vessels clink together. Finn takes my hand in his under the table.

"Tessa," Hayward says, turning to me in as the ruckus goes on around us. "Your first mission is to find the source of the disease. We need to know its origin. I hear you are familiar with the inter-authority comms system, should be an easy task for you."

My mouth goes dry.

They know no more than I do.

My heart sinks and hope of helping Clara shrinks. But maybe I can change that?

Sending notes to my sister is one thing. Finding the source of origin for a deadly infliction that is hardly spoken of in the city, is a completely different level of crazy. Classified-level crazy.

"I, ah—"

Hayward's brows lower, bushy with age, and now his grey eyes are homed in on me. The look of someone who is trying to decide if they made a mistake covers his lined face. I set my shoulders back and raise my chin. "No problem. Do I report back to you here when I'm done?"

"That won't be necessary. We have runners for that kind of thing, more inconspicuous that way. Let Finn know when you find it, and he'll be in touch."

So, I'm still not trusted—not fully at least.

I simply nod and after he searches my face for a moment, he turns back to his food. The woman beside him asks a question and he turns to give her his full attention. My shoulders slump and I grip my hands around my knife and fork. My appetite from earlier is nowhere to be seen.

"You alright, Tess?"

I glance up at Finn, worry contorts his eyes and mouth.

"Sure. Is it okay if we head back? I'm kind of wiped."

"Of course, let me say some goodbyes. You got your mission already?"

I tilt my head and raise a brow, as if he wasn't listening. "Yes."

"Good. I can think of a few places I'd rather be right now." The smile that splits his gorgeous face sends heat to my belly in an instant. He pardons us from the table, and I say goodbye to Hayward. We wander back to my quarters, through darkened alleyways and side streets.

"You're quiet," Finn says.

"Just thinking about the mission."

"Ah, you can have Amber help if you need to. Any other rebel is a resource at your disposal. A fact, I notice, Hayward left out."

"How do you know him?"

Finn stares ahead, our footsteps are the only sound filling up the silence. "He was my mentor when I first started flight training. When he semi-retired, he had already been initiated into the order."

"You started younger than me? Flying, I mean."

"I was still prepping for my final exams when I was chosen for early intake into the Aeronautical Elite core."

I did wonder how someone not yet thirty could be so superior to me. It makes sense now.

"Do Elites from other faculties find their way to the Order, or are you all filtered in from Aeronautics?"

"All faculties. It's a curation process. Many have come close to discovering us, only to be lead away. It's too important to keep our cover to let just anyone in."

"You let me in."

"Yes, we did."

"Why?"

"Because of your connection to the Sectors. Because of your assertiveness. I'm pretty sure that you not being afraid to break the rules for something, or should I say someone you love, made an impression. Around here, it's things, positions, success before people, before family. Sontaria is—"

"A crappy, shiny place?"

"Uncanny the way you see the world around you, Tessie. It's refreshing and everything this Ring needs."

"So, we do it together. Make things the way they should be."

Finn stops shy of the mouth of the alley we've been walking down, before the streetlight. His hands slide around my waist before resting on my hips. My heart rattles faster, and I breathe him in.

"You want to make a better world with me, Tess?"

A coy smile bends over my lips. "Amongst other things."

He chuckles, running is thumb over my bottom lip. "Other things, I like the sound of that."

"You should."

My hands twist in the opening of his shirt. We should go home. Hideaway until the world is desperate for us. Buy ourselves some time.

The people in the Sectors, the Province, my sister, they don't have that luxury. Every day that passes more innocent people die. As the privileged people of Sontaria carry on with their pristine lives, utterly unaffected. I break away and grab Finn's hand. "We need to get to work."

He runs beside me, all the way back to quarters.

But this time, I need his room not mine.

24

CLARA

EYES FULL OF FIRE, Nate glares at me. I stand, hands on
hips, giving him everything back two-fold. "How dare you
have an opinion on the people I care about, Nate! You've
been nothing but arrogant and horrible to me, my entire life!"

He inches closer, hands hanging by his sides, shoulders
working a deep heaving cycle, mouth pulled into a half
snarl. "Where do you get off telling me what I was like all
these years. You have no idea, Clara. You know nothing
about my life, about the people I care about, and even less of
a clue about whatever this is!" His hand waves between us.

I step back, mouth gaping. Is he actually telling me I
have this wrong. Whatever has happened between us in the
past twenty-four hours doesn't wipe out the last two and a
half decades. No way is he allowed to dismiss entire decades
plagued by the stupid, bully crap he pulled. He loathed me
until a few short weeks ago.

And . . . now!

He has the utter hide to tell me not to care about Ash. To move on!

"Screw you, Nate. If I want to have feelings for someone, I damn well will. None, and I mean literally NONE of this is your business."

He stills, before pulling back a little. The expression on his face is like I slapped him. Don't freaking tempt me, sweetheart. After a moment, he turns and walks from the dorm. I jerk when a noise comes from the bunk behind me. We were so busy yelling at each other, both of us forgot we weren't alone. Every set of eyes in the dorm is homed in on me.

Geez.

One of the guys stands and walks after Nate, tossing a glance over his shoulder. "You two should get your own room. Save the rest of us the drama, Bendall."

I gape at him, but school my face in an instant. Half afraid to turn back to my bunk I stagger backward until it hits the back of my legs. I drop down and shove my head in my hands. How the hell did that escalate so fast?

"He didn't mean it," a small voice says as the bunk beside me dips. I breathe through the fire currently trying to engulf my lungs and groan. We made absolute fools of ourselves. He definitely meant it. I'm certain.

The face of one of the latest recruits fills my gaze when I turn toward her. "Yeah, he did."

"Oh," she says, dropping her attention to her fidgeting hands in her lap.

"It's okay, we have been at it for years, nothing new. I'll live."

She looks at me and frowns. "Sometimes the people we love the most rile us up in the worst way."

"I don't—" I clear my throat and inhale, slow and deep. How do I put this. "Nate and I are not—"

"Sure, you guys keep telling yourselves that, at least it's entertaining."

I'm about to rebut when a cheeky smile splits her round face. Her blonde hair sits above her shoulders and her blue eyes are lit with mirth. She's pretty.

"Which part of the Province are you from?" I ask.

"Eastern, Emily Black."

"Clara. And I'm pretty sure you already know my last name. Southern."

"Oh, I can tell." She cracks up laughing, and I punch her arm playfully. She feigns hurt and rolls on the bed. I stand and offer her my hand. "Come on, let's grab some supper before those guys hog it all."

We walk to the mess hall. It's a ruckus as usual. Nate sits at a table with the guy who went after him. The second I pass the first of the tables, he tracks me across the room. We grab trays and load up our plates as much as the kitchen hands allow, dropping onto the closest bench seat.

"You and Nate grew up together?" Emily asks.

I shove a piece of bread into my mouth. It's half stale, but I don't care. I swallow. "Yep."

"Must be nice to have someone from home here in the Sector."

"Huh, you witnessed how nice it is. Nate and I have never got along. He's always tormented me in one way or another. I wish he'd leave me alone."

"Maybe he can't."

"What's that supposed to mean?" I pull a face so incredulous hers lights up.

"Well, it's possible he can't leave you alone. Have you ever thought of that? It could be entirely plausible he doesn't want to *not* be around you." Both her brows are raised in the are you picking up what I'm putting down here way.

I stare at Nate.

I mean, I have always loved looking at him. In my mind, it has always been a kind of hate to love, love to hate thing. We stare at each other briefly, holding the air between us hostage for a moment before he drops his attention to his plate. He mutters something to his friends and leaves the table, marching for the door.

"I'm not hungry," I murmur and push from the seat, following Nate.

"You're welcome!" Emily calls out from behind.

* * *

The training area is empty. The echoes of the punching bag being thoroughly annihilated snap through the cool air.

I pad across the grass to where the bag takes hit after hit. Putting both hands on the side, I hold it steady.

Nate's stare burns into me. I nod and he hesitates but throws another punch. Then another and another. The bag jerks with every hit as the vibration travels down my arms and into my chest—straight to my heart. A whole ten minutes pass before I say, "Nate, stop."

Punches keep coming. Sweat flies off his arms as they move. His neck and bare torso are slick, shirt discarded to the grass.

"Nate, please, stop."

He slows a little but keeps punching. Sweat rolls down the bulky biceps and over his ropey forearms. His dark eyes are trained on the bag and he's breathing heavy.

Releasing the bag, I slide in front of it, ducking as his fist goes for the bag, unable to slow the momentum.

"Clara! Dammit, I nearly hit you!"

He sways on his feet and sucks in long, ragged breaths. I push off the bag and file into his space, looking up into his brown eyes that are pure storm. "I'm sorry."

He swallows.

"For the last however many years, I *am* sorry, Nate."

His knuckles are red, raw. They must be stinging. He shakes them out and lets them hang, before closing his eyes. "Why are you sorry, Clara?"

"For not noticing you."

He huffs a laugh. "Yeah well. Acting like I hated you was easier than what I really wanted."

"I don't know if what you want is possible. I mean, I only stopped loathing you like five minutes ago, so you know."

He opens his eyes. "You did?" His lip twitches with the ghost of a smile.

"Yeah, I did."

"I'll take it. Although, I'm not sure we can be friends."

"Fair enough. You want me to stay away from you?"

He turns away and bends down to grab his shirt. But he doesn't turn back to me. Only stands rigid with his head down, like he can't look at me to process this. My gut flips.

"Nate?"

He hangs his head and sighs. "Go back inside, Clara."

"You coming?"

"In a bit."

"Okay, see you inside."

He doesn't respond when I walk away, so I pad to the dorm and busy myself with a shower. Once the last of our roommates have gone to bed, his is still empty. Wrapping a robe around my sleep clothes, I wander back to the training area.

Empty.

I make my way down the corridor to find the door to the stairwell is cracked open. Pushing through, I descend the stairs. I know where he is.

In the laundry room the linen is spread out like last time. Nate is sitting with his knees up, head resting on top, and arms cradling his head. His back is against the furthest of the oversized machines. Tentatively, I move to where he sits and kneel. I pull his hands down from his head. He lifts it, slow, like he already knows it's me. Stunning dark eyes look up at me, ravaged by devastation. My heart tightens.

"Hey," I whisper.

He sucks in a ragged breath. "Go back to bed."

"Nope."

"You have your life, Clara, and I have mine. There is no reason they have to mix. Not anymore."

Confused is an understatement. "What are you talking about?"

"If you can't see it, it doesn't matter."

I sit on the cold floor in front of him, wrapping my robe around my body, tight. I am not leaving until he tells me what has him so damn worked up.

"You'll freeze, go back to bed, Bendall."

"I'll go when you do."

"I don't sleep up there."

"What? Since when?"

"I never have. I come down here after lights out every night. The bunks are too soft."

What kind of household did he grow up in? "Too soft?"

"Not used to a bunk, is all. Plus, the laundry is not full of rank guys who snore. So it's a win, win."

Amusement wraps around my face, and a smile pops on his.

"Every single night, Nate?"

"Yeah."

"So, this is like your space?"

"I guess." His brows lower.

"No one comes down here? Or realises you're not in the dorm, ever?"

"Haven't yet."

"Oh." Glancing around the laundry room, it is quieter than the dorm. More private, for sure. There's only the two of us. How come I didn't notice Nate missing? Is that what he was talking about before?

Tracking my gaze back to his, I follow as his hooded eyes travel my body, his hands tangled in the sheets either side of him. I bite my lower lip, frowning.

"I should let you be then." The words are no more than a whisper.

I don't move.

I don't get up.

His stare burns into my skin.

If you can't see it, it doesn't matter. What can't I see Nate?

"What did I miss, Nate?"

He jerks back a little, folding his arms over his chest. "Forget it."

"Can't. It's going to keep me up all night. Knowing you're down here and I'm up there. All the while something I have no clue about is hanging between us."

"Okay. Tell me this, why Remmins?"

"What?" I straighten, hugging the robe tighter.

"You and Remmins. Do you like sleeping with guys ten years older than you? Or was he an easy target?"

Heat floods my neck and face as a gasp escapes my lips. "The hell?"

"There are plenty of willing guys in this Sector, apart from Johnson, you could have had your pick of them. You chose the supervisor."

"You really want to know why I like Remmins, Nate?"

"Enlighten me, please, Clara."

I stand and hover over where he sits on the sheets. He watches as I sway on my feet, exhausted from carrying around this heavy, hurtful thing we have had slung between us since we were kids.

"I liked Ash because he was kind. He was nice to me. Never humiliated me, hurt me, or made me feel small. The way you have my entire life!"

My robe opens but I don't even care. The cooler air has my nipples hard peaks. Nate pushes to his feet. A heartbeat later he is towering over me, inches away. His breath falls onto my face. His heaving chest almost brushes against me with every deep cycle.

"The only way I could ever get you to even notice me was with those things. It was a poor trade off. Your hurt feelings for little moments of your attention. Still, now, after weeks of trying to be what I thought you wanted, you *still* don't see me."

Dazed, I step back and turn to head for the door.

His hand grabs my wrist, spinning me back. I slam into him, and his hands cup my face, his lips sink onto my own with a kiss so raw, so overwhelming. Instinctually, my hands are on his jawline, then they disappear into his hair.

I melt into him for a second.

Breath stalled.

His heady scent, his warmth.

The all-consuming pull inside me to give in to him sees my mouth part to let him in. To give him everything I have. Electricity hums in my veins, heat rapidly swelling in my core. The ragged breaths that have rattled back into my lungs, are too short to be of use.

Wait...

Confusion tangles my heart with my mind. I push out of his hold with a gasp. My palm stings when it hits his cheek. I suck back a sob, and the burn of tears blooms behind my eyes.

His devastated face blurs as I turn for the door.

My heart cracks, a fraction.

Because those few seconds, where my body ached for the one man I've never considered, are the most I have ever felt for another person.

Ever.

25

TESSA

I BOLT up from sleep like somebody jump started my heart with bare live wires. Hand over my heart, I suck in a deep, steadying breaths.

Clara.

The disease only effecting the Sectors and Province is too suspicious. The higher the Elite score the closer we are to HQ. Information on it would be right under our noses. I know it.

I toss the covers off and fly out of bed. Sinking into my desk chair, I tap the Visi-Screen. The bright white and blue floods the room like artificial daylight. Blinded for a moment, I blink and rub the heels of my palms into my eyes to adjust. The blurry screen rights itself, and I tuck the chair in closer and settle in.

Scroll. Tap. Quick and precise I come to the comms trail for HQ. The same one I used the first time I sent a message to Clara. Somewhere down this rabbit hole I'm sure there will be a trail. Some small piece of communication that slipped through their firewalls.

An hour later, I have just that.

It's the last place I would have ever thought to go.

Leadership Elites.

The cursor of the Visi-Screen that indicates the start of the comms I have open dances a monotone two-step. Flash on. Flash off.

With a trembling finger, I scroll past the pleasantries and into the guts of the message. As I reach the last line, my breath stops altogether.

It's signed off by the General.

General A B Beswick.

The construction of underground factories, hydroponic agriculture and storage for centuries worth of precious metals. Why? The Sectors provide that. There has to be more to this. Unless . . .

I keep digging.

My body vibrates from overstimulation, hours of shocking findings and hopelessness. I plonk my elbows on the desk and slump with my chin on my laced hands. One last comms.

I type the line of code that Amber taught me how to crack and enter the sequence. Another message, the same as the tens before it, appears on the screen. This time schematics, along with protocol, are all I see when I scroll. It's biological. It's the disease. Leaning in, I study the text.

Virus.

Worse, a *synthesised* virus.

The city *made* it?

It's not just a natural plague they've harnessed. I push back on the seat and rub my face with both hands. This has to be hypothetical. Doesn't it? Continuing down the document I find timelines and dosages. In a red box, in all caps is a warning paired with a note.

The antidote to the virus, should it find its way to Sontaria, has been transported to a northern region, west of Ring 2. Three numeric codes and fingerprint ID matching is required to release the antidote. Precautions should be taken to ensure it is not required. Retrieval from its current location - highly dangerous.

What the *actual hell*?

They hid the antidote *outside* the Ring? In the Wastelands?

Why? I gape at the screen. Trying to grasp why the General would hide the only cure in a place no ring-dweller would dare go. Why he would do this at all. My eyes burn from hours looking at the screen. My back aches and my head pounds. I stand and wander to my window. The city, in all its glassy wonder, is lit up and sparkling. A pretty, pretty package for terrible things and terrible people.

A northern region, west of Ring 2.

Wastelands.

It's in the Wastelands so we can't get to it. No person from Province would ever dare chance the Wastelands. Not after the stories we grew up with. It's far too dangerous. Wastelanders are killers. Barbarians. At least, that's what they told us. The history and humanities lessons we were fed in school from a tender age fill every young mind. But . . .

Wastelander's are free.

"Never believe anything you see, half of what you hear, and absolutely nothing those city folk have to say." Dad used to repeat this time after time at the dinner table when Clara and I would come home with tales we had heard at school. Clara always had the best stories. Dramatic, funny, sad. My sister can make you feel, that's for sure. Right now, she is on the receiving end of an engineered virus set to wipe out our very own. Our families, our neighbours. The backbone of Ring Two is being annihilated. Sontaria is officially killing off its own people.

From everything I have seen, heard and read, they are eradicating Engineers and the Province. Every single last person who doesn't make the two percent cut. Their end game must be an Elitist society.

I pull up a schematic of HQ.

Leadership is the very top level. It has the highest security, as it should. Light aircraft, piloted by some of the most senior Aeronautical Elites, land on the top of the building twice a day. That I know from the flight rosters hanging in the debriefing room.

I could . . .

The screen beeps. Every message that I have open disappears all at once.

I was in too long. Hell, someone's found me. With a jerk, I stand and push the chair over and back away from the desk. Hands in my hair, I fixate on my door. Waiting for it to open. Surely, if HQ found out I was into classified documents, they'll come for me. I dash to the food dispenser, ready to hit the power button like Amber showed me in case I need help. I assume she meant the rebels would arrive.

When the door doesn't move, I pace the room. The gadget on my wrist lights up. A page from Finn. With a single tap I track his small white location indicator as it moves toward my building. I can't tell him to come. Any communication between the gadgets is monitored. So, quickening my pace, I try to will a way out of the hole I have dug for myself to materialise.

Nothing comes. A soft knock raps my door, and I rush to the peephole, heart flinging wildly. Finn's worried eyes search the door as I hit the access panel, and it slides open.

He's inside a heartbeat later, hand slamming over the panel to close the door.

"Tess, what are you doing?"

"I was trying to find the source of the disease." My words wobble, wracking with panic.

"Amber caught your little hunt. Luckily, she shut it down before it was flagged by her superiors."

I sink to my seat and shove my head into my hands, knees up. I am not cut out for this rebel life. My nerves are nowhere near hardened steel. But Clara. I can't let her be murdered, along with every last person outside the city.

"I found it," I mutter.

"Hey?" Finn pries my fingers from my face and lifts my chin with his hand. "Where?"

"The virus is synthesised. I tracked it to Leadership. The lab must be somewhere in HQ."

His face is slack with shock as he grabs my hands. "Tessie, you can't go in there. Let me relay the information to Hayward."

"No, it's my assignment and I will carry it out. I need to double check what I found is correct first. Then, you can tell Hayward."

"Promise me you'll stay away from the Leadership level. They won't bother banishing you to the Wastelands if you're caught. They'll execute you."

Finn's face is distraught. Eyes hunting for the answer he wants, grip around my face. "Please . . ."

"I promise."

I lie, right to his face. Sickness crawls up my insides, burning me like it should. As much as he means to me, I will not let my sister die. I will fight with my last breath to keep her safe. Her and every other person outside this city. I sink into the desk chair.

"Help me send a comms to Clara, Finn. She has to know this."

He straightens up and pulls me to my feet. Even when I'm steadied, he doesn't let go. Instead, he folds me into his arms, dropping his face into my hair. "I can *not* lose you, Tessa Bendall."

I hug his head with my arms, threading my fingers through his hair. "You won't."

Finn blows out a long, slow breath, he releases me and glances to the desk. "I'll log in. Save HQ seeing more activity under your name."

I nod and follow as he heads for the Visi-Screen. He sits and taps away. Comms fill the screen, and he hunts for Remmin's pathway, opening a fresh message. The tiny line at the beginning of the blank screen cycles through its own little heartbeat. Waiting. How do I say it? It has to be coded.

After a moment, and running a few versions through my mind, I decide to put the message inside an old childhood memory that Clara will definitely remember. It had Nate in it, and she hates Prendergast as much as she loves her family. It's intense what has lived between those two since we were little. Nate was always ruining something she was invested in. She will understand.

When I have tapped out the beginning, middle and end —with the what, how and why of this veiled story—I read it over.

There once was a boy who rued the day the girl was born. He was in every place she went. Mucking up every single thing she loved. He was like a scourge. He was not for the Province or the Sectors. He was special. NP, as the girl loved to call him, was not mother nature's work, he was pure evil. One day, the girl found him, in a place he wasn't supposed to be, and he spread ill far and wide, lest his home. He didn't need her anymore. And as she lay dying, surrounded by everyone she knew, her salvation only where no man would tread. NP looked down on her from his crystal palace and smiled. He had every-thing he needed without her.

Finn reads the message, raising an eyebrow. I chew my bottom lip. "Too obvious?"

"I don't think so. Remind me never to meet this NP guy."

I chuckle at him and lean over his shoulders, draping my arms across his chest. "He went to Sector One, so I doubt you ever will. Nate Prendergast has been my sister's nemesis since we were little kids. If there is anyone she could personify with this disease, it would be him.

She'll figure it out.

She has to.

26

CLARA

THE GIBBERISH IN my hand makes me want to laugh and cry. For so many reasons. I sit on my bunk, still in my uniform. The comms was under my pillow when I returned from shift. Without Remmins around, I am not sure who felt it was okay to slip the message through the system and into my hands.

Of course, Tessa would send a message that features Nate. I track back to the words. I know what she's telling me. The disease is from the city. The cure is in the Wastelands.

The general and his Elites are trying to wipe us out.

Trying to create a society where only the top two percent exists. Engineers, folks in the Provinces, may as well be cattle for all they care. Work horses that have proved too long in the teeth and need putting down. Why not banish every last Engineer to the Wastelands? The dead don't rebel. The dead can't come back to haunt them.

I push to my feet and wander toward the mess hall, stomach rumbling. The dining area is loud, despite the dwindling numbers. My thoughts go to Vivi. I pluck up a tray, slamming my eyes shut, trying to stifle the tears prickling the bridge of my nose. I open my eyes and shuffle along with the other Engineers, accepting grey rations into a cracked porcelain bowl.

I sit with some of the girls from the factory floor. They chat away, speculating about the origin of the disease. One suggesting the city will intervene and come to our aide. If they only knew.

I search the room for Nate. The usual group of guys he sits with are across the room at a far table. He isn't with them. I check every last table. He isn't here.

At all.

We only have twenty minutes to eat, he'll miss supper. I slide the bread roll from my tray into my pocket. The girls don't notice, still deep in conversation about the potential Sontaria officers who are supposedly coming to save us.

Idiots.

I finish and walk back to the dorm. With a quick pass through the men's side of the room, I pop the roll under Nate's pillow. Tired from a long, intense shift with Evans, I grab my night clothes and toiletry bag and head for the shower. Steam fills the small stall, and I step into the stream. The heat sends a crimson flush over my skin, and I rub the liquid soap over every inch of me, washing away a hard day.

Toweling off, I pull on my clothes. As the girls on my

side potter around getting ready for bed, I do the same. I lay back, muscles aching, and let my eyes drift shut. The lights are turned out an hour later and I'm still wide awake. Soft snores and chatter fill the room. I turn onto my side and shove my hand under my pillow. Another hour later, and roughly seventy-four tosses and sixteen turns, I sit up.

My mind is stuck on repeat. Playing my sister's story, which highlights all the ways I hate Nate, against the expression on his tortured face when he told me all he ever wanted was for me to see him. Heavens above, I'm a world-class ass.

I stand and pad to his side of the room, swiping the roll out from under his pillow, and head for the door. Stevens smiles at me, glancing at Nate's bed.

"If you want to fool around, Bendall, I volunteer as tribute."

"Shut up, Stevens."

Flipping him off with a middle finger, I stalk to the door and push through it quietly before padding to the stairwell on bare feet. A moment later, I open the laundry room door. The linen is arranged against the last of the machines on the back wall as it was last time, with Nate stretched out on top. His breathing steady. He's peaceful. Relaxed. Not the strung out, hostile version that I've been imagining in my head for the last hour.

Walking over the white fabric, I pad to where his shoulders lie. I wind on crossed legs to my seat, roll in hand. He doesn't stir. A small smile pulls over my lips. I wrap my robe around tighter and lay down on my side. I study the rise and fall of his breathing, the angles of his face, the lush, dark lashes resting against his cheek bones. How can someone spend that many years in pain, without a soul noticing? My breathing picks up, and I place the roll between us and close my eyes.

With a sigh, I slide my hands under my head and wriggle closer to his warmth. He releases a small moan, so I crack one eye. Dark brown eyes find mine as he rolls to face me, imitating my position. He releases a long breath, glancing at the roll.

"I'm sorry," I whisper.

He stares at me for a heartbeat. Strong arms tug me into his hold, and I huddle closer. He tucks me under his chin, and I breathe him in. "Me too, Clara."

I huff a laugh, what could he possibly have to be sorry about? I lay my palm on his collarbone, a finger tracing the angle. He pulls a sheet over us, and I let my eyes flutter shut again. Sleep beckons me, and I turn over. He shuffles closer, spooning me. The man in the story my sister told isn't this Nate.

He never was.

I hope that I have the chance to prove to him that there are people who care about him.

After everything we have thrown at each other, and been through, he has me.

I see you, Nate.

* * *

Amber light flashes around the laundry room. Nate jerks

awake, pulling me with him when he sits up. Darkness floods between the orange emergency light as it oscillates. The high-pitched screeching alarm sets my ears ringing as we jump to our feet.

Why is it so dark? The bunker lights should still be on. Emergency protocol dictates we assemble in the mess hall at the eastern side of the building. Nate staggers to his feet, pulling me up with him. "Stay here, I'll check it out," he growls.

"No way! We go together."

He turns back, the angles of his face lit up orange, hesitating a moment before rushing for the door. I swipe up the roll—he still hasn't eaten—and follow close behind. I slam into his back as he tugs the metal door handle. The door is locked.

We can't get out.

Is this a lock down?

"Dammit!" Nate shouts, turning back and sprinting to the back of the room, heading for a wall with a low-hung window. He has it open and is up on the work bench as I find him in the dim light.

"Here, I'll pull you up."

"I got it." I scramble up onto the counter, as he budges the rectangle window open. He crawls through, turns back and waits. The ground is only inches under the window. I crawl through and stand, dusting off my sleep clothes and robe.

Nate grabs my hand, and we run for the entrance of our

building. I pray the doors are not also locked. The ground is hard and cold under my feet, and I tighten my grip on Nate's hand trying to keep up to his long stride. When we reach the front doors, they're locked.

Spinning back, I glance around the facility yard. Lined up mere feet away are six black, armored vehicles. That's not right. Usually, only one or two are parked outside with a night guard posted at the front gates.

Nate rattles the big doors, but they don't budge.

Something is wrong.

"Nate," I utter.

He is trying to jimmy the lock. I have a bad feeling about this. I rest a hand on his arm, eyes fixed on the vehicles, praying nobody is still inside. "Nate, stop."

He turns back. "What is it?"

"There's too many trucks."

His gaze tracks from the vehicles to the post by the gates, usually occupied by the night guard. It's empty. My gut flips, sending my heart racing. "Something's not right," I whisper.

He takes a step forward, tilting his head, as if trying to hear or see better.

The second the screaming starts, and the pops of shots fired starts, fear floods up my spine. I grab Nate's hand and sprint from the doors toward the supply shed.

The continuous pop of the guns chases us faster. Panic claws my insides, stealing the air from my lungs. I set my eyes ahead. Forcing the doors open, we burst inside as I stumble over my own feet. Nate secures the doors behind us. What the hell just happened?

"They are taking out the entire factory. What the hell could be so important that none of us are allowed to survive?" Nate gasps, hands fisted in his hair, fear scrawled across his face.

My gut sinks like a stone in stagnant water.

Tessa's message.

The virus.

This factory was privy to leaked information. *I* was privy. And now an entire factory's worth of Engineers is paying the price.

"I—"

Nate swings around from his pacing and studies me. "What?"

"It's my fault." The words are so soft, they almost don't pass by my lips.

"How is this your fault, Clara?"

"Tessa, she—" I slide down the side of a stack of flour bags. My imagination fixing images of limp bodies and bullet-torn flesh.

"What are you talking about? There's no communication between the Sectors and the city."

I meet his stare as he takes a step back. "Clara. There is no communication . . ."

The words die in his throat when I raise my head and try to tamper the sob that rattles up my chest.

"What did you two do?" he whispers, disbelief fixing his face in a scowl.

The familiar feeling of him and I raging against each other, descends. "You are blaming this on Tessa and me?"

"You broke protocol, didn't you."

I can't respond. He's right, we sent comms back and forth for weeks. We used Remmins and whoever is on Tessa's side to break a law that has been upheld for hundreds of years. The only siblings to have existed for as long. The anomalies.

This is the consequence of our actions.

Not for a second, did I ever imagine Sontaria would take simple correspondence between two family members this far. We have been writing to each other for weeks now, which leads me back to the only possible conclusion. The Elites have been monitoring each move we make, each comms we send. That last one, with the not so cleverly coded message of the virus, that's what tipped them over the edge.

The ringing in my ears begins as Nate walks toward the door, hands behind his neck, breathing heavy. What happens when they discover he and I are not amongst the dead? If we're meant to be dead and not with the others, they will hunt us down.

What is happening to Tessa right now?

Nausea claims me, and I lose my stomach onto the cement floor beside me. Nate appears at my feet as I wipe my mouth and release a groan, clutching my stomach.

"We can't stay here. We need to leave, Clara."

"I know."

"They are going to realize in no time that we're not inside with the others."

I nod, staring at the cold cement between my dirty, bare feet. "I need clothes."

He disappears for a moment, returning with a bundle. Warm hands under my arms raise me to my feet. Nate swallows. "Do you want me to help you?"

My hands tremble. "I—"

I can't breathe.

My hands turn to claws as my breathing shatters. Spots flood the sides of my vision. Warm hands are around my face a second later.

"Breathe, Clara."

I try to suck in a breath. But I'm drowning. The tightness in my lungs is like a one ton stone.

"Clara. I need you to breathe for me."

I grip his shirt, and he folds me in close. "Nate?"

"Yeah."

"What have I done?"

"Come on, let's get you dressed. We gotta go."

His warm fingers push my robe off my shoulders. He dips his head, watching the material hit the floor. With quick hands he helps me out of the shirt and pants. For a small moment, I stand naked in front of him.

He swallows, his Adam's apple bobbing. Then the bra that he found is over my arms and he leans close, fastening the clasp behind me. Next, a shirt lowers over my elevated arms. It settles over my torso as he pulls it closed and buttons it up.

Lastly, I step into the pants he holds as he kneels in front of me. The warmth of his hand brushing the inside of my thigh. My heart flings, rattling my rib cage, as his forearms flex with every little movement he makes. Dressed, I find shoes amongst the supplies at the back of the shed. We pause at the door.

Nate's chest cycles in deep breaths as his hand rests above the handle. There's no noise outside.

"Can we make it to the nearest factory?" he asks.

"It's five miles. Run or drive?"

"Driving will draw too much attention. Run, I think."

I glance at his leg, his face remains stone as I say, "Solid plan."

"Which direction is it?"

"North, and the terrain is nothing major."

"Good. You ready?"

"No?"

He stares down at me. "We stick together, we both make it."

He bends down planting a kiss to my forehead. I swallow and hold his burning gaze when he says, "Just in case."

A wobbly smile pulls over my lips as he cracks the door open. The yard is quiet. The vehicles still in the same spot. We slip out and jog toward the double gates. Past the threshold a little way, I turn back. Officers in full black spill from the factory doors. Only a second passes before the yelling starts.

No! No, no, no, no, no.

"Run, Nate."

I sprint for the northern road. Nate close behind me. I glance back as the men clamber into their trucks.

"Whatever you do, don't stop running," I grit out.

Nate shakes his head, brows lowered. His stride overtakes mine, and he snatches up my hand as we fly down the dirt road. The roar of six military vehicles catches up fast, right behind us.

27

TESSA

THE DINING ROOM'S opaque white wall sconces flicker. The face of the pilot in front of me twists. The laxatives I popped into his drink work fast. The officer pushes up on shaky feet and I rush to his side, feigning concern. "Are you alright?"

Flight Lieutenant Peters blinks at me through wide eyes, before gripping the edge of the table.

"I—" He staggers forward.

Did I use too much?

Sliding an arm through his, I help him to the door leading to the corridor. He's sweating profusely. Okay, so half a bottle was probably too much. Mental note made. The officer clutches his stomach and throws a glance my way before slamming a hand into the door.

I release my hold on his arm, swiping my fingers across his hip as he disappears through the door fast. Sinking my hands into my pockets before turning back. Peters's access card wrapped between my palm and digits turns clammy in my hold. Slamming my eyes shut I say a little prayer that no-one saw me swindle a senior officer and Leadership Elite pilot.

Nobody bothers a glimpse in my direction, so I make my way back to my seat and finish my food. He will be in there for quite a while, gauging by the intensity of his reaction. Poor man, he has no idea. A sly smile pops over my face, and I tamper it. Tricking people and causing pain and discomfort is not something I'm willing to make a habit.

I set my cutlery down and make for the briefing room. The end-of-day flight to HQ leaves in fifteen minutes. I'm taking the spot of the Elite who is currently occupied. So, I slip into the pre-flight room and swipe the access card over the locker Peters owns. Donning a light-blue flight suit, which is luckily not much bigger than my usual uniform, I shove his helmet onto my head. It's too big, but I tighten the straps hoping nobody will realize.

Four other pilots file in, one by one. Two chat away about some new shiny toy they have qualified for. Most likely an extravagantly overpriced nicknack. I pretend to be adjusting my gear, as I check the heads-up display power level on my helmet. I have no idea how to use half of this tech.

I open the locker and pull out the flight gloves. The tactile fingertips of the silky fabric have been designed for quick movement, in case of an emergency. Leadership Elites are transported by only the most skilled pilots. Flight Control may very well pick up on the difference in my flying. And I pray I can go unnoticed until I land on the roof.

Here's hoping.

The door to the briefing room clicks and automatically slides open. We file in. I straggle at the back, head down. Every pilot is ready, helmet on, hands held out to their left, waiting. As the pilots walk through the doorframe one after the other, a green light scans each person. A small ping sounds after they are approved.

I search the small space. Another door on the opposite wall slides open allowing each Elite through as they are cleared and given their orders. The pilot in front of me crosses the threshold. The green light sweeps over him and the ping sounds. I step up, alone in the room now.

With methodical breaths, I will my heart to slow down. Hand held out, it trembles a little as my wrist gadget vibrates and flight instructions flash onto the screen. A direct input feed into the tech on my wrist. Wow. If I wasn't terrified of being caught, I could appreciate the brilliance of this system.

The swoosh of the automatic exit door startles me. I hold my breath and pad through it into the large hangar. The Leadership aircrafts sit on the top level, and I walk beside balcony rail past the smaller high-tech birds. Below, Elites mill about doing pre-flight checks and ensuring routine maintenance is to spec. I spot Finn and the breath gushes from my lungs.

He talks to another Elite, Visi-Tile in hand. He points to an aircraft and gestures as if telling them something needs fixing. I freeze, hands gripping the rail. If this doesn't pan out, I may never see Finn Matthews again. Emotion shrouds my senses. My grip tightens.

I can't lose my sister. This is for her. I would give my last breath to save hers. Finn Matthews is a want, not a need. I close my eyes, repeating that phrase. Hoping, if I say it enough times I will start to believe it. Jaw tight and teeth clamped together, I push off the rail and head for the craft.

My gadget vibrates.

Finn's paging me.

I should have been on the hangar floor with him by now. My afternoon flight out over the northern training area was cleared for take-off in thirty minutes. My solo flight. The moment every Elite pilot waits weeks for, sometimes months. Hopefully I will be back by then.

I can't think about that right now.

I can't think about Finn.

I step into the aircraft and slide into the pilot's seat. The entire machine is much smaller than my regular ride. With only a cockpit and two seats for passengers behind me. The inside of the fuselage is coated with protective, anti-radar, bulletproof metal lining. This bird must weigh out pretty heavy, despite its compact size.

The windshield in front of me is wide and, by the treatment that reflects across it in the daylight, also bullet proof. A small window sits to my left, at shoulder height. Big enough for me to check the surrounds below. With a wave of the access card, the craft purrs to life and the control panel slides toward me. The harness snakes around my torso, securing me tight.

"Welcome, Elite Peters. Outside air temperature, 75 degrees Fahrenheit. Air pressure, 1016hPa. Wind strength, 15 knots, north-north-west. Altimeter stabilized. Power source maximum. Enjoy your flight," the automated female voice spiels. Nice to see the superior pilots are spoon-fed the things the rest of us work for.

One finger on the control panel, sliding the power to maximum, I double check the clearance from air control. The route is preset, all I have to do is adjust for any anomalies or changes in wind speed and heading. The other aircrafts in the line-up lift off, one after the other, the wake of their disrupters rocks the small craft.

The radio crackles with air controls authorization as each one takes to the sky through the wide metal roof that has rolled back. The ceiling of the cockpit is glass, and I tilt my face up as the underbellies of the other birds rise higher and higher. Clouds skiff past the blue rectangle that the open top of the hangar affords.

My wrist gadget vibrates.

Finn.

Again.

I slide a finger up the panel and the disrupter changes direction, slamming its force into the floor below as the craft rises. I tilt it to the right a little. The other Elites mill about in the lower hangar. Then I see him.

I raise the visor on the HUD and Finn stares right at me.

The Visi-Tile in his hand falls to the ground, his face stunned.

An alarm sounds, with an amber light flashing on the dashboard to my right.

"Proximity warning," the robotic voice coos.

Dammit.

The right wing clears the opening of the hangar by half an inch. I shake my head and correct the craft, homing my focus to the tallest building in the city of glass.

Headquarters.

The city underneath swarms with life. Glittering towers with scurrying colorful insects under a well-lit microscope, it seems like, with the sun tracking toward the horizon.

The aircraft autopilot takes over as I turn it onto the heading for the HQ building. The seat reclines and the harness loosens. I check the dashboard for anything that could be of use. Only flight controls fill the small space. Nothing extra.

The first aircraft starts its descent and lands on the pad with a large glowing number one.

The second and third land in succession and I study their pattern. The autopilot warning dings, and the seat automatically moves forward, harness tightening. I hover my hands over the panel waiting to resume control.

DING

The power lulls momentarily and I slide the colored bar back to seventy-five percent power and steer the nose in the direction of the landing pad with the glowing number six.

The craft is small, every move I make is too much. The wings jerk down and up as I try to align with the center of the landing pad.

Crap.

Someone is bound to pick up on that. Or think something is wrong with Peters. Either way, this draws attention.

"Elite Peters, straighten and descend, clear to land," a male voice chimes in from air control.

Great.

I don't respond. It takes every effort to guide the small tin bird to the pad without any more messy maneuvers.

"Peters, respond."

"Wilco," I snap out in my lowest voice.

When nothing further comes and the bird is solid on the ground, I release a breath and kill the engines. The disrupters fade out with a whine, as I search the landing area. None of the other pilots are getting out of their crafts. How the hell am I supposed to make it inside without drawing attention?

Figuring it's now or never, I swipe a hand over the seat panel and the harness retracts. I rush from the aircraft, and march toward the door that leads inside. As I reach the shining silver door, it opens.

Leadership Elites file out, briefcases and Visi-Tiles in hand. Their uniforms, a light grey, still immaculate at the end of the day.

A man in his forties appears and turns back with a withering glare. "Why are you out of your aircraft, officer?"

"Pit stop," I utter, waving to the door, pressing both hands to my stomach.

He sighs, and grumbles something like *unbelievable, hurry up.* I dash through the door after the last of the Leadership personnel exit and track down the corridor.

I have less than five minutes to find that lab.

28

CLARA

NATE'S FACE hardens with every mile we run. His limp deepening the more terrain we cover. The air in my lungs burns more than the fire in his eyes every time he throws a glimpse back. So, I keep running. He slows, his limp making him sway with every step.

"Don't you dare stop, Prendergast. Not now."

He shoots forward.

Legs burning, I match his stride until we finally see the outskirts of the next factory. The massive twelve-foot wire fence is decorated with coils of barb along the top. The same layout as the factory we fled. A line of trees run around the eastern perimeter. I steer Nate toward them, desperate to crash and catch my breath.

Nate stalls to a stop under the cover of the first tree, its low hanging branches the perfect spot for conceal-ment from any vehicles that may fly past. We crossed the five mile stretch as the crow flies, but still, I search the compound of the factory for the six black military vehicles. Finding none there as yet, I drop beside Nate and dig my hands into my sides to quell the stitch that aches.

Nate's words, hard and short, break me from my breathless daze. "What the hell was in those comms between you and Tessa?"

Steadying, I lock my eyes to his. How do you tell the only friend you have left, that every single person they have ever known and loved is about to be wiped out. Genocide. *Elitist* genocide.

I decide on the truth.

"The illness that so many have come down with, lost their lives to, it's made by the city."

With Nate as my only ally left, I need him to want to fight this alongside me.

"What do you mean it was made?"

"Synthesized by Elites to wipe out the Engineers, every last person in the Sectors. And—and the Provinces."

He stares at me vacantly for what feels like an age before saying, "Maybe they should."

My mouth gapes, brows snapping down. Heat surges in my core. How the hell can he say that? His family, his own life. Are they not worth anything to him?

"How can you say that?"

He searches my face before he tracks his focus to the vast nothingness we crossed. "Not everybody had what you and Tessa had growing up."

"To wipe out every single person who doesn't make the cut as an Elite? That's pure evil. It's—"

"Inconceivable. Yet, they have a point, Clara. Misery only breeds more misery. I don't know—"

"What, tell me, Nate. How can you be confused about this?"

He turns on his seat and faces me square on. "But I don't want anything to happen to you, Clara. Or the people you love. So, I will help you in any way you need."

It occurs to me that this man, right in front of me, values his life so little. What brought him to this state of mind? Was it the accident with his leg in the Metal Sector? Or his childhood? Not being selected as an Elite? Because despite his long-standing annoyance with me, he has acted as if he thinks he's superior to the rest of us. I don't believe that. Not anymore.

"Nate?"

He is back to staring into the desert-like abyss. "Yeah."

"Look at me."

He dips his head and swallows. "Why?"

Lifting my hand to his chin, I force him to meet my gaze.

"Because I need *you* to see *me* when I say this." The words are soft. I drop my hand from his face, and he doesn't look away.

"I see you," I whisper. His jaw works, and he swallows. I suck in a breath. "I cannot do this without you."

The overwhelming need to be in his hold washes over

me. But I stay rooted to the spot. It would be unwise to complicate things further right now.

"Clar—" his voice breaks. "You, have me. For as long as you need."

I shuffle closer and press my forehead to his and utter, "You could have opened with that all those years ago, you know. The time we wasted, when we could have spent days together as friends."

He chuckles, as his hands come to rest on my shoulders. "I will always be in your life, in one capacity or another, Clara Bendall."

"Good," I whisper, breaking the contact and sitting back on my heels. "What do we do next?"

"Rally the troops? This factory site may let us in." He stands and drops a hand down. I slap mine inside it as he wraps his fingers around, tight. Grounding and solid, I hold it for longer than I should.

"We can only try."

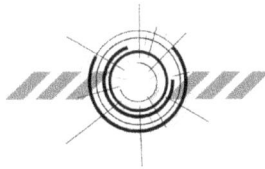

THE GUARD at the gate is nowhere to be seen. Nate scans the yard before the first large building that, if it is the same layout as ours, would be the dorms and first factory floor.

We walk in.

It's relatively quiet. Only the hum of machines behind

closed doors. It's almost like we are back in our own site, the format is identical. But it's not the same. The colors are different. We head directly for the supervisor's office. We pass a pair of Engineers that are no doubt on their way to breakfast, their confused gazes roam over our filthy clothes and worn-out faces.

A guard stands outside the supervisor's office.

"We're here to see the supervisor," Nate says, his tone is all business.

The guard nods and opens the door. An older man, grey hair and wrinkled face thinned from a hard life, looks up from the paper in his hands. A comms no doubt. I pray it isn't one about us. He stands and gestures for us to sit. We stand opposite his desk, and I try to find the words to tell him what I need to without mention of the disease.

"Well?" he snaps.

"We are from the site five miles south. Soldiers from Sontaria came, they killed every last person."

He stares at us, brows lowered as he folds his arms over his chest. And he opens his mouth, as if to say something and closes it again.

"Please, you have to help us." Nate takes a step forward. "Your site could be next."

The supervisors jaw works as he takes us in. "Carter!"

The door opens, and the guard outside walks in. "Yes, sir."

"Radio site forty-six. Request proof of life."

The guard plucks the radio from his shoulder and barks

out a one-liner. A voice answers on the other end. My gut falls. Who is answering? Who would have survived?

"Your little story has a few holes in it, officer."

"I swear, there was six military vehicles. Soldiers, in black uniforms, went in. There were gun shots and screaming. Nobody came out." I am up against the desk now, eyes pleading.

"You witnessed this also?" the supervisor asks Nate.

"It was exactly as Clara said. Twelve soldiers. Nobody came out after but the military officers."

Nate said my name.

"Stay here, I will find out what's going on."

The supervisor stalks out the door followed by Carter. The door closes. I sigh, slumping against the desk. The door clicks and the locking mechanism hisses, securing us inside.

Nate's wide glare burns into the door.

Oh shit.

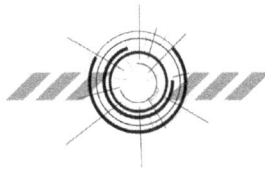

THE HOLDING CELL IS COLD.

Nate's head leans back on the wall, his arm around me. The only noises come from the breathing of two other Engineers, no doubt only in here overnight for brawling by the side-eye they continue to give each other. Footsteps, harsh and quick, snap toward us. I push out of Nate's hold, and he stirs awake.

"Someone's coming," I breathe.

He clears his throat and sits up, yawning, rubbing a hand over his stubble and I can't help but touch his jaw. He studies me for a moment. The door clunks open, sliding away to let the supervisor in.

Shifting my focus to the older, thin man, I stand. Nate pushes up and takes a small step forward, as if putting himself between me and the officer. "You can let us go. We've done nothing wrong." Nates voice is solid.

The supervisor clasps his hands behind his back and studies the two of us in turn. "Haven't you?" His eyes land on me.

Dammit.

The older man closes in on me. "You are Clara Bendall. Twin sister to Tessa Bendall, an Elite. Remarkable."

Hope rises for a single moment.

"That is, remarkable two girls could be so stupid. Did you think for a second, because you are *different*, you don't have to abide by the rules of this Ring?"

I gasp. "I—"

His hand shoots up. "Communication between the city and the Sectors has been prohibited since the inception of this Ring. The lives you have endangered breaking that one rule is profound. And now, you accuse Sontaria of mass murder."

He walks away, padding out a tight circle, as if pondering

his next words. The older man's eyes, lined with fire, home in on me. "So, now, General Beswick wants to speak with you. Then, you return to your site. And if you are to be found guilty of the slightest infraction, you will find yourself in the Wastelands, girl."

"Our site is Engineer-less. Haven't you been listening to a word we said?" I retort.

His hand strikes my cheek within the next heartbeat. I step back, soothing the burn that rises through my skin with my palm. Nate shoves me behind him. "Don't touch her."

"Young man, she may have ensnared you into her little game. But I will not hesitate to have you forcibly removed."

Nate's jaw clenches. "Are you daft? This is no game. Our site was executed!"

The supervisor pulls an incredulous face, huffing a chuckle. "I spoke to an officer over there, nothing was amiss, he assured me."

"Send a patrol to check!" Nate hands are in the air, palms up.

"Hold your tongue!"

Nate towers over the older man now.

"You're an old fool. You really think it won't happen to your site? Check for *yourself*!"

"Enough!" he hollers, seething. "Guards."

Three armed guards rush in, guns poised.

"Take him to another cell. Keep an eye on them both. We wait for the General's communication."

The guards man-handle Nate from my cell and into one

two doors down. His eyes stay fixed on me the entire way as he pulls against their hold. A guard hits him over the head, and he staggers forward before crumpling to the ground.

"Nate!"

Both cell doors are slammed shut. I grip the bars, air heaving from my lungs.

Nate grabs onto the bars and hauls himself up. "I'm okay, Clara."

My chin wobbles. The helplessness that washes over me, seeing him hurt and out of reach, is too much. Tears burn down my cheeks. This is all my fault. If I hadn't responded to Tessa. If I had followed the rules and kept my stupid head down.

"Hey, look at me Clara. Don't go there. We'll be alright."

I slide down the bars to my seat and shove my head in my hands. How will anything be right ever again. The perfectly structured world we have been raised in is breaking apart around me. The people I love dangled like the proverbial carrot on the end of a stick. The hunt, for something I have no idea how to find, is the only way forward. The odds are too great.

And I have no idea how I am going to escape this damned cell.

29

TESSA

BACK FLAT AGAINST THE WALL, I wait for the guard manning the stretch between me and the entry to the lab to circle back. From the blueprints I memorized last night, I should be able to at least steal a glance through the large glass viewing windows along the corridor by the door. The third floor from the top is nothing to look at. All white walls and sealed doors.

Footsteps, methodical and regular, close in. My only advantage is the element of surprise. That and the three self-defense classes my mother insisted Clara and I take when we were twelve. I think she only went to find ways to annoy Nate. I smile at the memory. Footsteps slowing by the corner, he's inches from where I'm concealed.

I slip around on fast feet. He startles and I slam my fist into his face. As he jerks back, I send another into his throat. His Adam's apple meets my knuckles. He gasps for air, doubling over, and I snatch the rifle from his hand and smash the butt into his temple. The guard sinks like a stone, hitting the wall on the way down, and I swipe up his access card.

I flip the safety on by the trigger, like my father did so routinely every day before leaving for shift along the perimeter as a Control Officer, and tuck it under my arm. Jogging down the corridor, I find the lab as it is on the blueprints, moving closer so I can take in the workings of inside. Three chemical Engineers, or simply scientists, work with their backs to me. Head downs, every type of safety gear covering them. Gowns, gloves, respirators, face shields and hair nets.

As if that will save them if they screw up.

I found it. I have my proof, don't I?

Maybe, maybe not.

Confirmation that the disease for the Sectors is what they're working on would be helpful. One of their Visi-Tiles, even better. Inside the first door is a containment, or quarantine space of some kind. Gowns and gloves, face shields and respirators hang in neat formation along one wall. Setting the rifle down, I push through the door.

Glancing over to check nobody noticed, I pull on one of each of the protective gear. I fasten the respirator to my face, and a small oxygen tank that I fix to my hip, but I can't find a way to turn it on. It's tight, and I'm breathing my own air.

Not ideal.

I set my shoulders back and slide a hand over the panel that opens the door.

It beeps at me, turning red.

Shit.

The door is shut tight.

Digging the guards access card out from under the gown, I press it onto the panel. It flashes blue as the door hisses and opens. The air changes around me immediately and I waste no time hurrying into the lab. The scientists don't bother looking up to see who has entered the space as one says, "if you're here for more of the antidote samples, we told you it will be another three days before the next batch is ready."

"Fine," I say, trying to sound official.

"Was there something else?" the gowned man closest to me says, as he peers away from the microscope that his hands are wrapped around. I rummage my brain for something that won't be seen as out of place but will give me an excuse to stay in here a little longer. Nothing comes.

His eyes narrow.

"I— um. Is there—"

"Wait. You're not Jenkins."

Astute, this guy. I would laugh if I wasn't completely void of oxygen and a way out.

"Jenkins sent me," I say, too fast.

"No, he didn't." The man releases his hold on the scope and moves closer. "This lab is classified space. How the hell did you get in here?"

With that the other scientists eyeball me with worried faces.

I step back, hands balling to fists. Pretty sure I can't take all three of them. And by the looks of the equipment and vials of liquids, breaking things in this carefully organized space would be a mistake. I back away in a hurry. One of the gowned and gloved officers swipes a button on the large overhead glass panel.

Alarms pierce the air. The noise is deafening, drowning out the shouting that ensues as I turn and run for the door. Outside the large windows that flank the lab six armed guards run for the lab. Dread winds a hot, sickening, molten river up my spine. The only way out is the way I came. Blueprints don't lie.

I didn't get a Visi-Tile.

Or anything else for that matter.

As I reach the door to the quarantine room, a rough grip grabs my wrist and I stumble forward. Another lands on my shoulder. I turn back and witness the disgust that scrawls over their faces. A moment later, guns point at my head, on the other side of the glass. The white gloved hands shove me over to the officers in the quarantine room.

The door hisses closed. They strip the gown and protective equipment from me until I'm left with only Peters's uniform. My ears ring, my hands tremble with every step down the corridor. Cuffed, hands at my front and in the rough hold of two officers, I am escorted. As well as a pair of officers ahead, and a pair behind. The radio squawks. The guard to my left answers it.

"Ten-four. Coming up now."

The alarms quiet and my ears ring all the louder. I stare ahead. Nobody speaks as we step into the elevator and the guard to my right taps the screen, choosing the top floor. The elevator glides upward. My stomach sinks.

Still, nobody makes a sound.

Nobody moves.

Until the elevator doors open with a swoosh and a soft ping. A bright, well-lit, wide corridor stretches before us. Frozen to the spot, I don't move. The grip around my arms tightens, forcing me forward. Lightning lances through my veins, sending fear rattling up my spine.

My chances of getting out of this are slim. And I'm glad that Finn and I had a few moments together. Still, overwhelming devastation creeps in.

I let the rebellion down.

More importantly, I let *Clara* down.

Tears swell, but I swallow tampering them. I will not cry in front of these people.

We come to a closed, white door, trimmed in silver. Most likely the precious metal that powers the city, or at least a mock version of it. The guard to my right radios a message through somewhere. When a short response returns, he pushes his shoulders back and reaffirms his hold on my arm. The guard to my left does the same.

Heart flinging against my ribs, with each too-shallow breath that's far quicker than useful. The door to the Leadership floor slides open on silent mechanism. Four large, white, oval tables fill the oversized room, two each side of the path we now walk, heading for yet another doorway.

This one is a double door with extensive security, double access panels on each side and a retina scanner, that I have only heard about in basic training. The guard to my right presses his thumb to the panel as he leans into the scanner, and the doors open swiftly. Only one large table sits in the center of this room. It's shining, metallic surface the only glistening thing in the room.

The General sits behind it. His black uniform, like his guards, is adorned with epaulets of silver. His greying hair is a salt and peppered version of light brown. His narrow eyes are dark and calculating. Homing in on me as we close the distance between him and the doorway.

The doors whisper closed behind us. I have to force air into my lungs. Prey trapped in the predator's lair. Stopping in front of the large table, the guards remove their hands from my arms and take a long step back. I glance at them before meeting the General's hard stare.

He doesn't stand, merely leaning back on his chair, hands steepled, elbows resting on the armrests of his chair. I don't dare breathe a word. Nothing can save me now. No counter information. No way of making my actions appear accidental. Nothing.

When I think he isn't going to say a word, he says, "Tessa Bendall. Aeronautics. And, *most importantly*, an anomaly in our carefully curated society."

He pauses. It's not the kind on silence you would offer to

fill. As he stands, he taps a finger to the Visi-Screen at a forty-five-degree angle on his desk and it disappears into the top. Now, he rounds the desk and comes to stand in front of me. At only a few inches from where I stand, he towers over me.

My hands tremble in the cuffs and I curl my fingers into my palms. I will not let him intimidate me. This man, who sees fit to exterminate his own people. For what? Academics and advancement? Where's the humanity in that?

"You despise me," he whispers.

A scowl twists my face, and he chuckles. Nothing about this is funny.

"Have you heard of the term, for the good of the many, Tessa?"

I fix my stare to the far wall.

He leans down and tilts his head. "Do you think that a life in the Province is something to aspire to?"

Still, I don't answer.

"Perhaps the Wastelands are more suitable?"

He tilts my head up with one hand, forcing my eyes to his. My skin crawls with the contact.

"Go to hell," I seethe.

He huffs a laugh as a smirk pulls over his lined face. "Hell is what happens when society is allowed free rein, girl."

"Is it? I wouldn't know. Free rein is a foreign concept inside this Ring, General."

"Perhaps, but it's better to have structure and peace, than

chaos and downfall. Nobody wins with that." He turns away, gesturing for the guards to wait outside. They leave without a word.

After the door closes, he turns back to me. "The Province and the Sectors are no longer a necessity to this society, to this ring. They have become a burden. One I intend to relieve the good people of Sontaria from."

I'm shaking my head, anger flying around my veins, fast. "You will murder thousands for the sake of the few. Where is the justice in that?"

"Justice is a side note when it comes to survival. And we *will* survive, Tessa Bendall. Not only that, we will thrive. We'll be light years ahead of any other ring in the entire Federation. Progress has a price. Fortunately for our Elites, it's one I am willing to pay."

"You can't do this. You're killing innocent people!"

I'm moving toward him but he stands his ground. "Innocent is in the eye of the beholder. Anomalies such as yourself and your twin will not be tolerated any longer. You will both be held here until we decide which path of correction is most suitable. For the Elite society, not for you."

"You—" Stars slide into my vision, and I sway on my feet as the ringing in my ears fades in once again.

He walks to his desk, pushing on a panel. It pops open and a vial sits in a small glass box.

My breaths shallow out. "No."

The General snatches up the vial, plucking a syringe from the space. He sinks the sharp point into the top of the vial. With the small container empty, he flicks the top of the needle. A drop flies from the top and he dodges it, jerking sideways.

Oh Heavens, please no.

I need to run.

To scream. To fight my way out of this. He closes in on me fast. My feet are cemented to the floor. I pull at the shackles around my wrists. The metal stings my skin and I stumble backward as my feet move.

The General grabs me up, slamming the needle into my neck. Blinding pain courses up my throat and into my cheek. I gasp for air, but none comes. The syringe depresses fully, and the General retracts his hold like he's been burned.

I sink to the floor. Cold marble bites at my knees with a crunch. Hand automatically over my neck, I crumple forward. A small parcel of air rattles down my airway.

Yelling and chaos starts outside the room. The General marches for a panel in the wall I didn't catch before. He presses a thumb to a slightly darker spot and the panel retracts. He plucks a pistol from its concealment.

The doors open, and the small bit of air I had managed to inhale dies out.

Finn stands, rifle aimed at the General, lips pulled into a snarl as he glances my way.

"Let her go." His voice is a raw growl.

"Another traitor. Let me guess, you are both part of that so called rebellion?"

"We are not rebels," I choke out.

Finn steps in front of me and I push to my feet. He shouldn't have come. Now, he is a dead man. We're both dead. The General doesn't move as Finn ushers me to the doors. I walk past the limp guards. The knot in my gut tightens. It was too easy. Finn walks in and I'm free?

I stagger down the corridor, Finn's grip on my arm.

Crack!

Time stretches out, stalling. My movements reduce to slow motion as I turn back to find Finn's pained face. Jerking to a halt, his fingers fall from my arm. He falters backward, dropping to his knees. The rifle in his hand clatters to the floor. Red soaks his shirt above his heart.

"No!" I scramble back to where he sways on his knees. The General stands in the doorway. His pistol still in his outstretched hand. I grab Finn's shoulder with my cuffed hands. "Finn! No!! Please . . . No."

"Tessie, I'm sorry."

"No, don't you dare. Stand up. Please, Finn. Get. Up!"

He tries to push up, lifting a leg to push up with.

Crack.

He lurches forward as another bullet claims his other shoulder.

"Noooo!"

He falls to the ground, face first with ragged shallow breaths. I launch to my feet and rush the General. He fires another shot. It sails past my face. Burning starts on the tip of my ear. Warmth trickles down my neck. I leap and crash into him, cuffed fists first. He falls to the floor, hands hitting

304

at my face, sending one after the other. I waste no time, sinking both fists into his windpipe.

He gasps, bucking on the ground.

Rough hands grab me from behind and I'm hauled off. The General recovers, wobbling to his feet. Every breath he takes, raspy and shallow. The grip on my arms tightens. I struggle in their hold. "Take your hands off me!"

"Hold her," he croaks.

I try to spin around, desperate to see Finn, but black uniforms occlude my view.

"Finn," I sob.

The General moves closer, boots scuffing over marble, as I turn back. The fire in my veins has liquified to lava. Pure hatred pouring out with every ragged breath.

"You will have the rest of your three weeks to think about every choice you have made, Miss Bendall. Along with the fact that you killed your friend here. Then, you will die a slow and painful death. There's your justice."

My mouth gapes. I want to throw some kind of retort at him. Nothing comes as I turn back to stare at Finn's limp body being dragged from the corridor.

The next few moments hardly register, as I'm tossed into a bare, white room. Four locks on the other side of the door hiss closed. I slide down the wall with a cry that would wake the dead.

Heavens above, what have I done?

30

CLARA

IT'S BEEN three days since Nate and I were thrown into the holding cells. Nobody has come. Nobody has asked any more questions. With every day that passes, the sinking, rotten feeling that something is terribly wrong, buries deeper and deeper. I can't keep the thoughts of my sister from my mind.

Tessa is in pain. *I can feel it.*

The cold stone smarts my back, and I roll over. Nate is asleep, two cells down. The night guard on duty is slumped over in his chair. His loud snores echo through the long room of bars. The door opens and two officers spill inside, he jerks awake with a mumble.

They talk a minute before all three make their way to my cell. I push to my feet, stretching out each aching limb in turn. My stomach grumbles but I ignore it. Standing with my hands by my sides, I brace for the next bad thing to happen.

My cell door opens, and an officer walks to where I stand. "You're with us."

Nate is standing now, hands curled around the bars. His face is stone, but the worry that laces his stare strings my already thundering heart along faster. I don't move. The officer grabs my arm, pulling me from the cell. I tug on his hold, trying to put distance between us. But he doesn't falter.

Nate moves to the gate of his cell as we walk past. "Clara."

I meet his gaze, his face is as strung out as mine, now twisted with fear. Shoved down the corridor, we turn and make for the office of the supervisor. This time, when I enter, the screen on his wall is turned on. Static scrolls over it as we come to a stop in front of the old man who has kept us for days with no word.

"Come to your senses? Did you see for yourself?" I hiss. The grip on my arm turns painful and I shoot the guard a withering glower.

The supervisor steps around, out from behind his dark and comes to stand on my other side. "No. You have an appointment with the General."

His burning stare is harsh. Spiteful. His eyes narrowed; lips curled into a snarl. The screen squeals and the static disappears as the General fades in. He's sitting behind a desk. Hands steepled, propped on elbows on his desk. His black uniform is immaculate. The same as the ones the officers wore that slaughtered our factory. Eyes piercing through me even from the other side of the screen, I swallow and air lodges around the stone in my throat. I curl my hands to fists. So, this is the man who thinks killing thousands of innocent people for his pets is acceptable. I return fire, with a glare so fueled with hate, my face aches.

"Clara Bendall. You are the spitting image of your sister."

He's seen Tessa?

"Tell me this, Clara. When you decided to break rules that have been held since the inception of this Ring, what did you think would happen?"

"Go to hell," I grind out.

He laughs, his hands fall and slide off the desk as he leans back. "The same sentiment I received from your sister only a day ago."

"What . . ."

My mouth gapes, fear spirals up my spine at a rapid rate, stealing the air from my lungs. He frowns now, as if deciding whether to change tactics. He taps something and another screen view takes over half of ours. The whimper that leaves my mouth is followed by my knees buckling.

Strapped to a white bed, is my sister.

Unconscious.

Pale.

"No!"

I struggle against the hold of the guard.

"This is what happens to citizens who don't follow the rules, Miss Bendall."

I drag in ragged breaths, forcing myself to stand tall.

"What about the Engineers and officers at our factory? What rules did they break?!"

He leans his head back a little before saying. "You know which ones they broke."

The grip on my arms loosens a little. *Now* they believe me! For Heaven's sake.

"The rest of the Sectors? The Province? The Federation of the Americas will not let you—"

"The Federation will *not* interfere! This ring is ours to govern as we see fit. The society we aim to mold is of *our* making. Whatever decisions we make, whatever actions we take, are well within the right of the Leadership of this ring. Now, back to your predicament."

"I will never help you."

He huffs a bored laugh. "I neither want your help nor need it. Hand yourself in, and your sister will receive the proper treatment she needs to live. Don't and she will not."

The disease takes two to three weeks to kill someone. I saw it with Vivi. With others who fell ill and took far too long to die. At least I thought that then. Now, it buys me two weeks to decide. To find another solution. One that will stop the General and his plans for mass genocide.

"Fine. But I come to you. I make my own way."

"I thought you would say that. Twins really are incredibly similar." He nods to the supervisor beside me.

I turn to find the older man holding a syringe. What? No. I can't help Tessa if I have the virus. The needle stings as it buries deep into my upper arm. The minuscule amount of liquid carries a small silver dot.

"This ensures you do it fact come to me, as you say, making your own way. The tracking device you now have in your arm allows me to find you anywhere in this ring. This conversation does not leave this room. Failure to keep this classified will see all three of you executed. Am I understood?"

"Yes, sir," the guard snaps.

"Of course, General," the supervisor says, but his words are weak.

"Release her, and her friend, with supplies. I will see them in a matter of days. In the meantime, production will continue until further notice." He is looking directly at the supervisor now, as if they had simply cleared up some routine piece of business. Not a life and death situation that he is holding over their heads.

Both hands drop from my arms, and I falter backward. The General holds my gaze. "See you soon, Clara Bendall."

Without a word I turn and run from the office. A minute later I'm at Nate's cell. He is breathing hard, searching me for damage.

"They didn't hurt me. We have to leave."

"Let them both go," the supervisor says from the doorway. The day guard, looking far sharper than his predecessor rushes the cell and releases Nate.

"Clara, what's going on?" Nate says.

"I'll tell you on the way."

Donning the two heavy packs the guards prepped, we run from the building like it's exploding around us. We clear the site, and I grab his hand and haul him toward the group of trees we hid out in last time. He crowds me against the trunk of one, before wrapping me in his embrace. "Don't ever do that to me again."

His Adam's apple works as he tightens his hold, sinking his head into my hair. Closing my eyes, I melt into his arms as the first sob spill over.

My sister. How can I save her and let the world burn?

Someone has to do something.

The General cannot be allowed to murder thousands of innocent people. I sob into his shirt until it's damp. Nate doesn't let go until I wriggle, desperate for a lungful of air. Pushing my hair from my face, he tucks it behind my ear. "Where are we going? What did they—"

"Tessa, they gave her the disease, I have to hand myself over or she dies."

"No. Please tell me you won't do that. Then you *both* die."

"What choice do I have?"

"Anything is better than you dead, Clara."

"If I don't, I will lose my sister. He—"

"He? The General?"

I nod.

Nate's face is crumpled. "What is it?"

"He confirmed that he plans to wipe out all the Sectors, and the Province."

"That's insanity. The Elites are not going to witness that and not care."

"By the time they do, it will be too late."

"There has to be another way. The Sectors and Province outnumber the Elites. Burn the city to ashes. All their tech and resources."

"Ashes." I scan the vast, empty landscape around us. The thin grey plants that struggle to survive in the arid ground. "Ash."

"Usually what comes after fire."

I catch Nate's confused stare. "Ash, he can help."

"Remmins?"

Eyes wide, I nod. I look up to the sky, placing the sun and calculating direction from here. I need to make it to the outer wall. Need to find Ash. I take off running southwest. No footsteps sound behind me, so I turn back. "Come on!"

I have one week, ten days tops, to find Ash Remmins and the cure. Another week to return to Sontaria, to my sister. Everything else, how to stop the General, how to save every last soul of this ring, I will have to figure out as I go.

Nate thunders up beside me. We run.

Hard.

Fast.

Together.

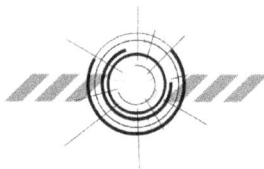

SELECTED

THE PACK on my back is heavy. My arm aches where I cut out the tracking device two nights ago, leaving it in the dirt by the outskirts of Sector Two. As far as the General is aware, we are camping there and considering our options. But that ruse won't last for too long. I rub the sore spot, pushing on.

Nate's three-day stubble from the cells has turned into a six-day starter beard. I kind of like it. Despite being literally running for our lives, and in the middle of nowhere with the future of everyone I know hanging over our heads, I'm happy right now. A little stressed, but happy. A whole lot messed up over the way I feel about Nathanial Prendergast.

I'm supposed to hate him.

He's supposed to hate me.

That is the way it has always been. The last three nights when he has wrapped his body around mine, to save me from freezing with the outside elements, all I have wanted is to roll over and plant my mouth on his. To put my hands on his body.

". . . Clara, did you hear what I said?"

"Huh? No sorry, what?"

He stares down at me, and a small smile tugs up on that gorgeous mouth and my already dry throat turns parched.

"Look ahead." He nods to in front of us.

The wall.

It's high. Like twenty feet high. No convenient doorway with a neon sign that flashes *Wastelands - this way*. How rude.

"Do we climb over?" I ask.

"We don't have rope, or anything, to scale a solid wall for that matter."

"We will have to hunt for a door. Split up?"

"Nope," he shakes his head, face turning serious. "We are not doing that again."

I huff a laugh at his intensity and nod. Course not.

"Hopefully, we find one soon then." I walk to the north, closing in on the wall as I scan every inch we pass, looking for some kind of marking or sign. Or actual door.

Nate is quiet.

I stumble over a rock, dirt flinging up from the toe of my boot. A steadying hand rests on my shoulder. "Give me your pack, it's too heavy."

"I'm fine, Nate. Besides, you have a heavy one also."

"Yeah, but I'm much bigger than you."

I turn back to slap him only to find his crooked smile, eyes laced with jest. Wall who? I walk on and he files in behind me. Hope he's liking the view; I snort at my own ridiculousness.

Nate laughs and mutters something I can't make out.

Urgh, when all this is over, I am definitely climbing him like a tree. Now that his meanness has all but dissolved, he is downright gorgeous. Sharp words gone, and insults all dried up, he is *something*.

I run my hand along the wall hoping to catch a crack, a depression, or anything that would indicate an exit.

My mind flicks back to Ash.

The memories of him and I stir more emotions, and they collide with every feeling I have when I take in Nate. I'm so torn.

When my fingers brush over a gap, I almost miss it. I jerk to a halt, stopping a pace short of Nate, before turning back.

Inches from him, eyes burning into his, I whisper, "Found it."

"I see that."

But I can't move.

I can't.

The two packs strung over his shoulders fall to the ground. His hands cup my face.

"Nate—"

His lips crash against my own a heartbeat later. He's hot, hungry. I need more. Running my hands up his neck and into his hair, he picks me up, planting me on his hips.

I wrap my legs around his waist. My back slams into the wall, and I whimper. Still needing more. Tracing my hands down, I explore the toned warmth of his body. He breaks away, eyes searching mine.

"Cara, I—"

I press a finger to his lips as Ash's face blooms in my memory. "Please, don't."

He tilts his head, eyes narrowing. "Don't what?" His grip loosens.

"Never mind, I just got carried away. Put me down, Nate."

Hurt and desperation flood his eyes. My heart aches, all

too tight. I slide down the wall, as he lets me down, and something behind my back clunks. I turn back and we step away, my gaze hitting the ground.

The stone of the wall slides to the side and splintering light pours through the space as it widens.

"We really found it," I breathe.

Nate clears his throat. "Let's find Remmins then." He walks past me, shoving my shoulder as he slips through, ducking to clear the opening. I stare at his back, my breaths still ragged from moments ago. The image of my sister pale and limp on the white bunk burns in my mind. Thoroughly and utterly ripped in two, between what I have to do and what I want to do, I step through the doorway and into Wastelander territory.

Hold on Tessa.

Continue the story with book two ~ Sacrificed

CONTINUE THE STORY...

SACRIFICED

R M MULLER

ACKNOWLEDGMENTS

Nothing challenges your mettle like writing a novel. And it shouldn't be done alone! So here is my list of thank-yous in no particular order . . .

To all the writerly friends that have encouraged me through the journey of creating something from nothing, you are absolute legends. My patient and very grammatically correct mother, who read early editions that now make me cringe.

To my girls, for letting me bounce plot ideas and scenes around with them, and always giving me very honest (read: blunt) feedback. My husband, who interest in books is nonexistent, but listens when I prattle on about imaginary people and places, nonetheless.

Thank you to every reader who has found themselves on this page (and perhaps in these pages), you are truly rockstars!!

ABOUT THE AUTHOR

Perched on a thin limb in a tree that had stood for decades, was a skinny, little farm girl. Her focus was solely on the scrappy notebook and pencil in her hands. Oblivious to the swaying branches around her and the voice of her mother calling her down, she scratched out a story. For the first time her imagination made it to paper, and she was obsessed. Rose-Marie is a mother to four vivacious daughters, wife to a grazier, sister, daughter, etc. Stories and her little bunch of humans keep her alive and give her purpose every day, and the reason she spends a disturbing amount of time with imaginary people, in imaginary worlds, most days.

Milton Keynes UK
Ingram Content Group UK Ltd.
UKHW021940281024
450365UK00018B/1195

9 781763 549616